"While pulp fiction, which peaked from the '30s through the '60s, has been rehabilitated in the past decade, this revival has not benefited the genre's female practitioners. . . . Kudos, then, to the Feminist Press, as it launches the 'Femmes Fatales: Women Write Pulp' series in an effort to spotlight forgotten women writers."
—*Time Out New York*

"There's another kind of woman in pulp noir fiction: the kind bold enough to write it in a man's world. They not only wrote noir thrillers but in the other pulp genres as well — sometimes using male pen names to sell more books. The Feminist Press, like a good private eye, has tracked them down. . . . Check out these queens of pulp." —*Minneapolis Star Tribune*

PRAISE FOR *BUNNY LAKE IS MISSING* (1957)

"A super psychological story of terror and suspense."
—*St. Louis Post-Dispatch*

"Evelyn Piper . . . master of taut and impelling writing, compresses the events of a single evening into a headlong story of nerve-wracking tension, psychological validity and emotional drive."
–*Oakland Tribune*

"Ranks high among the season's most compelling breath takers."
—*New York Times*

"A beautiful job . . . frantic scenes of action, contagious terror and near hysteria." –*San Francisco Chronicle*

"Ranks high and hair-raising as a psychological thriller."
—*Pittsburgh Press*

"Original . . . exciting . . . well written." —*The New Yorker*

BUNNY LAKE IS MISSING

FEMMES
WOMEN WRITE PULP
FATALES

BUNNY LAKE IS MISSING

EVELYN PIPER

AFTERWORD BY MARIA DiBATTISTA

FEMMES FATALES: WOMEN WRITE PULP

THE FEMINIST PRESS
AT THE CITY UNIVERSITY OF NEW YORK
NEW YORK

Published by the Feminist Press at the City University of New York
The Graduate Center, 365 Fifth Avenue
New York, NY 10016,
www.feministpress.org

First Feminist Press edition, 2004

09 08 07 06 05 04   5 4 3 2 1

Originally published in 1957 by Harper & Brothers.

Library of Congress Cataloging-in-Publication Data

Piper, Evelyn.
    Bunny Lake is Missing / Evelyn Piper; afterword by Maria Dibattista— 1st
Feminist Press ed.

    p. cm.
  Includes bibliographical references and index.
  ISBN 155861-474-5 (pbk. : alk. paper) — ISBN 1-5581-475-3 (cloth : alk. paper)
    1. Upper East Side (New York, N.Y.) Fiction. 2. Mothers and daughters—
Fiction. 3. Missing children—Fiction. I. Title.

  PS3531.I76B86 2004
  813'.54—dc22   2004009621

The Feminist Press is grateful to Sallie Bingham, Laura Brown, Jean Casella, Jan
Constantine, Blanche Wiesen Cook, Lis Driscoll, Barbara Grossman, Nancy
Hoffman, Florence Howe, Betty Prashker, and Susan Scanlan for their generosity
in supporting the publication of this book.

Text and cover design by Dayna Navaro
Printed on acid-free paper by Transcontinental Printing
Printed in Canada

Women write pulp? It seems like a contradiction in terms, given the tough-guy image of pulp fiction today. This image has been largely shaped by the noir revival of the past decade—by reprints of classics by Jim Thompson and best-sellers by neo-noir writer James Ellroy, the rerelease of classic film noir on video, and the revisioning of the form by Quentin Tarantino. Fans of such works would be hard pressed to name a woman pulp author, or even a character who isn't a menacing femme fatale.

But women did write pulp, in large numbers and in all the classic pulp fiction genres, from hard-boiled noirs to breathless romances to edgy science fiction and taboo lesbian pulps. And while employing the conventions of each genre, women brought a different, gendered perspective to these forms. Women writers of pulp often outpaced their male counterparts in challenging received ideas about gender, race, and class, and in exploring those forbidden territories that were hidden from view off the typed page. They were an important part of a literary phenomenon, grounded in its particular time and place, that had a powerful impact on American popular culture in the middle of the twentieth century, and continues to exert its influence today.

Pulp fiction encompasses a broader array of works, and occupies a more complex place in the literary, social, and commercial culture of its era, than the handful of contemporary revivals and tributes to pulp suggests. Pulp emerged as an alternative format for books in the 1930s, building on the popularity of pulp magazines, which flourished from the

1920s to the 1940s, and drawing on traditions established by the dime novel of the nineteenth and early twentieth centuries. The dime novel had developed the Western, the romance, the sleuth story, and the adventure story as genres, with narratives geared largely to young readers, in particular on the frontier. Pulp magazines, needing to compete with early motion pictures and to connect with an urban audience, offered similar stories with an edge. Grouping fiction or believe-it-or-not fact under themes like crime, horror, and adventure, magazines such as *Black Mask*, *Weird Tales*, and *Dime Adventure* demonstrated the existence of a market for inexpensive and provocative teen and adult reading matter. The move to book-length narratives provided an expanded scope for a voracious literature rooted in American popular culture, reflective of American obsessions, and willing to explore American underworlds.

Printed on wood-grain, or pulp, paper, and cheaply bound, the books were markedly different from hardbound editions. These first modern paperbacks served different purposes, too—entertainment, thrill, or introduction to "serious culture"—and were presumably read differently. Books intended for the pulp lists were undoubtedly produced differently, with less time given to the writing, and less money and status accruing to the authors. As pulp publishers grew in number (Fawcett, Pocketbook, Bantam, Ace, Signet, Dell), economic patterns emerged in the treatment of authors and texts: pulp authors often received one-time payment (no royalties); editors focused on keeping books short, tight, and engrossing; and author identity was often submerged beneath the publisher's pulp brand name and the lurid cover art that sold the books. Some pulp authors used pseudonyms to conceal an everyday identity behind a more saleable one, often of the opposite gender. Georgina Ann Randolph Craig (1908–1957) wrote prolifically as Craig Rice. Some used several names, each evocative of a genre they wrote in: Velma Young (1913–1997) published lesbian pulp under the name Valerie Taylor, poetry as Nacella Young, and romances as Francine Davenport. Eventually some contemporary authors emerged as brands themselves: a Faith Baldwin romance was a predictable product.

At the same time, classics and contemporary best-sellers were reincarnated as pulp, as the format absorbed and repositioned literature that might otherwise have been inaccessible to working-class readers. Pulp publishers seem to have selected classic fiction with an eye to class politics, favoring, for example, the French Revolution and Dickens. They tended to present science as an arena where good old-fashioned ingenuity and stick-to-itiveness win the day. The life of Marie Curie was a pulp hit. When classics were reprinted in pulp editions—for example, *The Count of Monte Cristo* or *The Origin of the Species*—author identity might move to the fore on covers and in descriptive copy, but in becoming pulp the works acquired a popular aura and gravitated into pulp genres such as adventure and romance. Again, when new titles like William Faulkner's *Sanctuary* or Mary McCarthy's *The Company She Keeps* were issued in pulp editions, the cover art planted the works firmly in pulp categories: ruined woman, Southern variety; the many adventures and many men of a fast city girl. The genre, more than the author's name, was the selling point.

As the stories in pulp magazines were marketed by themes, so book-length tales were distinctively packaged by genre—Dell used a red heart to mark its romance line, for instance. Over time there were Westerns, science fiction, romance, mystery, crime/noir, and various others to choose from. Genres were to a large extent gendered. Crime/noir, for instance, focused on a masculine world of detectives, crooks, femmes fatales (positioned as foils to men), corruption, and violence, all described in hard-boiled prose. Romance focused on women's problems around courtship, virginity, marriage, motherhood, and careers, earnestly or coyly described. Since genres were gendered, the implied assumption was that men wrote and read crime/noir and women wrote and read romances. In fact, this assumption proves largely false.

Because pulp genres tended to rely on formulaic treatments, it was not difficult for writers to learn the ingredients that make up noir or, for that matter, how to write a lesbian love scene. The fact that authorial name and persona were rarely linked to real-life identity further permitted writers to explore transgender, or transgenre, writing. In so doing, they might self-consciously accentuate the gendered elements of a given genre, sometimes approximating parody, or they might attempt to regender a genre—for instance, writing a Western that foregrounds a romance. These freedoms, combined with the willingness of pulp publishers to buy work from anyone with the skill to write, meant that women had the chance to write in modes that were typically considered antithetical to them, and to explore gender across all genres. Leigh Brackett (1915–1978), a premier woman author of pulp, wrote hard-boiled crime books, science fiction, and Westerns, in addition to scripting sharp repartee for Bogart and Bacall in *The Big Sleep* (director Howard Hawks hired her on the basis of her novel *No Good from a Corpse*—assuming she was a man, as did many of her fans). Other women authors wrote whodunnit mysteries with girl heroines, science fiction battles of the sexes, and romances that start with a Reno divorce. Women wrote from male perspectives, narrating from inside the head of a serial killer, a PI, or a small-town pharmacist who happens to know all the town dirt. They also wrote from places where women weren't supposed to go.

Notoriously, pulp explored U.S. subcultures, which then often generated their own pulp subgenres. Where 1930s and

1940s pulp depicted gangster life and small-town chicanery, 1950s and 1960s pulp turned its attention, often with a pseudoanthropological lens, to juvenile delinquents, lesbians (far more than gay men), and beatniks, introducing its readers to such settings as reform schools, women's prisons, and "dangerous" places like Greenwich Village. These books exploited subcultures as suggestive settings for sexuality and nonconformism, often focusing on transgressive women or "bad girls": consider *Farm Hussy* and *Shack Baby* (two of a surprisingly large group in the highly specific rural-white-trash-slut subgenre), *Reefer Girl* (and its competitor, *Marijuana Girl*), *Women's Barracks, Reform School Girl,* and *Hippie Harlot.* Other books posited menaces present in the heart of middle-class life: *Suburbia: Jungle of Sex* and *Shadow on the Hearth.* A growing African American readership generated more new lines, mysteries and romances with black protagonists. Though the numbers of these books were fairly small, their existence is significant. With a few notable exceptions, African Americans were almost never found in pulps written for white readers, except as racially stereotyped stock characters.

While a strengthened Hays Code sanitized movies in 1934, and "legitimate" publishers fought legal battles in order to get *Ulysses* and *Lady Chatterley's Lover* past the censors, pulp fiction, selling at twenty-five cents a book at newsstands, gas stations, and bus terminals, explored the taboo without provoking public outcry, or even dialogue. (Notably, though, pulp avoided the four-letter words that marked works like *Ulysses,* deploying instead hip street lingo to refer to sex, drink and drugs, and guns.) As famed lesbian pulp author Ann Bannon has noted, this "benign neglect provided a much-needed veil behind which we writers could work in peace." Pulp offered readers interracial romances during the segregation era, and blacklisted leftists encoded class struggle between pulp covers. The neglect by censors and critics had to do with the transience of pulp.

Circulating in a manner that matched the increasing mobility of American culture, pulps rarely adorned libraries, private or public. Small, slim, and ultimately disposable, they were meant for the road, or for easy access at home. They could be read furtively, in between household chores or during a lunch break. When finished, they could be left in a train compartment or casually stashed in a work shed. Publishers increasingly emphasized ease of consumption in the packaging of pulp: Ace produced "Ace Doubles," two titles reverse-bound together, so that the reader had only to flip the book over to enjoy a second colorful cover and enticing story; Bantam produced "L.A.s," specially sized to be sold from vending machines, the product's name evoking the mecca of the automobile and interstate highway culture; Fawcett launched a book club for its Gold Medal line, promising home delivery of four new sensational Gold Medal titles a month. To join, one cut out a coupon at the back of a Gold Medal book—clearly, no reluctance to damage a pulp volume would impede owners from acting on the special offer.

The mass appeal of pulp proved uncontainable by print. Characters and stories that originated in pulp soon found their way onto radio airwaves (e.g., *The Shadow*), onto the screen in the form of pre-Code sizzlers, noirs, and adventure films, and into comic books and newspaper comic strips. Through all these media, pulp penetrated the heart of the American popular imagination (and the popular image of America beyond its borders), shaping as well as reflecting the culture that consumed it.

Far more frequently than has been acknowledged, the source of these American icons, story lines, and genres were women, often working-class women who put bread on the table by creating imaginary worlds, or exploring existing but risky or taboo worlds, to fulfill the appetites of readers of both genders. But these writers, and the rich variety of work they produced, are today nearly invisible, despite the pulp revival of the last decade.

This revival has repopularized a hard-boiled, male world of pulp. Today's best-remembered pulp authors are not only male but also unapologetically misogynistic: pulp icon Jim Thompson's *A Hell of a Woman* and *A Swell-Looking Babe* are not untypical of the titles found among the noir classics recently restored to print.

In fact, it is interesting to note, even in a broader survey of the genres, how many male-authored, and presumably male-read, pulps were focused on women (remember *Shack Baby* and *Reefer Girl*)—a phenomenon not found in the highbrow literature of the period. Men even wrote a fair number of lesbian pulps. But more often than not, the women in these books are dangerous and predatory as well as irresistible, exploiting men's desire for their own purposes. Or they are wayward women who either come to a bad end, or come to their senses with the help of a man who sets them straight (in the various senses of the word). Some critics have noted that such female characters proliferated in the immediate post–World War II period, when servicemen were returning to a world in which women had occupied, briefly, a powerful position in the workplace and other areas of the public sphere—a world in which the balance between the genders had been irrevocably altered.

In contrast with these bad girls and femmes fatales were the heroines of traditional romance pulps, most of them relentlessly pretty and spunky girls-next-door. They occupied the centers of their own stories, and navigated sometimes complicated social and emotional terrain, but in the end always seemed to get—or be gotten by—their man.

Given this background, and given the strict generic dictates to which all successful pulp writers were subject, did women working in undeniably male-dominated pulp genres such as crime/noir write differently from their male counterparts? And did women writers of formulaic romances, both heterosexual and lesbian, reveal the genuine conflicts facing real women in their time, and explore the limits of female agency? They could hardly fail to do so.

Relatively little scholarship has been done on pulp fiction; less still on women writers of pulp. It is not possible to speculate on the intentions of women pulp authors, and few would suggest that they were undercover feminists seeking to subvert patriarchal culture by embedding radical messages in cheap popular novels. Yet from a contemporary vantage point, some of their work certainly does seem subversive, regardless of the intention behind it.

Women writers provided the first pulps with happy endings for lesbians: Valerie Taylor's *The Girls in 3-B* is a prime example of this suprisingly revolutionary phenomenon, and still more intriguing for its contrast of the different options and obstacles faced by heterosexual and homosexual women in the 1950s (with little doubt as to which looked better to the author). The femme fatale of *In a Lonely Place,* the luscious Laurel Gray, has brains and integrity, as well as curves—and in the end, she is not the one who turns out to be deadly. In fact, Dorothy B. Hughes's bold twist on the noir genre can be seen as addressing the crisis in postwar masculinity, with its backlash taken to the furthest extremes. The protagonist of Faith Baldwin's *Skyscraper* is typically pretty and plucky; she longs for domestic bliss and she loves her man. But she also loves the bustle and buzz of the office where she works, the rows of gleaming desks and file cabinets, the sense of being part of the larger, public world of business—and she epitomizes a new kind of heroine in a new kind of romance plot, a career girl with a wider set of choices to negotiate.

These premier books in the Feminist Press's Femmes Fatales series were selected for their bold and sometimes transgressive uses of genre forms, as well as the richness of their social and historical settings and their lively and skillful writing. We chose books that also seemed to have some impact on public consciousness in their time—in these cases, rather inexactly measured by the fact that they crossed over into different, and even more popular, media: Both *In a Lonely Place* and *Skyscraper* were made into films. And we can only speculate whether *The Girls in 3-B* played any part in inspiring *The Girls in Apartment 3-G,* the syndicated comic strip about three young working women (heterosexual, of course) living together in New York City, which debuted in 1961.

The enormous popularity of the Femmes Fatales series's first season, in 2003, confirms readers' intense interest in these rediscovered queens of pulp. In 2004, the series expands to include a second book by the incomparable Dorothy B. Hughes: *The Blackbirder*, a World War II espionage novel with a unique hard-boiled heroine. It also includes two books that achieved fame, again, primarily through the films they inspired. *Now, Voyager*, the renowned romantic melodrama that gave Bette Davis her favorite role, deals directly with issues of women's emotional, sexual, and social autonomy. The fascinating psychological thriller *Bunny Lake Is Missing*, made into a supremely creepy (and cult classic) film by Otto Preminger, introduces a hardboiled mom, who must rapidly transform herself from a handwringer to a gunslinger when her daughter is kidnapped.

In the past three decades, feminist scholars have laid claim to women's popular fiction as a legitimate focus of attention and scholarship, and a rich source of information on women's lives and thought in various eras. Some scholars have in fact questioned the use—and the uses—of the

term *popular fiction,* which seems to have been dispropor-
tionately applied to the work of women writers, especially
those who wrote "women's books." The Feminist Press
views the Femmes Fatales series as an important new initia-
tive in this ongoing work of cultural reclamation. As such, it
is also a natural expression of the Press's overall mission to
ensure that women's voices are fully represented in the public discourse, in the literary "canon," and on bookstore and
library shelves.

We leave it to scholars doing groundbreaking new work
on women's pulp—including our own afterword writers—
to help us fully appreciate all that these works have to
offer, both as literary texts and as social documents. And
we leave it to our readers to discover for themselves, as we
have, all of the entertaining, disturbing, suggestive, and
thoroughly fascinating work that can be found behind the
juicy covers of women's pulp fiction.

> Livia Tenzer, Editorial Director
> Jean Casella, Publisher
> New York City
> July 2004

This time when Blanche came in the woman was alone in her vegetable store. Waiting for the woman to pick an apple off the shining pyramid of them, Blanche could not help glancing at the dark corner where, each evening until this one, the boy had leaned against the dusty potatoes and stared at her.

The woman lifted an apple off the pyramid, near the base. "He isn't here. Eddie. My boy."

"Oh, is he your son?" There was no resemblance at all to this big, firm, healthy woman. Opposites, Blanche thought. "I think I saw your son this morning." The woman suddenly pressed the apple to her breast. It was a startling gesture.

"You saw Eddie? Where?"

"Outside my house." Blanche took a dime from her purse.

"Did he say something to you?"

"He couldn't. I was inside the glass doors. I was in the lobby waving good-by to my mother."

"So he found out where you live and all!" She bit her lip. "After that—did you see Eddie after that?"

"I'm afraid not." The boy Eddie was in some trouble. He looked like trouble, Blanche thought. "The minute a taxi came for Mother, I went upstairs again."

"You come out again, didn't you? Did you see my Eddie when you come out?"

"No. I took my little girl to school when I came out next and I was in a terrible rush. Is there some trouble with your son?"

"You're the trouble, Missus! Eddie and his papa had a terrible fight last night. Over you," she said.

"Me? But Mrs.—"

"Negrito."

"Mrs. Negrito, I've never even spoken to your son."

"You think you got to speak? You didn't notice every night how he ate you up with his eyes? His papa noticed!"

"I'm very sorry, Mrs. Negrito." Blanche held out her hand for the apple, remembering the boy's narrow, deep-set eyes, the feverish way he wet his lips, the way he kept them slightly apart. "I have to go now."

Mrs. Negrito clasped the apple. "It's because Eddie never had a girl. You know! George shouldn't have gone at him so hot and heavy: 'An apple a day keeps the doctor away. An apple a day keeps Eddie away!' You know. Because you buy that apple every time. 'You going to stand there till that apple drops down, Eddie? You'll wait until she drops for you, Eddie?' Oh, my God," the woman said, "he got Eddie wild! 'You'll see if I'm waiting until she drops,' Eddie yelled. Because Eddie's little and quiet, George—my hubby—he doesn't know!" Now, giving up, Mrs. Negrito put the apple in a paper sack and took Blanche's dime at last.

Blanche repeated, "I'm very sorry, Mrs. Negrito. I won't come here again." The woman looked at her as if she had said something very stupid, shrugged as if she had come to her senses much too late.

She would not buy Bunny's apples in that store so the incident was over. When she came out of the subway, she would walk down Lexington Avenue a way and not go down Eighty-sixth Street at all. Blanche walked quickly, holding the paper sack away from her body as if it contained something that might soil her suit, and because she was holding it that way, as if it could drip, she understood what had happened in the vegetable store on Friday evening. As she left, she had heard the big man, Mr. Negrito, laugh behind her, and then Mrs. Negrito had gasped, so sharply that she had turned her head to see. The three of them were just standing there staring at the pyramid of apples, but now she knew what Eddie had done in retaliation for his father's teasing. He had spat at the apples. It had been spittle she had seen sliding down the shining flanks of the apples. Holding the paper sack away from her, Blanche went to the curb and dropped it. She brushed her hands together and told herself to brush off her mind, too, wanting nothing of the apple thing to touch Bunny.

If she hadn't allowed plenty of time, that vegetable woman would have made her late, but it was just five now.

Just in time, Blanche thought, seeing the other mothers going into the red door of the nursery school. She went in also and stood looking at the darkish hall with the two old wooden benches along the wall on which the others had seated themselves. One of the women, wearing bright blue slacks, shoved closer to her neighbor on the bench and made a place beside her.

"Come and join the rest of us stage-door Johnnies."

Blanche smiled gratefully and sat down.

"Boy or girl?" the woman in the blue slacks asked.

"Bunny's a girl. Felicia, really; I just call her Bunny."

"Is Bunny your only one? Don't answer that! I can see by the stars in your eyes that she is. Look at her, Maeve; she can't wait for Bunny to come down those stairs!"

Maeve, wearing oxford-gray slacks, grinned. "Wait until you have three little bunnies in the old hutch! You won't be so anxious!"

"There couldn't be three like Bunny." Blanche looked at her wrist watch. It was five after five. "Except for one week while I was looking for an apartment for us, this is the first we've ever been separated. And Mother was with her then. This is the first Bunny's ever been with strangers."

"Have patience, have patience. They're supposed to be down by five and don't think the teachers aren't as anxious as you are, but you know the little darlings when anybody's in a hurry! Sometimes it takes an extra ten minutes for the poor teachers to clean them up enough for us to recognize our precious angels when we see them!"

Blanche looked at the hall again and it seemed dirty to her. She told herself that the boy Eddie had done it. When he spat at the apples, he dirtied the whole city for her, that was it. But the impression remained. The walls were brilliantly blue, but the paint was so lumpy that it seemed as if someone had simply painted the bright clean colors right over whatever had been underneath; that dirt, insects, mouse droppings were permanently fixed in the paint like flies in amber. She said to the woman in the bright blue slacks, "This is a good nursery school, isn't it? I just moved into New York two weeks ago, and all I know about the school is from the brochure, really."

"Well, my oldest, Petey, went here all last year and I didn't get any complaints." She pulled a face. "Of course, at the time Pete could only speak about ten words, so you wouldn't exactly call him a very reliable reference!"

"Don't look so *serious*, Mrs.—?"

"Lake," Blanche said.

"She's just teasing you, Mrs. Lake. It's a fine school. Miss Benton is pure Boston—you can rely on good old Boston any time. Your little girl will be fine here."

Another woman leaned across so she could see Blanche. "Any school that will keep my Jerry safe and happy and out of my hair from nine to five, five days a week, is okay by me. I have a pair of fourteen-month-old twins under-foot at home and that's about all I can take!"

"It's talk like that, Alice, that gave that Ford woman her high opinion of us!" She said to Blanche, "There was this teacher here last year who honestly thought we weren't fit to be mothers!"

"Ford wasn't fit to be a teacher. They got rid of her, thank goodness!"

"Some people don't approve of nursery schools," Blanche said. "My own mother doesn't."

"Nonsense. It's the best place for them. Keeps them safe and keeps them happy."

Safe and happy, Blanche thought. Of course. The two women in slacks started to talk to each other and, so she wouldn't seem to be eavesdropping, she took the letter from Chloe out of her purse. There hadn't been time to read it that morning. It was one of those envelopes and stationery in one, blue and flimsy. Blanche tore down the sides where it was perforated and crumpled the strip of paper in her hand. As she reached for some place to throw the strip, Blanche saw the red-headed boy near the door and smiled at him. He blushed. (About ten. Shy, Blanche thought. When Bunny is ten, she'll be shy, too, maybe. Right now, of course, the whole world's her friend.) Blanche smiled at the red-headed boy again and began to read the letter:

DEAR BLANCHE,

Married to a strange Englishman three whole weeks and still ecstatically happy except that I miss you and Bunny so much. Gavin and I talked about Bunny all across the wide Atlantic. He was terribly taken with her and *teddibly* disappointed that you wouldn't let us have her the way your mother wanted. Much as I love Bunny, I would have been disappointed if you had. Bunny belongs to you. Not that I had any hopes—that was pure mother and not her girl Blanche! You stick by your guns, old thing! Certainly, as your mother says, Bunny needs a father, and—as I'm discovering every minute—a husband comes in right handy, but he'll be Mr. Right and not Mr. Albert Stakely Wrong! Gavin is concerned about you all alone in the big city, but you won't be alone long. All the world loves a lovely, and you're a lovely, Blanche. Will write again as soon as I meet Gavin's folks—excuse me—Pater and Mater!

With all my love,

CHLOE WRIGHT BAINTER

Blanche, smiling at Chloe's letter, looked up and saw that the red-headed boy had come up to her and was staring.

Gray Slacks said, "It's not your fatal beauty, Mrs. Lake. Chrissie is here to collect his little sister but what he is really interested in collecting is stamps."

"Would you like this one, Chrissie? It's from England." She was about to tear off the corner with the stamp on it, but the boy stopped her. He collected *covers*, he said.

"Envelopes," Gray Slacks explained.

"I got three hundred and four."

Chrissie was looking hungrily at her letter from Chloe. The nice woman in gray slacks was watching. Blanche hesitated. As Chloe had written she was alone, and even a letter from a friend— But that was silly. This nice woman might be her friend if she didn't show herself up too stingy to part with a letter.

"Do you have a pencil?" she asked Chrissie.

When he gave her one, she crossed over the body of the letter. "Personal," she said to Chrissie.

"Yeah," he said. "Thank you."

"Here they come now," said the gray-slacks one.

Blanche looked up and saw, at the head of the stairs, a young woman in an orange smock which shone like a lantern. She had two children by the hand and behind her trooped the others, each wearing blue jeans and a little jacket. They looked adorable, Blanche thought.

The bright blue slacks narrowed her eyes. "Those are the big boys and girls."

The description "big boys and girls" would have made Blanche smile except even they seemed so tiny to be sent off to school that she felt a sudden fear of having left Bunny, so much smaller, so much more helpless. "How old is yours?" she asked.

"Petey's five. There he is now! Hi, Pete! Timmy's three. June sixth. Just got in under the ropes, Timmy did."

"Bunny was three in April."

"An old lady."

"She looked such an infant when I walked out and left her. Her eyes were the biggest thing about her. I have to, though. I have a job."

"In an office? Maeve, remember when you had a job? Nine to five? And got paid for what you did? Remember when you had holidays, Maeve?"

"Do I! Don't let Emily get you down. This is a fine school and they do wonders for the children. You'll see. Hello, Chic," she said to a little boy in a red corduroy jacket and a red beanie. "Your mom's outside with your sister and the baby buggy."

"All the other mommys are outside," the teacher said. "Everybody in our group has a mommy outside waiting. You remember from last year, don't you, Anne? Don't you, Perry?"

"Outside," Perry said.

"Big as a penny," Blanche whispered to the gray slacks, "and cute as a button." But not beautiful like Bunny, she thought, and glanced toward the stairs again, for as the wavering line of children went out into the street, she could hear fresh sounds from upstairs and looked into the dimness eagerly. She wondered if it would be all right to ask Bunny's teacher—how ridiculous—Bunny's *teacher*—how Bunny had taken her first day in school. Had she made friends? (Made *friends*—Bunny!) Had she eaten the strange food for the first time without Mommy there to tell her stories—and drunk milk out of a glass that didn't have a bunny rabbit on it? Had they taken the chill off the milk? Had bunny managed to take a nap on one of the small cots she had seen this morning? Blanche was so glad she had gone back, even though they were so late, when they discovered that Bunny had forgotten her cuddly toy she always went to sleep with. And had Bunny been a young lady all day and had she wet again?

"Now there's Timmy. Hi, Tim, how's the boy?"

Timmy was coming downstairs holding the low rail with one hand and a little girl's hand with the other. Not Bunny, though. "He's so sweet," Blanche whispered. He had a most solemn expression.

"I'll swap sight unseen for your little girl. Which is yours?"

Blanche stood up and moved toward the stairs a little: Not the children holding to the orange-smocked teacher's hands. She could see traces of tears on the boy's face nearest her. Did that mean that only the crybabies got to walk downstairs holding on to Teacher? Oh, brave little Bunny! Not the two children after that, not with Timmy. Seven, eight, nine, ten. "How many are there in the group?" Ten, the brochure said.

Oxford-gray Slacks moved toward her Timmy. "Ten. Ten nursery-school pupils to one teacher; that's the law in New York City, isn't it, Miss Green?" She kissed Timmy's cheek. "Are you *sticky*, kid!" Timmy still clung to his partner's hand. "Look, Miss Green, just like his old man! Timmy doesn't want to let go of his new girl friend!"

"Timmy and Bessie have been good friends all day. The rest of the mothers are outside. Come on, people!"

Blanche started to ask Miss Green about Bunny but the boy who had been crying began again, so she stepped back toward the wall. Gray Slacks, having detached the girl friend's hand, lifted Timmy and set him down on the bench and was smoothing down his curly hair. "Bunny wasn't there," Blanche said.

"Not there? Probably overslept then. They nap after lunch and if the little ones oversleep, Miss Green would let them have their sleep out. I stopped her letting Petey because then I'd never get him off at bedtime."

"It would be a miracle, Bunny napping. I don't think she's slept during her nap time once in six months."

"Wet, then." Gray slacks moistened a handkerchief and applied it to Timmy's sticky cheek. "Wet and rewet, maybe. Did you bring enough extras for her?" She pulled the corduroy beanie down on Timmy's head.

"I didn't bring any extras," Blanche said.

"Didn't they *tell* you? Well, your living doll must be upstairs waiting to dry out, then. I tell you what, you can take a set out of Timmy's cubby." She saw that Blanche didn't understand. "That's what they call them—cubbies, cubby-holes. Each child has his own. They're marked with the kids' names. Aren't they, Tim?"

"That's very kind of you. I'll get them back by morning."

"It's darn funny you weren't told. With the Threes it's the first thing to remember. I mean—after all—"

"I suppose they did and I forgot. I'll go up and get Bunny. One flight up and to the right."

"Two flights up and to the left."

"But I distinctly remember—I guess Bunny's in another Three group. There they come now!"

"Those elephants? That's a Five, I think. No, there's only one group of Threes. Third floor and to the left. The Threes use the roof garden up there instead of the yard or the park; that's why they put them up there. Well, so long—and you take an outfit of Timmy's." She lifted the little boy down. "Let's get out of here before that troop of elephants tramps us down, Tim. Run for your life!"

The little boy screamed for joy and ran off after his mother, whose wide rear, outlined by the tight pants, wriggled as she ran. "I like her," Blanche thought, watching them. The little boy, Timmy wasn't afraid of a herd of elephants while his mother was with him. Now that the children had come closer, Blanche could see that they were older than Bunny. She waited while the children lunged past her noisily. This teacher was older, too. She looked tired; the brilliant orange smock, apparently a uniform for the teachers, was not becoming. "Excuse me," Blanche said. "Isn't there a Three group on the second floor this year?"

"Topside." She jerked her finger up. "Threes topside, right, Marie? We stow the Threes topside, don't we, Marie?"

She was talking as much to keep the thin little girl whose hand she held busy as to answer Blanche. (The little girl's mouth was trembling as she watched her classmates tumbling out of the door.)

"Marie, this mommy's little—"

"Girl," Blanche said, starting upstairs.

"This mommy's little girl is stowed away topside. Wait a minute!" Blanche stopped. "Aren't the Threes down yet?"

"They're all out, just Bunny isn't because she wet her clothes." She was sure of this now.

"Didn't you bring any spares?—to stow away topside, Marie!"

"Marie enjoyed the word; that was why this teacher kept repeating "topside." It showed how sensitive the teacher was to the little girl, Blanche told herself, approving. "I'm afraid this mommy forgot. I won't forget again." She touched Marie's soft hair as she passed her.

"This mommy's going to try to improve—topside!" She tapped Marie's white forehead softly and grinned, and Marie rewarded her with a shaky smile.

"That's the way! Now, Marie, let's go into the office and we'll put you to work while we wait for Mommy."

Orange Smock opened a door to the front of the hall and she and Marie went inside. Marie, Blanche told herself, trusted

Orange Smock; you could see that. The building was very quiet now with the children gone, and dim for all the brave colors. This was an old brownstone house—fireproofed (the brochure had stated) and renovated, but they hadn't improved the hall very much. Modernized where it *counts*, Blanche thought, put the improvements where it *mattered*. The room in which she had left Bunny had been beautifully light and airy. (But surely not on the third floor? Of course it had been on the third floor if the teacher said it was. She had been so rushed this morning and so nervous about leaving Bunny for the first time that she simply had not counted correctly.)

When she reached the second floor, she was certain that this was where she had left Bunny this morning. Blanche paused, then shook her head. Could it have been—mustn't it have been because she and Bunny had come so late? The teacher who had called—Miss Ditmars—had said that they did not want the little ones upset on this first day at seeing a mother just after their mothers had left, so the teacher must have told her to leave Bunny in what was the room where the older children were, on this floor. She started up the next flight. Leave Bunny on the second floor. Deposit child here. Child deposit. Child safety deposit, Blanche told herself.

It was because this was the first day and so much had happened that she felt nervous. "And darling, when I stood there in the hall and saw all your little classmates coming downstairs and you weren't with them—" NOT TO BE SAID TO BUNNY! What a terrible thing to say to Bunny! Darling Bunny with her big brown eyes and the twitchy button nose.

Blanche turned left to the front of the building and stood for a moment outside the door marked CHILD PSYCHOLOGY, waiting, so that she wouldn't appear breathless and anxious when she saw Bunny. Then, because it was so quiet in the room when she threw the door open that she could only think of Bunny being put to bed for punishment—because Bunny wasn't happily playing with the blocks Blanche had seen in the morning, or with the finger paints or the plasticine, or any of the equipment the brochure had listed—she called, "Bunny! Bunny!"

The room was empty.

No. The teacher must have put Bunny in one of the little cots which were around the corner of the L-shaped room. (And not for punishment! Never, never had she given Bunny the idea that bed was punishment, and certainly a nursery school—) "Here's Mommy, darling! Darling, we're going to borrow dry clothes from the little boy named Timmy!" She hurried across the linoleum floor. "And after dinner we'll wash them and then we'll put them on the radiator to dry—"

The cots were set in stalls, each with a low enclosure so that the children who wanted to could really get to sleep, the brochure had said. Bunny must really be asleep.

Although she intended to wake Bunny, now she whispered her name. Under that mound of green blanket? "Bunny?"

There was no one under the green blanket.

Blanche called out, "Bunny!"; then, hearing how shrill her voice was, added, "Come out, come out wherever you are! Bunny—that's a game Mommy used to play. *Do you know that game, Bunny? 'Come out, come out, wherever you are?' Do you know that game, Bunny?"*

Blanche went out of the Threes room and down to the second floor, to the room on the right. She had brought Bunny to the Fours on the second floor. She had left Bunny there because the teacher had told her to leave Bunny with the Fours. (After all, three in April—whereas that little Timmy hadn't been three until June sixth!) Bunny would be right where she had left her.

Blanche opened the door to the room on the right. In this room the children had "co-operated" to build a—something— of blocks. (Bunny would tell her what it was supposed to be.)

"Here's Mommy, Bunny! What is that—*thing*—the children built in the middle of the floor?"

She went out into the hall again and threw open the door of the room to the left. "Are you in here, Bunny?"

They wouldn't just give Bunny another child's dry clothes without his consent. So when Bunny wetted and there were no dry clothes for her to get into, they had to take poor Bunny out of her group.

Children were very possessive about their own things. Not that she needed to read that; even Bunny was possessive about her things. Bunny's dwess. Bunny's *tschair*. Bunny hadn't got over not having her things in New York yet. But even so, Bunny would give any child anything of hers if she was asked nicely. (You certainly are a doting mother, aren't you?)

She would find Bunny in the office where the pale little Marie child had been taken to wait for her mother.

Marie was sitting behind the big desk happily stamping PAID over a huge sheet of newsprint spread before her. The teacher was at the window now, smoking a cigarette. She glanced up quickly as Blanche entered, then turned away again. (Looking out the window for Marie's mother, wishing Marie's mother would come and take her child home? Well, here was Bunny's mother come to take *her* child home.)

Bunny was probably in the room behind the sliding doors.

"*Your* mommy will be here soon, Marie. You get the paper all stamped up, won't you? Miss Benton isn't here, if you want her."

"No, it's Bunny I want. Don't you remember? You told me in the hall about the Threes being— topside?"

"Of course. It's kind of dark in the hall and I didn't—This is my first day here. I'm fresh from the Walton School in Chicago. The cement hasn't hardened on our building yet— not that there is any—cement, I mean. All glass, of course. But, of course, what counts in a nursery school isn't the bricks and mortar, is it?"

Blanche said, "Of course it isn't." She gestured toward the sliding doors. "Have they put Bunny in there?"

"The kitchen and pantry are in there."

"But she wet—and—"

"You're the one who forgot to bring the extras? Oh, and she wet—then she could be in the infirmary. No, we call it the 'quiet room,' don't we, Marie? Bunny must be in the 'quiet room.' It's on the second floor, rear. I'd show you but I don't want to leave Marie alone."

"Of course not." But who was with Bunny? Second floor, rear. I went right and left, but not rear. Blanche smiled at Marie and went upstairs again.

The quiet room was quiet and empty. Although there was no suggestion of hospital about the small room, which had a cot with a cheerful plaid throw over it, and a wicker chair and a table and gaily flowered draperies on the narrow window, "hospital" was what came to Blanche's mind. The teacher in the office didn't know about it because they wouldn't have come into her classroom and told her that a little girl called Bunny in Group Three had been taken sick and rushed to the hospital. The doctor had been called in and that was why the director, Miss Benton, wasn't in her office. The director was the one who had taken Bunny to the hospital. They had tried to call her at home, and, of course, no one was there. (She had decided not to give them her business telephone until she could explain about that.) She hurried back downstairs to the office.

Blanche's voice explaining her theory to the teacher was enough to frighten Marie, who stopped stamping PAID, threw the stamp on the floor and climbed off the chair.

The teacher (as Blanche was happy to see, visualizing the director comforting Bunny in the hospital) scooped Marie up into her arms and, retrieving the stamp from the floor, sat down at the desk with Marie in her lap.

"Let's keep our voices even, shall we?" She renewed the ink on the stamp, stamped PAID hard, then held out the stamp to the child. (Marie had her thumb in her mouth.) "Why do you think hospital?"

"Well, she isn't here. Bunny. Anywhere I can see."

"Gently does it!" Gently, she took Marie's thumb out of her mouth. "Which group did you say she was in?"

"Bunny is three."

"Three is Ruth. She left, but—just a minute— You still have that corner to fix up, Marie." She looked down at the child, noticing that her delicate mouth was quivering. "Could you sit with Marie, Mrs.— "

"Lake."

"Mrs. Lake, you sit with Marie and she'll show you how to use the PAID stamp. Marie, you'll show Bunny's mommy, won't you?" She stood up and waved Blanche into the seat, then put Marie on her lap. "Please show Bunny's mommy—I think Dorothy is in there having a cup of tea. She lives out in Scarsdale and waits for a certain train, anyhow. I'll get Dorothy, maybe she knows—while you show Bunny's mommy how to stamp, Marie."

Blanche hugged Marie, because she could feel her trembling. Marie had outgrown her baby fat; such a thin, rigid little girl! Blanche could feel her bones. She held Marie closely and dropped her chin gently onto the small, smooth head the way she did with Bunny sometimes. All little girls had hair like silk. All little girls sighed when they relaxed in your arms.

The door slid open and a young woman came out. "I'm Dorothy Klein. I'm afraid I don't quite understand—"

"I'm Bunny's mother. Bunny Lake. I can't seem to find Bunny anywhere in the place."

"Bunny?"

"Felicia."

"What's the matter with Bunny? Bunny's a fine name! Bunny isn't in my group and I thought that the Threes were all on their way home—"

Marie screamed.

"I'm sorry," Blanche said. "I must have squeezed her too tight. The Threes aren't all on their way home, Miss Klein. Bunny isn't."

Marie's teacher said, "Dorothy says your Bunny couldn't be with Louise Benton—the director, Miss Benton—because Dorothy knows definitely that she's at an agency trying to promote a cook. The one who was supposed to be here today didn't turn up and there was quite a mess. It doesn't seem likely that Miss Benton would take your Bunny along to the agency with her—" She saw Blanche bite her lips. "I suppose she *could* have—"

"Why would she do that?" Dorothy asked. "Where's Elvira?" "Gone home. And what would a Three be doing with the Fives? They'd murder her!"

"Do you think they did?" Blanche shook her head, laughing at herself. "I don't mean *murder*, of course. I mean unless I'm mistaken I did leave her in the wrong room with the bigger ones." Now she wasn't laughing. "Do you think they could have hurt her?"

"All I have to do is open my big mouth! Now, Mrs.— "

"Lake," Blanche said. "Lake."

"We do believe in a certain amount of freedom here, Mrs. Lake, but we certainly don't permit Fours or Fives to beat up on a Three!"

"I can't get over the idea that Bunny's been taken to a hospital."

"Without notifying you?"

"Parents are notified before anything is done to any child." Topside glanced out of the window, grabbed up her coat from a chair and thrust her arms into it. "There comes your mommy, Marie!" She said to Miss Klein, "I'm afraid some other arrangement will have to be made about Marie after today. I have to get to 108th Street three times a week." She showed her teeth. "Pyorrhea! Isn't that the mostest? Dorothy will get your trouble straightened out, Mrs. Lake. You have to hang around anyhow, don't you Dorothy?" She buttoned Marie's jacket and scooped her up. "Come on, we'll beat Mommy to the door." She carried Marie off and they heard the door slam.

"Of course!" Dorothy said. "I know! Gosh, I should! It's happened before! Someone else called for Bunny!" She shook her head affirmatively more vigorously, to override Blanche's headshake. "Take my word for it, Mrs. Lake, some member of your family came and took her home and there you'll find her all anxious to tell Mommy about her first day in school."

"Nobody would have—"

Dorothy snapped her fingers at Blanche. "Right? I can tell by your expression that somebody would have, after all!" She walked toward the room beyond the sliding doors.

"I suppose it is *possible* that my mother could have—"

"Your mother did! I haven't taught for six years without knowing what grandmothers can do—their range is enormous!" She went into the other room and came back with her pocketbook, coat and hat. "You go on home and—if you'll take my advice—give your mother hell. If she just came here without a word to you and nipped Bunny up without so much as a by-your-leave she should be given hell the first time, or it will go on happening."

She put the hat on. "Grandmothers have their uses and their abuses. Now, if you'll excuse me, I have to get my train at Grand Central or my mother will give *me* hell!" She held the front door open for Blanche. "Your mother will tell you that she never thought for a minute you'd be upset—suddenly couldn't wait to hear how her grand-daughter made out and got her afore you!"

It was sunny and October out on the street. Blanche stood still. Miss Klein gently pushed her by the shoulder, nodded and hurried off.

The way home lay in the same direction Miss Klein had taken. Blanche had to walk west to First Avenue, but she didn't want to keep the teacher any longer. She walked slowly to give Miss Klein a head start, and then began to run.

Something had made her mother change her mind and come back to the city. Any number of things could have, Blanche thought doubtfully. Once I know what it was, I'll know that it was sensible—that I should have thought of it at once. And, if she had come back—as Miss Klein suggested— How furious Mother would have been when she came back and saw the mess I left this morning in the kitchen. Mother wouldn't admit it, but part of the reason she must have decided to call for Bunny would be to have someone (even Bunny) to complain to. Mother doesn't realize how much she complains about me. "Bunny," Mother would say, "how in the world will Mommy manage when Granny is gone for good? Granny goes away and look how Mommy leaves this kitchen."

"Mommy," Bunny would have repeated. It would be all that she could understand of what Mother was saying. Bunny's tiny perfect mouth rounding, saying "Mommy."

"You see what all this talk about being able to manage without me comes to, Bunny?" Mother would have said, plunging the breakfast dishes into the dishpan of soapy water as if she were drowning them.

Bunny would be waiting for her. Blanche caught a glimpse of the white fur in the toy-shop window. "My pussy!" Bunny had said, pressing her nose against the window in an ecstasy of longing. She would buy it for Bunny now. She would go into the store now and buy it for Bunny, put it into her arms. ("Oh, Mother!" Blanche whispered, running again. "How could you do this to me? Didn't you realize what it would mean for me to come for Bunny and not find her there?")

"Do you realize what things mean to me?" Mother would say. The white crescents of anger would appear around her nostrils as they always did when they got onto that subject. "Do you realize what it means to me not to be able to hold up my head with my oldest friends? Forcing me to tell lies all over the place! Making me want to sell my own house where I've lived ever since your father and I were married! Needing to leave the place where your father is buried! Don't you talk about not realizing things to me."

No, don't talk about not realizing things. Best not to reproach Mother for taking Bunny without letting her know. Best not to buy the toy now. Waste time buying toy. Best to hurry home as fast as she could and hold Bunny tight in her arms and let her cheek slide against her silk hair as she had done with Marie.

Blanche heard her heels on the pavement and they seemed such a slow beat. Surely she could run faster than that?

The self-service elevator was there for once, waiting, which looked as if Mother might have been the last person who used it. Most of the people in this house didn't bother to press the button after they got out of the car, but Mother did. When Mother had come in, she must have lifted Bunny up and let her press the 5 button to take them up, and then let her press the M button, and that was why the elevator was waiting now. Mother was always sweet to Bunny. Mother had stood there patiently while Bunny watched the indicator light flash on in each of the little numbers. Mother had taken Bunny home from school because she loved her.

Blanche leaned against the back of the elevator, wishing it weren't so slow. She rang the doorbell of the apartment and waited, quietly, so that she would hear the footsteps inside, but then called out, "I've got my keys, Mother, don't bother!" She gritted her teeth because her hand shook so badly that she could not open the catch of her pocketbook. "It's Mommy, Bunnsy! It's just me, Mother!" She bit her lip and leaned her elbow against the side of the door to steady her hand, thinking that if anyone came out of the other apartments on the floor, they would think that the new sublet tenant of 5A was a fine one, coming back home so drunk at six o'clock in the evening that she wasn't even capable of unlocking her door! "Bunny!" she called, throwing the door open. "Bunny! Mother!"

—————————

"I should have telephoned," Blanche thought. "Oh, why did I come all the way back? I should have telephoned first!" She would have to telephone the school now. Even though what was hardest was to be still even for a minute, she would telephone first. She walked to the telephone and lifted the receiver, then put it back. She didn't know the number.

Blanche hurried to the rickety little desk to find the letter from the Benton School which had the telephone number printed on it—quicker than the directory with her hands so—

Not quicker, she thought, pulling at the right-hand drawer, which didn't open easily. She had pulled it evenly, of course; the next thing would be the loose knob coming off in her hands. Always, always when you were in a rush! Telephone book, she thought, and picking it up dialed Information and then propped the phone between her shoulder and her neck so that her hands would be free to turn the pages. So thick, Blanche thought, so many people in Manhattan. "I want the number of the Benton Nursery School on East Eighty-third Street," she said, turning pages as she spoke. A race between her hands and Information. She got there first and hung up. How annoyed Information would be.

The telephone rang and rang. "Tele*phome*," Bunny said when ever she heard theirs ringing, and grinned proudly, showing all her perfect teeth, because she really knew better. She just said "telephome" because it made Blanche smile.

Blanche slammed down the receiver. Could Bunny have wandered out of the room that morning? Could Bunny have tried to follow her when she left? Unwilling to be deposited? Before the teacher came from around the L part? Because, if she had, before the teacher had even seen her . . . So that the teacher thought she had kept Bunny home after all? She should have talked with the teacher then and there, even if she was late, even if it had all been arranged so carefully. The children had seen Bunny; there had been several of them there—but too young to report? Even if it had been the Fours (but why the Fours?) she had left Bunny with, they were surely too young to report that a little dark girl had been left there by her mother while the teacher had been busy in the L part of the room. Too young to know that Bunny should have been stopped when she walked out after her mother?

But even if no one had seen Bunny going down—where? Down too far?

"One—two—eight, ten," Bunny always counted, going carefully downstairs.

Down one flight too many? There must be a basement in that horrible old brownstone house. Suppose Bunny had gone down into the basement? Fallen down the steps?

Why hadn't she searched the place except for the class-rooms?

She saw the policeman directing the traffic on Lexington Avenue. If no one was in the building when she reached it, she would get that policeman. Mother used to frighten her about policemen, telling her that they would put her in prison if she was such a bad girl, but the once she had heard Mother saying that to Bunny she had stopped that. So Bunny wouldn't be afraid of a policeman.

Because Blanche wanted it so badly, as she walked—since by then she had had to stop running; her lungs were bursting—she could see the black of Bunny's hair against the blue of the police-man's uniform as he came up the cellar steps carrying her. "Here's your little girl safe and sound," he said, and Blanche saw Bunny's starfish hand reach up to touch the policeman's shiny buttons. Bunny wouldn't be afraid when that policeman found her, and Bunny wouldn't have been afraid of the dark cellar either the way she, Blanche, used to be scared of the dark. Bunny had always had a night light, so Bunny wouldn't have been afraid to go down into the dark cellar. And that is why a three-year-old child, perfectly conscious, completely unharmed, could have stayed in a dark cel-lar patiently waiting.

"I wouldn't have believed it possible," the policeman would say, looking down at Bunny's dark hair resting against his uni-form and at her little hand admiringly fingering the brass but-tons. "Honestly," the policeman would say, "I wouldn't have believed it! You could have knocked me over with a feather when I saw her sitting there, not a scratch on her—"

The front door of the school was locked. Blanche, leaning against it, breathing with difficulty, pressed the bell and kept her finger on it.

"I wouldn't have believed it," the cop would say.

Did she believe it? Could she believe it? Safe and sound? Not a scratch on her? Blanche counted twenty-five as slowly as she could and took as deep breaths as she could before she began running for the policeman.

The people in New York City were no different from the people in Providence. Heads turned as she ran by, but in Providence someone would have asked her why she was running and could they help. Here, it seemed to her, now, the staring people were kept from asking by the fear that they would be made fools of if they should ask; that it would turn out to be some kind of trick, some new advertising scheme, some joke on them. But the police would help her, she thought. "Officer! Officer!"

He heard her voice above the traffic and, directing it, moved toward her. While she told him, he took her arm to hold her up.

"My little girl is locked up in the school and I can't get in."

"You go to the precinct station. Get in a cab. Sixty-seventh Street."

"Officer!"

"Lady!" He gestured. "I have a job here!"

"She's only three! *Three!*"

"Three years old? In school?"

"Nursery school!" Blanche reached for the arm that was supporting her and began to pull at him. "The Benton Nursery School on Eighty-third Street. Hurry!"

"I can't leave my post, lady. Go to the— Okay," he said. "Okay." He took one more look at the cars behind him and began to walk rapidly, speaking over his shoulder. "Okay, I'll put in a call at the box for you."

"No! You come!"

"Miss, I can't. This isn't life and death, Miss! They won't be but a couple minutes. There's the box, see?" He opened it and kept his back turned, not wanting to see her face any longer than he could help. "You go to that school and someone from the precinct station will be along." With great relief, he heard her running steps.

When Blanche got back to the door, she began to bang on it. In the back of her mind she remembered a movie she had seen about people trapped in a mine—and when they heard the banging from above— She could not feel it as her fists smacked the wood.

"What is it?" a woman's voice asked from the sidewalk.

"Search me!"

"What's your trouble, Miss?"

"My little girl—"

"Locked in the school?"

"And where was she so the kid *got* locked up? Late? Couldn't leave the television set! Call themselves mothers sending tiny little babies to school! All day long, too!"

Blanche began pounding with her palms instead of her fists, but she could hear the woman on the pavement anyhow.

"If anything's happened it's a judgment, that's what I say! That's what they learn them in college—how to drop their kids and leave them for others to take care of—"

"I got a cat does that—"

The voices stopped when the policeman came.

"You're not going to get anywhere that way," he said, meaning the banging, but he would not take Blanche's word that there was nobody inside to answer it, and rang the bell himself.

Finally the policeman tipped back his hat and looked doubtfully at the thick door. "I'll see if there's a window open in the rear. You wait here. Generally, in back—"

Blanche could not understand where he was going, but one of the women explained to the others that the cop was going into the next house and get to the back yard over the fence.

"Probably bust the fence down—"

"Naw, that's the firemen do that!"

"How come a kid came to be locked in, anyhow?"

"Call themselves mothers and don't care enough to take care of their own, that's how. Some people don't deserve to have kids!"

But a school is where you leave children, Blanche thought. A school is where children are safe. Nothing happens to children in school. Everyone— Blanche turned around to see who had been saying the terrible things: a man, a woman with a bulging paper bag of provisions. "I have to work," she said to all of them. "I have to work"—she stamped her foot—"and Bunny's an only child— No one to play with—"

"Always excuses!"

It was the one with a baby carriage—hard line of mouth. She stood there, shaking the baby carriage, rattling it.

"If I was the Lord God, I'd be plenty sick of hearing excuses!" She turned the carriage so abruptly that the infant rolled onto its side.

Blanche said to the woman with the bag of provisions, "I think she must have followed me out of the room and gone down too far—"

"You mean into the cellar? *Rats!*"

"Rats wouldn't hurt a kid that age, only the tiny kids— Rats wouldn't— Oh, for God's sake," she said to the one who had said it. "Rats! Honestly!" Because she could not help, she moved off, too. This was the woman with the bag of food.

"If it was anything like that, she'd have yelled plenty." The man was sorry he had said that. He couldn't leave, however, until he saw the door open and the policeman's face appear.

The policeman dusted his pants with his cap, put it on and let Blanche into the hall. Blanche saw the line of benches again, the lumpy blue paint.

"Now, where's the cellar door?"

As Blanche ran along the hall she called out that she didn't know. There was a door and she pulled at it but it was locked. The next door was locked, too, but the policeman saw the key hanging from a hook high up near the ceiling.

"It's locked so I don't see how your kid could— Wait a minute, they could have locked up when they closed the school." When he got the door open, he reached in and found the light switch. "You wait here. You wait here," he repeated.

Blanche saw that the policeman was not sure what he would find and began to call "Bunny, Bunny, Bunny!" as he walked downstairs. When there was no answer, she listened to his deliberate steps, then peered down the stairs, holding on tight.

The cellar, which wasn't large, was clean and tidy. At the street end, where the faintest light came from a small barred window, was a heap of coal. The policeman, Blanche saw, was rolling some coals away from the bottom of the heap with the tip of his heavy shoe. It was as if he had touched Bunny with his shoe. Blanche moaned, ran downstairs and, shoving at the shoe, began to roll the coals with her hand; then she stopped. "How could a little girl of three get under coals?" she asked, brushing off her filthy hands, almost smiling. The policeman had walked around to the other side of the coal heap and was staring down at it thoughtfully. Then, as she watched, he took up a shovel which had been leaning against the wall and dug it into the coal heap, lifting a shovelful. "Not with that! Not with that!" Blanche tried to pull the shovel out of his hands.

He set his chin. "Get out of my way, lady!"

He meant that if Bunny was under the black coals, the

shovel wouldn't hurt her. Blanche fell down on her knees and began rolling the coals again frantically. "That's crazy," she said, pulling down the coals, talking over the roll of them, the dig of his shovel and his grunt as he lifted a shovelful, "that's crazy because this isn't an abandoned cellar where someone could— This is a respectable school," she said.

But the policeman continued shoveling until he made sure; then he walked away from the flattened coal heap and, as Blanche watched him, set the shovel between his knees and wrapped a handkerchief around his hand, then jerked the furnace door open. "Don't!" she screamed.

"Lady— I told you to stay outa here!" The policeman thrust the shovel in among the glowing coals and moved it about. "Okay," he said, slamming the door and turning his red face toward her. "Thank God, lady! Don't cry! I had to make sure; you can see that, can't you, lady?"

———

The cellar door shut with a bang and they heard the key turn in the lock. The policeman's hand went to his holster. For a moment, before the voice sounded, Blanche knew from the look on his face that the policeman believed that this was a part of it, part of what had happened to Bunny, but then the voice said, "I warn you down there. The police are on their way!"

The voice was prim and precise. It sounded uncomfortable with the words it was using.

The policeman's face cleared and he took his hands off the holster and wiped off the sweat which had formed on his forehead. "Open up!" He took Blanche's arm and led her to the steps. "You don't have to get the police; this is the police, lady."

"You can't expect me to believe that!"

"Yes, I expect you to believe that!" The policeman pushed Blanche up the stairs and banged on the door. "Open up!" He gestured to Blanche, grinning, then lifted his foot and kicked at the door. "Can't you hear the flat feet, lady?"

"This is not funny."

"You're going to look funny if you call the cops, lady. Open up! Open up!" he shook his head. "Go outside, there must be one of those people out there left. Go ask if a cop didn't come in through the back."

"No. We can't wait here wasting time," Blanche said. "Ask her who she is. Who are you?" Blanche asked. "Is that Miss Benton? She's the director of the school," she explained to the policeman. "Miss Benton? This is Blanche Lake speaking. We can't wait locked up in here."

"I'll go out and ask.'

"Then, go on!" Blanche banged her palms against the door and pushed, as if she could push Miss Benton away through the wood. They heard diminishing footsteps, then the front door closing. Blanche stood that way, her palms against the door, her face resting on her hands. Suppose all those people had left? How long did New York people wait for anything? Always in such a hurry. Perhaps she should have insisted that Miss Benton call the police; perhaps that would have been quicker. Every time she chose the wrong way, the slower way. She hadn't searched the building thoroughly. Perhaps in one of the cots she hadn't examined. . . . Suppose, because her mother had left her for the first time, Bunny had—retrogressed, as the psychology book put it, was sleeping the way she used to when she was an infant? She used to be able to do anything in Bunny's room when she was an infant and she wouldn't awaken. (Retrogression often occurred after a shock, the psychology book said. Worse retrogression than this, much worse. Grown children forgetting how to talk—) Well, if only Bunny was sleeping now it wouldn't matter so much that her mother made stupid choices. Blanche saw Bunny's sleeping face as she had seen it so often when she went in to make sure she hadn't thrown her covers off. She put her hand to her forehead and felt the grit on it. Her hands must be black with coal dust. She must not touch Bunny with the coal-heaver hands; only the softest, cleanest, most gentle hands should touch Bunny. "Oh, God," she prayed, "don't let any hands have touched Bunny!"

"Don't break down, lady," the policeman said. "You'd be surprised how many lost kids we get! Take it from me and when you find her, just harden up your heart and give her a good walloping! You might *want* to give her an ice-cream soda, but a good walloping—"

"Bunny?" She smiled at him because the word "walloping" in connection with Bunny was so preposterous.

"You see?" The cop asked no one. "You see? Here she comes now!"

The key turned and the door was opened. "Please excuse me," Miss Benton said. "I'm so sorry," she said. She was a small young woman with documentary features. It wasn't only her lineage which had given her the clear eyes, the good nose and the firm mouth, but the life she had had and the life she intended to have. Everything about Miss Benton was a credential. "When I came in and heard noises in the cellar— Why those people out there on the sidewalk let me walk into the building without—" She caught Blanche's gesture of impatience and stepped to one side. "Your child was locked in here after school? I simply don't understand how that could have happened." She stretched out her hand to help Blanche. "This door is always kept locked, so she couldn't have been down there. If only I had been here— Did you search the building thoroughly? Although I really don't see—"

"Just the classrooms and the sickroom. The office."

"Perhaps in my apartment? I live on the third floor. Although, as I said, I really don't see—" Now Blanche was standing near a light. "Which child is this?"

"Bunny Lake."

"I will go up to my apartment and look there. Wouldn't you like to wash? There's a—" She waved and started for the stairs.

"I'd like to go through the place myself," the policeman said.

"Please do."

"Yes." Blanche touched his arm as he passed her. Miss Benton had moved to the side of the stairway so the policeman could go up first.

"Did you call her? What did you say her name was?"

"Bunny. Bunny Lake."

"Bunny Lake. The first day! As if the first day weren't sufficiently hectic, the cook doesn't turn up at all. Bunny!" She began to go upstairs. "Bunny! Come out, Bunny!"

Blanche followed them up. When she reached the landing she could see how the policeman was staring at whatever it was the Fours had constructed. Miss Benton brushed past her.

"Wait. Let's look inside the cubbies. Curled up?" She skirted the construction carefully. "I suppose it could happen! Oh, the cubbies have no doors," she said, looking back over her shoulder at Blanche. "Please don't imagine Bunny locked in a cubbie!" Her voice was muffled as she bent over the first locker, stirring the clothes in it. "But if she did curl up and pull the clothes over her—" She went to the next locker and paused there, and, as if Miss Benton could have missed Bunny, Blanche went to the first cubbie after the director. (It was a matter of not wanting any hands but her own to touch her child.)

"Like a babe in the woods, sleeping under—leaves," Miss Benton concluded, straightening up.

The policeman was examining the windows in the room.

He shoved one open and looked out. Blanche stood perfectly still until he pulled the window down again and turned away from it.

"The washroom?" Miss Benton said. "Although, again—" She went to the washroom, however, and the policeman followed her.

"Ain't that something now!"

Blanche hurried, but the policeman was only talking about the row of low white sinks with the mirrors above them. There were ten hooks set into the wall. Ten brightly colored towels hung from the hooks. Blanche had found towels for Bunny with rabbits on them. Every single time she was washed in New York, Bunny had fussed about not being dried with her own towels. "Oh, hurry," Blanche said.

The three of them went through the school part of the building and then into Miss Benton's apartment, which consisted of two rooms on the top floor (to the rear of the Threes' big room). There were a living room, a small bedroom and a kitchenette with no windows in it, made out of a closet. "Hurry," Blanche said.

The policeman even pushed his way his way up and out onto the roof but he did not find Bunny up there.

"I was fairly certain she wouldn't be here," Miss Benton said, talking over her shoulder as they walked down the last flight of stairs, "but of course we had to—" She opened the door of the office and waited for Blanche and the policeman to precede her. "Now, I think we'll have to concede that somehow or other—" She turned to Blanche questioningly.

"Bunny. Her real name is Felicia."

Miss Benton frowned. "We must concede that Bunny left the building, somehow or other."

"After me? This morning?" She spoke as if she had not considered this possibility herself. "You mean this morning and that she's been lost all day? Where is she then, Miss Benton?

Where is she then?"

"At some police station, I would say."

"Could be," the policeman said. "Anyhow, that's the next thing. Get Missing Persons on it."

"Maybe they have her already," Blanche said. "They might not have been able to find out—Bunny thinks one number is as good as the next— One *street* number," she said, almost smiling. She pushed the telephone toward the policeman because he could do it faster. "Here, call them." Bunny, she thought, would be sitting on a golden-oak bench. The policeman would be at Bunny's feet, *all* the policemen! They would ask her where she lived, and she would say, "One-two-eight Street. *Five* street." And she would smile at them. No work done that day, Blanche thought. They would have fed her, and her face would be smeared with the ice-cream cone the police traditionally fed lost children; her hands all sticky with it. She would be lying asleep on the golden-oak bench. (That was best because no amount of ice cream or attention from strangers could have kept her interested so long.) Asleep, yes, on the bench, so that she wouldn't even know how long her stupid mother had gone around in circles. (When Blanche was just a bit older than Bunny was now, she had fallen out of a canoe—so Mother said. She didn't remember it and Bunny wouldn't remember today.)

It seemed to Blanche now that she had not heard the thick front door close behind her when she had hurried out of the school that morning. So Bunny could have pushed it open or—*so tiny*—squeezed through.

"That's it," the policeman said.

"I was in such a tearing hurry to get to my job. I haven't been there long enough to rate many privileges, and I had to ask them to be let off early today. We were so late, anyhow, and of course I'm supposed to be at my desk by nine thirty. I simply raced down your stairs and out on the street without looking back or even closing the door properly."

Miss Benton put her fingers to her lips.

Policemen, like others who are supposed to be tough, are notoriously softhearted. Probably he only suggested a good walloping because he couldn't wallop. Probably spoiled his own. "I love them," Blanche thought, smiling at the policeman. "Guardians of the—" He was shaking his head at her. "They haven't got her?"

"What we want is a complete description." He put the telephone against his chest. "You tell me, I'll pass it on."

Blanche tried to be as accurate as possible. "About thirty-seven inches high. She weighs thirty-two pounds. Black hair. Brown eyes."

"Scars?"

"No scars. Of course no scars!"

"Any identifying marks on her?"

She shook her head.

"When last seen, wearing—?"

"Wearing? I took her little sweater off for her. She can't really dress herself. Wearing—a yellow linen ruffled dress with white appliqués." She showed the policeman on her own suit, just above her knees. "Rabbits appliquéd." Why was Miss Benton frowning at her? "What is it, Miss Benton?"

"Wasn't she wearing her jeans and a T shirt?"

"Wearing a yellow linen dress. Oh, God," she said, "a child is supposed to be safe in school! School is where you leave children so they will be safe!'

Miss Benton came to her. "Please, don't! Nothing like this has ever happened here before. We've had the usual amount of trouble, but—" Her clear voice wavered. "I have known of several cases where children did get out of nursery schools— perfectly reputable ones. It could happen, but—oh, dear," she said, "I know how you must feel!"

"Do you?" Blanche shook her head. "Anyhow, now isn't the time. What do we do now?" she asked the policeman.

"We get a snapshot and bring it to the station, lady."

Miss Benton nodded. "And while you're gone I'll call the staff. I'll leave urgent messages for the ones who haven't reached home yet. Ruth, for example, has to get out to Scarsdale."

"The other one went to her dentist. She has pyorrhea."

"I beg your pardon? I'll find out whether they have an idea how this—and I'll call you. Wait! What police station are you going to, in case I get some news right off?"

"One fifty-three East Sixty-seventh. Regent 4-1897."

Miss Benton wrote that down on the edge of the sheet of newsprint with PAID stamped over it. "I don't trust my memory. I am one of the unfortunates who have to mark everything down."

The policeman pulled at his tunic as he waited for Blanche to go out of the front door. "I must be dreaming," Blanche thought as they walked toward her apartment. What could be more dreamlike than this walk down the street with a tall policeman? And, as in dreams, the faces you passed, all strangers, all strange, turned indifferently toward you and then indifferently away, and the policeman didn't speak again after he had asked where she lived, and she didn't speak, either, because what was the point in a dream when salvation only lay in waking up?

Blanche and the policeman waited for the self-service elevator to come down. A man and a woman, stepping out of it, glanced at Blanche and her policeman, but since she was as much a stranger to them as she had been to the people she passed in the street, it did not seem more outlandish to them than to the others that she, Blanche Lake, should be with a policeman.

"Floor?" He held his index finger poised over the row of buttons.

"Five. Fifth." This has been the first elevator Bunny was ever in. *First*, not *last!* "I have my key." The policeman took the key from her and inserted it into the lock and opened the door for her. Blanche ran past him. "Bunny! Bunny!" When there was no answer, she said, "I just hoped."

"Sure. Now, let's get that snapshot."

"It's not a snapshot. It's a cabinet photo. Bunny was two then, her second birthday. One of those colored enlargements. I gave it to Mother." ("Do you imagine I'm going to stick it up on my mantel for everyone to see?" Mother had said, Mother had wept. But when Mother came here, she had brought the cabinet picture with her.) "It's in my mother's room." She showed him the way. "You look and I'll look." Because it wasn't on Mother's dresser. "About like this." She framed the picture in the air.

It didn't take very long to search her mother's small bedroom or much longer to go through the rest of the apartment, but they could not find the picture of Bunny. "I guess my mother took it with her this morning." She does love Bunny, Blanche thought. See how she loves Bunny, taking that picture with her. "My mother had to go home for a few days and she took Bunny's picture."

"Okay. Anyhow, a more recent snapshot would be better."

"I don't have any." Blanche saw the policeman's surprise. "I have hundreds back home, a whole album, in fact, but I didn't bring it. The kind already made up and you paste snaps in and the birth certificate and you write things—that kind. We just moved here two weeks ago and I left the album in storage. Not here. I had Bunny," she said, "I didn't need—"

"I like to carry them on me," the policeman said. He did have children, then. "Too bad. They like to have a snapshot."

Blanche put her hands down on the table over which she had been bending. "How many little girls of three are lost? The picture doesn't matter so much, does it?"

"Well, they like to have one. I know, I know," he said hastily, because she was going to tell him about the album of them in storage again.

"Now what?" she asked, realizing, because the pain in her chest had returned, how wonderful the twenty minutes had been when it was only a photograph she was trying to find. The policeman was scratching at the back of his head behind his ear, staring around the room and scratching at the back of his head as if something puzzled him. "Now what should I do?"

"Sit tight. I'll go back to the station. You give me your number. They'll call you the minute they have something."

"Oh, please! I'll call them! Please give me the number." The apartment, which had seemed pleasant up to now, was a dreadful place. She ran to the telephone and found the pad. (Bunny had scribbled on the first ten pages. "Don't," she had said. "Naughty, Bunny!") "Please, may I have the number? I just can't stay here. Maybe I should, but I just can't. I'll go ring doorbells near the school. How far could she get, after all? Maybe someone saw her."

"You check in at the precinct station, though. Maybe they'll have something for you, real soon. Missing Persons will be out, lady, and they're pros."

Blanche thanked the policeman and let him go without her because she could see how uncomfortable she made him. He didn't know what to say to her. She pulled off her shoes and hurried to the closet for her moccasins. It wasn't the comfort of the low heels so much, but to eliminate the tapping of the high heels of her pumps. The tap tap behind her was her fear stalking her, tap tap. Bunny. Tap, tap.

She shoved her feet into the moccasins. "You've got to go into every house near the school. Start on the opposite side of the street. Perhaps someone was looking out a window. Do New Yorkers ever look out of windows the way we do back home? New Yorkers," she told herself firmly, "are no different from anybody else. In New York City, just like any other place, there's always someone to see when something happens. The difference is that New Yorkers might not be so quick to do something about what they see."

Oh, God, she thought, there's always someone to see. You read about it in the papers all the time. Maybe they'll talk to me where they wouldn't go to the police. You read about that in detective stories. People who have something to fear from the police. People who just naturally distrust the police. And that street is slums, really, she thought. The school building was really just a slummy building renovated, only different from the four others like it in the row because of what had been done to it. Slum people would be just the ones not to want to talk to cops. "Tell me," she would say. "I'm her mother. Tell me!"

"And then you can cry," she told herself. "When it might help loosen someone up, I will let you cry. But not now."

The very first person she asked, the superintendent of the tallest house on the block, told her about the old man who lived on the top floor of the building just opposite the school. This old man, the superintendent said, stayed glued to his window as if he were paid to do it. He gave her the address and told her top floor front, but he came out after her as she hurried toward the house, to tell her his wife had just reminded him that the old man was a night watchman and would be gone now.

"No use in ringing," he said, seeing her finger press down on the bell. "No use you ringing!" he repeated, speaking louder, as if it were her ears which were deaf to this destruction of hope.

But he *had* followed her to the house to tell her. *Not* indifferent. But he *had* known the habits of a neighbor. New York like home. But he had spoken to his wife about Bunny immediately. No more hearts of stone than any hearts anywhere.

After the first house, Blanche timed herself. A house took twenty minutes, most of which was spent knocking at doors, or explaining that she wasn't selling anything. (When they would open the door wide enough to really look at her, she didn't have to explain that.) It took such a short time to say no, they hadn't seen any little girl.

After each house, she promised herself, she could call the police station.

"No, Ma'am," the policeman said the first time. "Don't you worry, though, we'll get your little girl for you."

The first few times, the policeman sounded very sympathetic, but then he became curt with her. She was becoming a nuisance with her calling, she supposed. When this was all over, she would apologize for having been a nuisance. She would bring each of the policemen a nice gift. (They couldn't call her gratitude bribes—not when they had found Bunny for her.)

Then the policeman asked her to hold on.

Blanche felt her heart thump and opened the door of the booth to give herself air. Her head fell forward and the bump of it against the telephone booth brought her to. "Yes," she whispered. "Please!"

"Mrs. Lake? This is Lieutenant Duff speaking."

"Duff. Have you got her there? Bunny? No? But you've heard something. Someone—"

"Mrs. Lake, who is your nearest relative?"

"My mother. But she's out of the city today."

"Okay, then, who's your family physician?"

"She's hurt! She's hurt! What is it?"

"We don't have any news for you, Mrs. Lake. I want to contact your family physician. You go on home now and I'll send your doctor over, see?"

"I thought you had her! I thought you'd found her!"

"If you'll give me the name of your—"

She had a picture of Dr. Freundlich shaking down his thermometer. "I haven't a family physician in New York."

"The little girl's doctor, then."

"Bunny hasn't a doctor in New York, either. She's only been in the city two weeks."

"None, eh? Well, in that case, I have a list of doctors, Mrs. Lake. You're not doing yourself any good carrying on. You take my advice—"

"What good are you doing? What good are you doing?"

"We're doing everything we can, this end. Look, Mrs. Lake, you take my word for it, what's the sense carrying on? We're doing everything possible here. Now, you want to co-operate, don't you? Then you go on home and let me— Wait. Who else in the family?"

"Bunny," she said. "Bunny. Bunny."

"Yes, yes, sure. I mean the baby's father. Where is he?"

"I don't know where he is. He doesn't know where I am. He hasn't my address in New York and there's no way he could get it. Please, please, please, forget about the baby's father!"

"Okay. I get it, but I mean somebody to look after you now. You need someone."

"I need Bunny. I don't need anyone. Find Bunny."

"Give me your mother's address. Where she is."

"No. She's out of town. She can't help. That's just wasting time. Please don't waste time. Please, please! Mother won't know where Bunny is!"

"But she could tend you."

"I will not give you Mother's address to waste time on. So you think you're doing something. I'm Bunny's mother. You spend your time on Bunny."

"That's just what we'll do, but— Listen, you don't want to keep calling this way. You want all our lines to be open, don't you?"

"I see. Oh, I'm sorry! I'll hang up. I'll come in next time. I won't telephone again."

"Yes," he said. "You come in. Ask for Lieutenant Duff."

Before she left the drugstore Blanche ordered a cup of coffee at the soda fountain. She reminded herself that a drugstore was sort of a neighborhood club. She told the soda jerk about Bunny and his eyes filled with tears.

"Gee, that's lousy, that's lousy," he said.

"Would you just ask everybody who comes in if they saw a little girl alone?"

"A little girl alone if you're lucky," the soda jerk said. "Hey, Miss!"

If the man two stools away hadn't been quick, he wouldn't have caught her. "You're a damn fool, Joe! Boy, are you one damn fool!"

"Should I throw water on her? What do you mean 'damn fool'? Wouldn't it be lucky if she was alone and not with some of those sex fiends you hear about?"

"Wet that towel. I'll hold her." He pressed the towel against Blanche's face. "See if you can get some of that coffee down her, Joe. That's the best thing, coffee."

"Some sex fiend couldn't have got her ten minutes after she sneaked out of the school?" He held the coffee to Blanche's lips. The man holding Blanche tilted the cup further. "Shut up, Joe."

"Like that case was in the papers?"

Blanche pushed at the coffee cup with such force that the man holding her released her.

"Go wan, drink that hot coffee, lady. That's the best thing. Drink it down."

Blanche saw how the soda jerk's hand shook holding the coffee cup. His eyes, bright with tears, dark with terror, stared into hers, and she could not stop looking at him while she swallowed a little of the coffee. The soda jerk couldn't talk, the man who had held her was drying his hands on a paper napkin, the voice she was hearing came from a man hunched over a plate at the other end of the soda fountain.

"Kid'll go with anybody. You got to train them up not to. Kid'll go with any Tom, Dick or Harry, it's their parents' fault."

Teach Bunny she lives in a jungle terrible with wild beasts? Teach her to be afraid? "You're wrong," she said, pointing to the tears in the soda jerk's eyes. "People aren't like that!"

The man at the end of the soda fountain shoved his plate away. A big bulky man in a red Eisenhower jacket. "Where do you come from, lady?"

"From Providence."

"Maybe in Providence," he said.

Halfway to the door, Blanche remembered that she had not paid for the coffee and took a dime from the change she had put into her suit pocket for the telephone calls.

The soda jerk made a pass in the air with his hands. "No." His hand shot up. "On the house," he said.

But she would not let him do that. He did that because he thought that Bunny— She came back to the counter, defying the bulky man hunched at the end and the one who had held her, and the dark, terror-filled eyes of the soda jerk, laying the dime down so that they could all see it.

He was picking rotted grapes off the bunches of them, but when he saw her undoing her apron, he stood up. "Rose, where you going? It's not nine yet, Rose." She was folding the apron. "Rose, I already told you. I'm sorry I rode Eddie."

"I'm going to look for him. In case you want to eat you got what Eddie didn't show up for in the icebox."

"He's a little kid you got to look for him? First you tell me he's no little kid, I shouldn't have rode him, now you're going out looking."

"He's no kid, Georgie, is why I'm looking."

"Why?"

"You didn't know my first husband, George." Mrs. Negrito pulled off the sweater she wore in the place, and hung it in the back room. "There's certain things about my first husband, Emilio, I never told no one. So Eddie is like Emilio. You, George, you're big, you make a big noise, but you're not like Emilio."

"But, Rose—"

"But Rose!" She began to walk toward the door of the store.

"Maybe I'm going to make a big noise now, Rose. Maybe you better stop, look and listen. I'm your hubby now and I say you stay here. I'm not going to close up alone and I'm not going to eat from the icebox, either."

"George—I told you. He was right outside her house this morning."

"So he was outside her house this morning. If she's old enough to give Eddie hot pants, she's old enough to take care of herself. Eddie's no baby and she's no baby." He pulled off his dirty white coat. "Rose, you going to be Georgie's baby or not, Rose? You going to or not, Rose?"

There was a grocery store just around the corner, and Blanche hurried to ask them in there. When the woman who kept it said they stayed open until ten, she asked her to question anyone who came in to buy. "Please ask if they've seen a little girl in a yellow dress, alone—" Blanche swallowed—"or with someone."

The woman promised that if any customer had any information she would call the police station immediately. "I got three of my own, grown." She called after Blanche. "I got two grandchildren."

After the grocery store, that was the formula: after they said they hadn't seen Bunny alone—or with anybody—to ask them to question those they talked to and to report anything to the police station on Sixty-seventh Street. Everyone Blanche asked, once he understood what the trouble was, said he would. Everyone was sympathetic. They all wanted to help find a helpless little girl.

Nobody would hurt a helpless little girl. Nobody.

Rose let George take her home to the apartment. She told herself that George was right, George had sense. The girl wasn't a baby. The girl had sense. The girl had nothing to do with Eddie and that poor little pussycat when Eddie was a kid. And, anyhow, she told herself, that was when Eddie was a kid.

When Blanche had been in love with Bert, when she had waited day after day for his letter, she used to go for a long walk just before the mail was due. She wouldn't let herself go to the post office and ask for a letter until a certain time after the mail had arrived. It made waiting for the next mail that much shorter.

She would not let herself go to the precinct station until she had gone into ten more houses.

When Blanche walked into the police station, the relaxed tempo of the place struck her. But ridiculous, she told herself, to have expected them to be scurrying around like the Keystone Cops in the revival movies on television. *Calling all cars! Calling all cars!* They had done that already, she told herself. The moment that policeman had phoned in, the ones who looked for lost children had gone out looking for Bunny, in cars and on foot, so much more efficiently than she had been able to search, really thoroughly. This is routine to them, she thought. They must have found so many lost children before this. "Lieutenant Duff, please. I'm Miss Lake." She was accustomed to men looking at her, but not this way, she thought. Why was the policeman looking at her this way?

Ridiculous to expect Lieutenant Duff to be standing before a map, crossing out house after house, street after street, narrowing down the search, closing the net. "That is a movie idea," she said to herself. "In real life they sit at a desk reading the *Daily News*."

"Lieutenant Duff, I'm Blanche Lake."

He folded his paper. He was not put out at having her see him reading his paper so that proved he was doing everything possible. "Have you heard anything? Yet," she added, to show she had faith in the police.

He shook his head, standing up, leaned over his desk and pulled a chair forward. "I'm glad you came, Mrs. Lake. Sit down. Mrs. Lake, in my opinion, you should let us contact your mother."

"Please!"

"Somebody then. No? Okay, now I'll give you a list of the doctors around here, and—"

"Hasn't Miss Benton called you? The director of the school?"

"Now, why do you ask that?" He spoke very clearly as if he believed she was deaf. "Why do you ask if she called?"

"She said she would telephone her teachers and ask them. Could they tell her anything?"

"No, they couldn't tell her anything, not a thing." He saw how her hand went to her throat. "She's keeping in close touch," he added, again speaking very clearly.

"Keeping in close touch"—it sounded as if there were all the time in the world! Haste makes waste, Blanche told herself. (Mother always said that. "Haste makes waste, Blanche. You don't get anywhere flying around like a chicken with its head cut off!") Head cut off—Blanche jumped off the chair. "Don't just sit there! Oh, God, you mustn't just sit there! Those policemen outside standing around and looking— This is a helpless child, don't you understand that?"

"Now, Mrs. Lake, those guys out there are doing their jobs."

"I'm sorry. Of course, there are others looking for Bunny! That policeman who came to the school and looked. Is he out looking for Bunny?"

"Klein? Yes, ma'am, Klein's out looking for her. You just leave the looking to Klein—and the rest of the boys. Now, I'm going to give you the list of doctors and you pick one out that looks right to you and we'll run you over to see him." He fished two sheets of flimsy out of the drawer of the desk and flattened it on the desk top near her, but she would not look at it. "Now, come on, what good is it banging your head against a stone wall?"

"Blanche, talking to you is like talking to a stone wall." Blanche took the paper and looked at it. Dr. Granit, Dr. Greenspan. She had forgotten why the policeman had given it to her; when she remembered she handed it back. "Lieutenant Duff, I don't want a doctor! Lieutenant—don't you have any children of your own? Then you *know!*" He had nodded. He pushed the papers back toward her again. "Or your wife knows." Perhaps men didn't know.

"This little girl means a lot to you?"

"—a lot to me—a lot to me?" Men didn't know. "Bunny is—she's my baby, my baby! Oh, ask your wife if you don't know. Ask your wife what it means to lose your baby!"

"It's a terrible thing to lose a baby."

"Ask your wife." Because of the way he said the words.

"You ever lost a baby before? I mean, did you have a child that passed on, that's what I mean?"

"I have Bunny. One child. Do I have to lose more than one before you pay any attention?"

"Just asking," he said. "I mean— Look," he said. "What's the use of talking; you need a doctor. Where are you going?"

"Home," she said bitterly.

"That's the spirit. Go on home. Get something to eat in you. Have a nice hot dinner; that's what you should do, have a nice hot dinner. You don't need to reduce like my wife, do you? So you can have a nice hot dinner. Half the women's troubles these days come from that reducing, if you ask me. You trust Officer Klein; you liked him, right? Just remember Officer Klein and the other boys in the squad are out looking for your little girl so you can go home and have a nice hot dinner."

She did not notice that now she was talking the way he did, slowly and clearly. "I have only one trouble. I have only one child. I have not lost a child by death. I lost a child this morning in school." She heard the policeman asking if they could run her home but shook her head and walked out. When she went into the outer room, the policemen there looked at her that way again, but nobody said anything and nobody stopped her.

The police, she reminded herself, could think about good hot dinners because the police were organized. There was probably, she thought, a master plan for finding little girls, and each policeman had his duty and went about it like the firemen did when there was an alarm. Officer Klein wasn't hanging around that outer office to stare at her; Officer Klein's duty was to be out looking and that's what he was doing and so were all the other Officer Kleins. It comforted her to remember Officer Klein's tall strong body and the way his muscles had bulged out his tunic when he shoved the door to the roof open. It comforted her to remember the expression on his face. Officer Klein cared about Bunny being lost. (And so did the other officers whose duty it was to care.) She hailed a taxi and went home.

The first thing, now that she was home, was to make a cup of coffee. And, perhaps, toast? She would never get the toast down, Blanche thought, going into the kitchen. It was odd to see the mess she had left it in that morning unchanged. At first Blanche did not know what the slight sound was; then she recognized it as a sigh. She was sighing. "No," she told herself, "stay in the kitchen. Don't run. Open the tap. Put water in the kettle." (Up on a high shelf where Bunny couldn't reach them, matches.) "Light the range. Water on. Measure out the coffee, two spoonfuls to the cup, twice as strong as usual very good idea." The smell of the coffee, usually so delicious, made her queasy. Chocolate instead? Quick energy? Her hand reached up toward the box of milk chocolate, but that was Bunny's box of candy, up on the high shelf where she couldn't reach it. Two squares daily for Bunny.

Blanche's gorge rose, this time because—to have been so careful about such a thing as chocolate and to have walked out this morning and left Bunny— But that was because it was a school, Blanche told herself. All mothers left their children in school. Her own mother had left her in school.

She forgot about the coffee and hurried to the telephone. She turned the torn-off pages with Bunny's scribbles on them face down. Now she recalled that Bunny had also scribbled on the letter from the nursery school which had the telephone number of the school printed on it. Because Mother had been telling Bunny that school was where you learned to read and write, and telling Blanche at the same time that it was ridiculous to put Bunny in a school. Bunny, irritated by the voices, had scribbled all over the letter to show her grandmother that she could, too, write. The pencil had crumpled and torn the paper so the letter had been thrown out.

And Blanche had not jotted down the school's number when she had called it.

For a moment, she could not remember whether it had

been quicker to look up the number or ask Information. (She almost went into a panic because she could not remember that.) Look it up, then. Better to do something than to wait. Her fingers were as stiff as twigs. She found the number and dialed it. Suppose Miss What's-her-name is up in her apartment and it is a different number? I can ask Information if it is a different number. Director of the— Suppose I forget her name the way she couldn't seem to remember mine? "Miss Benton? Hello, Miss Benton. Oh, I'm so glad you're there! This is Blanche Lake."

"Hello, there! How are you feeling?"

I don't need to tell her how I'm feeling with Bunny lost. It's just a thing one says. "Fine," she heard herself saying, because that was quicker. "Miss Benton, I've been running around trying to find Bunny like a chicken with its— Stupidly. I want you to give me the names and telephone numbers of the mothers in your school, please. Start with the ones in the room where I left Bunny. I will ask them to ask their children— One of them probably saw where Bunny went when I left. I know they're all too young to have tried to stop Bunny. I'm not blaming the children, for goodness' sakes! But if their own mother asks them *calmly* about the little girl in yellow who—"

"I'm certain that won't help, Mrs. Lake."

"You can't possibly be certain! Children notice a lot more than one thinks; at least I've discovered Bunny does. Many times—some other time I'll argue about that. I'm sure you know they do as well as I do. Better," she coaxed, the flattery coming because she could sense the director's opposition. She picked up the pencil and pulled the memo pad to her. "I'm ready, Miss Benton. For the names and telephone numbers," she reminded.

"Now, Mrs. Lake, you must be reasonable. I can't do that, Mrs. Lake. I can't have you worrying my parents."

"You think any parent would *mind* being worried? You think any human being would consider this being 'worried'? To try to find out if one of the children—"

"The police, Mrs. Lake—"

Blanche had to think a minute to get past the impenetrable surprise at being refused; then she nodded. "Do you mean that the police have already questioned them, is that what you mean?"

"That's it, Mrs. Lake."

Questioning the mothers had been high up in the master plan the police had, see, and she had just thought of it! "Of course, but, anyhow, I would rather—"

"This was earlier, Mrs. Lake. By now the children must be asleep." She laughed. "At least I hope they are."

"If they don't want to, they don't have to wake their children. I can't make them wake their children, but I can ask!"

"I can't do it, Mrs. Lake. You must leave it to the police. They've already questioned my staff."

"Your staff! Your staff! I can't believe that the mothers would mind if I asked them to just calmly question—" That nice woman in the oxford-gray slacks; she would help. Blanche saw the woman running, her wide rear wobbling. That nice woman wouldn't just sit back. That nice woman would run all around New York if she knew. Did she know? "Are you sure the police have questioned them, Miss Benton?" And the others on the bench in the hall. They'd been nice, too. Given the chance, they would help, too. "Are you sure you haven't convinced the police that none of the children could possibly help so why bother the parents? You certainly wouldn't want them to know that Bunny was allowed to wander out of your precious school and get lost! You'd be afraid that if the parents found out they wouldn't leave their children in your precious school again—for fear they wouldn't find them when they came back for them!"

"If you're going to be abusive, there's no point in our continuing this conversation, Mrs. Lake."

"No point! No point!"

"I believe you should be under a doctor's care, definitely!"

"How dare you?" Blanche said. "This is your school Bunny was lost in. How dare you? What is the matter with you?" Silence. "Miss Benton! Miss Benton!"

"Mrs. Lake—"

"Don't you dare use that tone to me as if I were insane! Of course I'm beside myself, so should you be beside yourself. You're the director of the school! What kind of director are you, anyway?"

"I'm not using any tone, Mrs. Lake. Mrs. Lake, please do listen to me. A good friend of mine is a physician. He knows about this dreadful thing. I can't tell you how relieved I would be if you would see him!"

"What can he do?"

"He can—"

"About Bunny."

"Mrs. Lake, I don't think it will serve any purpose for you to call the parents in the school, but if Dr. Newhouse thinks you should, I will give you the list. This should show you I have complete confidence in Dr. Newhouse."

"All right. If he hurries."

"He is here with me, now. We've been talking about you. He'll be right over. Oh, wait, Mrs. Lake, what is your address and telephone number?"

"But you have it."

"Downstairs. In the office where we keep our files. I'm up here in the apartment now. I don't want to waste time going down and—"

"Oh, of course." She gave Miss Benton her address and telephone number.

"You'll be there?"

"Yes." Coffee. She put the telephone back. Coffee. Now she could hear the water boiling on the range because it was so quiet in the apartment. She longed for noise, real noise. If there were no sounds except that water boiling and the sound of her sighs to press against the New York streets, the outside noises would burst in the walls. Like the atom bomb explosions, she thought. On her way to the kitchen, she stopped at the window, seeing how night had settled down. She told herself that it was just as true now as earlier that Bunny wasn't afraid of the dark. It was no darker where Bunny was now because it was night than it would have been in the dark cellar. "Make day," Bunny had once commanded imperiously, meaning that she, Blanche, should pull up the Venetian blinds and let the light in. And, "Let there be light," she had said to Bunny, laughing, jerking up the blinds in a gorgeous clattering gesture, as if she really were God. "Oh, God," she said, falling on her knees, "help me find Bunny, God, please!"

She got off the floor, telling herself, coffee, to make coffee, good, strong, black coffee which would not remind her of the weak stuff in the drugstore or the soda jerk who had said that Bunny might not be alone in the dark. This coffee needn't remind her of that coffee.

The kitchen was full of steam because the water she had put up had almost boiled away. She would have to add some and start again. Blanche went to the bread box and took out a loaf of waxed-paper-wrapped bread. At first, she merely held the loaf, poking the nail of her thumb through the waxed paper; then she pulled out two slices and, doubling them over, crammed as much of the bread as she could into her mouth. She was ravenous, she thought, chewing frantically, stuffing more bread in before the first mouthful was down, staring at the kettle, willing it to boil. A watched kettle never boils. (Mother.) A watched telephone never rings. Blanche stayed in the kitchen with the kettle because that was the lesser of two evils.

Evils. Evils.

The steam was coming up out of the spout; not steam from an earth that was hell, not from hell on earth, merely from the kettle.

Coffee, Blanche told herself, and carefully, not spilling a drop, poured the boiling water into the dripolator and sat down at the kitchen table.

Drip. Drip. Drip.

The Chinese torture, she thought; a constant drip of water until you went mad with it was the Chinese torture.

Torture. Sex crime.

"No," she whispered, and quickly wrapped both her hands around the coffeepot, to feel the too hot, to be burned, not to think. And then the doorbell rang.

———————

He was so—tidy—Blanche thought when she opened her door and saw him standing there, smiling not too broadly. The smile in place, she thought, like the crease in his dark gray slacks. Involuntarily, her hand went to smooth down her rumpled and coal-smeared blue jacket. He wore a blue cashmere sweater with a darker blue scarf neatly tucked into the neckline.

"I'm Dr. Newhouse. Miss Benton asked me to—" He saw her frown. Like thunder, he thought, darkening her beauty and making it ominous. Because she is beautiful, he thought, and remembered Louise saying, "She's really lovely, Dennis. I think I'm rather stupid to send you to rescue such a lovely damsel in distress." But he had told Louise—and it was the simple truth, he thought—that he was certain she knew him well enough to feel perfectly secure about him and beautiful damsels in distress, *after hours*, "Helping damsels in distress after consultation hours," he had assured Louise, "would be a busman's holiday."

He smiled at Mrs. Lake. "Miss Benton is very much concerned about you. She asked me to come and see if you were all right."

"I'm trying to be." She stepped back and allowed him to come into the apartment. "I just have to remember that the police are out looking for Bunny, don't I? And that the best thing I can do is keep out of their way and not disturb them."

He closed the door softly and went to the most comfortable-looking chair and patted it suggestively. "And one other thing to do while you wait is calm down."

"Of course."

But she frowned at the chair. He went and led her to it.

"It will only upset Bunny if I throw a scene when they bring her back. Yes, of course," she said, obediently seating herself, "I'm going to try to calm down."

"Good." Her hands clasped each other on her lap, clung to each other. Poor kid. Moving unhurriedly (she was exhausted), he chose a seat where she did not have to look at him. "Let's talk, then." He sat in his consultation room, waiting for her to talk, but she was silent. He could see her lips, the line of them in repose. Eloquent, he thought, just as they are. Not needing, he thought, the thousands of words, the hundreds of thousands of words. (As if, he thought, it could be done without words. With mirrors, he thought.) He leaned forward inviting her to speak.

She understood. "I'm afraid I can't—*discuss*," she said.

She had a mouth for marble, Dennis thought; that is, he

could see that mouth in marble, the sweet, deep curve of it arrested. She had a mouth like the one on that head of a girl found drowned in the Seine he used to have a cast of. In his room in medical school. He would hear the other students going out to make a night of it and he would get up restlessly and walk around his small room. He would touch the marble lips of the girl and sigh and go back to his desk again. Dennis told himself that this was what happened when a person kept her trap shut with him, just because he got so damn much talk in his line of business! "Of course you can't *discuss!* Naturally, you can't do that. Talk about anything that comes into your mind." Now he could see her lips trying to smile, modeling a smile for him. "Just say anything that comes to your mind, anything at all." He leaned his head back out of her line of vision and pressed his thumb and third finger against the ethmoid bones in response to the sensation there which always accompanied tension. He was, of course, trained to be observant of his own reactions as well as those of others, and he wondered why he should feel tense. Because his plans had been disrupted this way? On Monday evenings he had dinner with Louise and tonight they intended to catch *The Gate of Hell* at the Sutton. So rigid that any disrupting influence caused tension? But how else could he manage? It was all very well to be flexible, but within limits. He had to keep within strict limits if he was to spend his time the way he wanted to. Could the tension, he wondered, pressing hard on the eth- moids, be guilt toward his patients, because if he was to give them his full attention tomorrow (and Tuesday was his heavi- est schedule) he should be—*rigidly*—carrying out the usual Monday-night procedure? He had to smile at that. But selec- tion, he told himself firmly, did entail a certain amount of rigidity. You could not let yourself be shifted by every wind— by every smile, he corrected, smiling. Nor could you help everybody. He had chosen his obligations as well as his pleasures. It was natural that he should feel this tension because his Monday evening with Louise was being loused up this way. "I beg your pardon?"

"I said you sound like a psychiatrist."

"How did you guess? Have you had much experience with psychiatrists?"

She said, "Providence isn't exactly darkest Africa."

"Providence, Rhode Island?"

"That's where I was born. I haven't lived there for three and a half years. Bunny is three," she said.

He saw her blush and throw her head up.

"In case you didn't notice the connection between Bunny's being born and my leaving Providence; Bunny is illegitimate. That's why I had to go away."

"I see."

"I suppose you think that's awful!"

"Haven't they heard in Providence that psychiatrists don't think anything is 'awful'? If anyone can reserve value judgments, psychiatrists should."

She said, "Should!"

"Where did you go when you left home?"

"I had a teacher, my favorite teacher, and she moved to—a small town. I wrote her when I knew I was pregnant. You see," she said, "my mother didn't reserve value judgment! Mother does think it's awful about Bunny."

"She does?"

"She does, yes. She thinks—well, never mind Mother."

"The lieutenant from the police station told Miss Benton that you won't give him your mother's address."

"Why? Why should Mother have to go through with—this waiting?" She paused. "I suppose you've guessed the other reason I won't let them tell Mother." She waited for him to speak, but he was silent. "Of course you've guessed! Because she'll blame me. Because Mother will say this is my fault!"

"Your mother will blame you?"

"If she could help— Do you think that would stop me if she could help? Do you think anything would?"

She was out of her chair. She was standing over him. She thrust her hand through her hair and he thought he could hear it crackle. That kind of hair. "I'm not thinking anything, Mrs. Lake. Why do you think I'm thinking anything would stop you?"

She looked at him, shrugged and went back to her seat.

"Tell me about this teacher."

"She didn't think I should be stoned through the streets with a big red letter 'A' embroidered on my bosom, that's all."

"The father of the child?"

"The father—" She grimaced. "The father was married. He still is married," she said defiantly.

The head going up again, making a taut and beautiful line from her throat to the tip of her chin. "Still is married," he repeated.

"He has a lovely wife and four children and it wasn't his fault any more than it was mine and he didn't want to marry me any more than I wanted to marry him."

"It was just one of those things?"

"Just one of those things. It happened and we were both very sorry, but why should his wife and the children suffer for what I did?"

"You're very generous."

"Oh, he probably wouldn't have, anyhow. All I would have accomplished would have been to break up his marriage and hurt the children. When Chloe—that's my English teacher's name—said I should come and stay with her, I did."

"I see."

"Bunny was born there and we lived with Chloe. She was wonderful to me. Nobody knew."

"You didn't want anybody to know?"

She said, "Of course not! Of course not!" Her voice trembled and her hands moved away from each other and each of them clenched. "Having Chloe was very lucky for me."

Dennis looked at the clenched fists. Not as lucky as all that, maybe.

"Chloe had a little house and when Bunny was six months old she made me go to secretarial school and then, when I was trained, Chloe found this nice woman to come in and take care of Bunny while she was away and I got a job, too, so I could start paying my way."

The old expression "the woman pays" flashed through Dennis' mind, because she did, of course. Because this was payment. Friend or no, lucky or no, broad-minded or not, this girl believed she was a wicked girl and that she *should* be stoned through the streets with a big red letter "A" on her bosom. (He could see the rapid rise and fall of her bosom, so agitated by just recounting this story.) "That seems to have worked out for the best, then. Why did you come to New York?"

"Chloe got married," Blanche said. "She met this Englishman and went to live in England."

"And left you alone?"

"My goodness, you sound as if she shouldn't have. Of course she should have married Gavin. He's very nice. And I wasn't alone. I have Bunny."

"Of course. Bunny."

"Chloe's husband wanted to adopt Bunny. He wanted to take Bunny to England with them. He fell in love with Bunny. Everybody does." She jumped up. "That would have been good for Bunny, wouldn't it have? To have a mother and a father?"

"Children can use a mother and a father."

"You think I could have given her to them, too! Just like Mother!"

"Your mother wanted you to give Bunny away?"

"For her good! How do you think I feel when Mother says 'for her own good'? Don't you understand, Mother thinks Bunny is wrong. Not what I did, only, but Bunny, too! And that's not so!"

Now she was wringing her hands. Little soft hands wringing like the hands of heroines in old-fashioned books. "That is not so?"

"Of course not so! It can't be so! I mean God wouldn't let an innocent child—I mean, the sins of the fathers—we don't believe in that, any more, do we?"

Don't we? he thought, while shaking his head at her. Don't we? He wondered what guilt could be more racking than this which made this girl feel she had been damned until the third generation. To fight such a guilt would take a giant. Hercules would stagger under a load like that and now, although he had thrown his head back and had his eyes closed, he could still see the delicate body, the narrow wrists and ankles, the sloping shoulders and the small, soft hands wringing. Not Hercules, Dennis thought. No.

"Mother thought it was a gift from heaven, Chloe and Gavin wanting to take Bunny, because, then— You see there's a boy from Providence— He'd marry me in a minute. We'd been going around for a year before— He's forgiven me for what I did—" She frowned.

But you haven't forgiven yourself for whatever you did, Dennis thought. No God so implacable as self, he thought. No God, anywhere, so lacking in mercy.

"Bert's an engineer. He went and got this job in Sao Paulo where nobody would know. Sao Paulo in Brazil. I thought he was so marvelous when he would—honestly, I just worshiped him because he knew and he still wanted me, but he wanted me to give Bunny away, too. He leaped in the air when I wrote about it. I never thought for one moment he would, I just wrote about it, and how Mother—"

"So you wouldn't marry him?"

"No," she said. "I wouldn't."

He had no idea, of course, whether any of this was the truth, but the shame was true and the guilt (for whatever sin) was true, and that was enough. She suddenly parted her hands and, as he watched, rubbed them down her sides, frowning. He had seen so many look at their hands after rubbing them the way she was doing—He had seen people trying to wash their hands of so many sins, and how rarely they could do it, he thought. Now she was pacing up and down. "Do I smell coffee?" he asked.

"Coffee? Oh, I was just going to have some."

"Could we both?" He stood up and walked toward a door in the room.

Blanche said, "That's Mother's bedroom, the kitchen's the other door— No the *other* door!" Because now he had gone to her bedroom. He stood there looking in at it.

"That's my bedroom."

"Of course. Sorry."

By the time he joined her in the kitchen, she had poured two cups of coffee for them.

He picked up a cup. The coffee was very black.

"May I have some milk in mine? If you have it, of course. Silly of me," he said, going to the refrigerator. "Where there's a child there's always milk."

"Yes, and Mother always has her hot milk at night." She watched him pouring milk into his coffee. "Mother wouldn't sleep a wink, she says, if she didn't have her hot milk before going to bed." She put down her cup without tasting the coffee. "I don't think I can get it down."

"Try." He drank some of his coffee. "When did you eat last?"

"I was stuffing bread into my mouth when you came."

"Good."

"Good? When did Bunny eat last? When did Bunny eat last? I can't talk any more! I can't."

"Please try." She shook her head. "There are a couple of questions I think I should ask you. Tell me, do you think there is any possibility that Bunny was kidnapped?"

Why did she think of the spittle sliding down the apple? Because it was dirty, because it was filth, and an apple, fresh and rosy— Because spittle sliding down an apple was like a kidnaper's hands on Bunny. She shook her head. "Why should Bunny be kidnapped? I haven't any money."

He came to her, lifted the coffee cup and held it to her lips. "Well, it occurred to me, those people you mentioned, the ones who want Bunny so badly—the school teacher and her husband—do you think they could have—?"

She had sipped at the coffee and had to swallow it before she answered. "They're in England. I told you."

"Sure? Are you positive? Perhaps they just made you believe they were in England." He watched her carefully.

She took the cup from him and set it down. "I had a letter this morning and it was from England. I read it while waiting. Waiting," she said again, and her hands flew to each other.

He took her hands. "Are you sure it was from England? Can I see it?"

"Chloe said she had known that I wouldn't give Bunny away."

"Let me see the letter."

She shook her head. "I gave it away." She felt how his hands, holding her clasped ones, jerked suddenly, and looked at his face in surprise. "I was reading it in the hall of the school and this red-headed boy who collected stamps wanted it, so I gave it to him."

"Red-headed kid of about ten? Two front teeth missing?"

"You know him?"

"Yes, he's a patient of mine. Chrissie Robbins, a sibling-rivalry case. There's a little sister in the first group in Benton School. He's calling for her these days—we want him to be her superior, but he still prefers his imaginary companion. Chrissie invented this boy for himself, Calfit. Funny name, Calfit."

"Invented?"

"Haven't they heard about imaginary companions in Providence? It happens more often than you think and is perfectly okay unless there is a confusion between reality and—" She pulled her hands away. "What is it?"

"I don't know." She left him and walked to the door of the kitchen, looking out into the living room.

"There even was a play where a man invented— Did you ever see *Harvey*? The movie, perhaps? About an imaginary rabbit?" The word had hardly left his lips, she had hardly had time to make the connection: Rabbit, Bunny: Bunny Rabbit, when he felt the hot sting of her hand across his cheek. He turned away, furious with her because the tears had come into his eyes. They always did when he felt pain unexpectedly, and emancipated psychiatrist or no, this embarrassed him. He got himself under control and turned back to face her. "Why did you do that?"

"I'm sorry. I shouldn't have, but—" She gestured. "Oh, because she isn't asleep in the bedroom where she should be— You made me feel she was—erased—with your invisible rabbits. I couldn't help it. Oh, please, I'm sorry," she said. "You're being so kind and here I—I'm always doing things I'm sorry for!"

"Are you?" I'll bet you are, he thought. He hadn't even heard her moving across the floor then. She was one of those girls who go from stillness into sudden motion. Cats, he thought. He said stiffly, "You were saying?"

"No, I can't talk any more."

"We were talking about this letter from England that you gave Chrissie. Talk, Mrs. Lake, it is much better than thinking. Tell me about coming to New York."

"You're being very kind," she said. "I know you are, and I am afraid of being alone and thinking. Oh, I read *The New York Times* and answered an ad for a job and they wrote me, so I came."

"Job?"

"With McClellan and Forrestal. They're in the Empire State Building."

"What was wrong with the job in—wherever it was? You're being rather mysterious, aren't you, Mrs. Lake?"

"*Miss* Lake. That's why. There was nothing wrong with my job but you make more money in New York, and if I wasn't going to marry Bert— There's more future to jobs in New York. Don't think I'm a career woman. If I could, I'd stay home with Bunny, but I have to support us. Anyhow, New York is so big that it's easier not to have people know about you. You reminded me of Bert," she said. "That was part of the reason I slapped you. He wanted us to wipe Bunny out of existence, too."

"So when you slapped me, you were really slapping Bert?"

"Yes, you were just an innocent bystander who got in the way."

"Don't give it another thought. It's an occupational hazard; psychiatrists are always getting one kind of slap or another meant for entirely different people."

"But you're not my psychiatrist."

"Let's talk as if I were. Is it that which makes you want to hit out? People wiping out your child as if she didn't exist?"

She said, "And how would you feel if your child were lost and somebody—"

Her hand made the most exquisite outflung gesture of despair. He wondered if she had ever studied ballet.

"I cannot talk like this calmly! I can't sit here talking. I don't know what I'm saying because—underneath—all the time—" She laid her hand on her breast. "No, there's one thing I want to ask you—" She waited for his permissive nod. "When I was waiting outside the school for the policeman to come there was this woman. There were a couple of people behind me on the sidewalk and I could hear them talking about Bunny. This woman said it was like a *judgment*.

"I turned around—her voice was so—awful. She had a baby in a carriage and she kept shaking it. Rattling it. She said mothers who didn't stay home and take care of their babies— it was a *judgment* on them."

"Perhaps she was referring to herself, Miss Lake. People often do, don't they? From your description of her treatment of the baby in the carriage—'rattling' is very vivid—perhaps she wanted to shake her own baby out of her life and attributed her desire to you. Or perhaps she was jealous. There was a teacher in the Benton School last year who was jealous of the parents because she couldn't have a child of her own, and she projected abominations on their heads—" But she wasn't interested in the teachers in the school; she was merely waiting for him to be done, so she could continue.

"She did mean it would be a judgment of God on me if something happened to Bunny, didn't she?"

"Perhaps."

She came and stood very close to him, whispering, "You see, before I was sure that Bunny was coming, I prayed not to have a baby. I was so frightened."

"Frightened," he said, encouraging her to go on, because she was obviously having difficulty.

"Terribly frightened," she whispered, as if it couldn't possibly be spoken aloud. "I prayed not to have a baby."

"Yes, you prayed not to have a baby? I see, you mean that if the baby is gone now, you have no baby?" Her skin had turned chalky white. "So your prayer is answered?"

"That's superstition, isn't it? That's not religion! To believe that God would answer a prayer that way? That would be savage, wouldn't it? I mean, whatever punishment I deserve, Bunny doesn't—God wouldn't hurt a little child!" She didn't wait for him to agree or disagree, but challenged, threatened. "I would never believe in Him again," she said, "never!" She saw how he shook his head, how he smiled. "But I heard her saying it was a judgment every time I thought of a new horrible thing that could be happening to my baby. That's what's been driving me crazy," she whispered.

If George reached out and grabbed her again just when she got to the edge of the bed, she would go crazy. Emilio used to do that when Eddie was little. Eddie would yell in his crib and it wouldn't wake Emilio. Nothing woke Emilio once he got off, but when she'd roll away to go to the kid, that skinny arm of his would reach out and grab her. Like a cat with a mouse. Like Eddie that time with the black pussycat.

The way to keep the springs from creaking was to press down the same time you got up. She didn't do it right, and the springs creaked. Let him wake up then, Rose thought. She stood there next to the bed with her hands on her hips. I've been a good wife to him. If I want to get up from the bed and go find Eddie, I got the right!

"You lay there sleeping, you big lug, but me I laid there thinking about Eddie. Because I know Eddie and you don't, Georgie!"

She felt her way across the room to the chair where she had thrown her clothes. It was because she was scared she *didn't* know Eddie, how far he'd go. Her own kid.

But she knew he had less than two bucks on him, and she knew the fellows he went with, where they hung out. In that bowling alley near Third.

All she wanted to do was find out where Eddie was so she could rest herself. All she wanted was so Eddie would really say to her the way she'd been saying to herself laying there next to Georgie, "You're nuts, Mom. You honestly thought because George rode me that way—?"

Because Eddie had found out where the girl lived. Because why else was he hanging around her house, for the air?

"You're real nuts, Mom."

"Because of that pussycat, Eddie." Because he had stretched out on the floor with it, playing. Laying on the floor with it. Because he got a piece of rag from the kitchen and tied it on a piece of string and played so nice with the kitten. Because the kitten got tired playing with the string and went under that table they had with the long cloth on it, and Eddie went under the table after it. And then the string.

But the girl wasn't a dumb little pussycat. Any girl knew better than a dumb little pussycat.

He put the coffee cup back into her hands and she did drink some of it, although it had, of course, become quite cold. He told her that she must stop blaming herself. "Suppose you try to blame someone else. Do you think that the boy who wanted to marry you— The child stands in his way, doesn't she? Do you think that it is at all possible that he could have come to New York?"

"From Sao Paulo?"

"It doesn't take too long by plane."

"Bert doesn't even know where I live in New York."

Something in the way she held her head made him ask the question. "But there is somebody who does know where you live?"

She said, "Yes, somebody does."

He asked her to tell him and she told him: A boy in a fruit-and-vegetable store to whom she had never even spoken. Who had never even spoken to her; who, according to her, had simply leaned against a bin of potatoes and stared at her. (He had those swimmy eyes. Feverish, she called them. He wondered whether the boy in the greengrocer's could be nearsighted. Couldn't this possibly explain the quality of his stare? Didn't nearsighted people often stare like that?)

"You don't think I should call the police and tell them about him?"

"No, I don't. I wouldn't bother the police with that."

"I suppose not." She sighed. "I suppose not. Of course not. It was you who made me think about him. I wouldn't even have thought of such a thing if not for you." She had the feeling that he wanted her to accuse someone of kidnaping Bunny. Not to make her feel silly, she told herself, but probably because now she was supposed to feel that whatever else she might be imagining was equally as ridiculous as the theory of the boy in the fruit-and-vegetable store. Well, she thought, looking at Dr. Newhouse, he looks satisfied anyhow. She went to the telephone.

He heard her explaining to the police how terrible it was just to wait, asking if she couldn't go along with the policeman, go along with Officer Klein, for instance. She listened to what they said and then hung up.

"Detective Klein is looking for her. He's a detective. He's out looking and they can't reach him until he calls in. I can't seem to reach *them*. There's a kind of a *wall* between me and them," she said.

He saw her walk to the table and pick up her pocketbook. "Where are you going?"

"Out looking." She held out her hand for him to shake and he took it. "Thank you for trying to help me. It was very kind of you." She pulled her hand away and walked to the door, then paused with her hand on the knob. "They don't seem to *feel* it," she said. "As if it weren't important. They seem to be taking it in their stride so." She opened the door. "How can a little lost girl be routine to anyone?"

He followed her as she hurried to the elevator. "What is your plan?"

She pressed her finger on the bell. "Plan? Like what to do when the atom bomb strikes?"

She was making fun of him, he thought, of the prim way he had said that. Dennis felt himself blushing, because it was true, he thought. At least that was what he felt every time he read or heard some of the civil-defense stuff. Laughable, it seemed to him, too, for that was what she meant by her remark. Canute commanding the waves to stop. Ant citizen hurrying around carrying off microscopic crumbs in the face of monumental disaster.

"All the plan I can think of is to keep moving," she said bitterly. The elevator came and she stepped into it. "I'll keep moving and I'll keep asking."

She moved and he moved with her. She stopped people and asked them, and he waited in back of her while she received the completely negative answers. She must have been in the drugstores already because she just walked in and the pharmacist and the soda jerk began to shake their heads. When she came to the brightly lighted bowling alley, she stood for a moment staring up at the huge neon sign in which a bowling ball rolled perpetually toward pins which fell to rise again. She seemed puzzled, as if she could not believe that any mechanism should be working tonight, and he could understand that, too, he decided. (How transparent her face was!)

He followed her into the bowling alley and watched her as she moved along the benches which lined the wall and questioned the men and women sitting there. He saw the heads shake and then, as she passed on, the eyes following her. She had reached the last of the benches when he saw her stop. Her hand went to her mouth and then she ran, stiffly, crookedly, as if her legs were both stiff and too loose, to a tall blond man who was lifting a ball out of the rack. She pulled on the man's arm, and they stood staring at each other, then, as she ran toward the door, the man turned back to the alley and, without pausing for preparation, bowled the ball. His arm had moved viciously, as if he wanted to knock down not only the pins but the whole alley, although only one pin toppled. Somehow, the sound sickened Dennis. He did not rush after Blanche, and because he was standing there, he saw the dark woman's face after Blanche brushed past her. He saw how the dark woman stared after Blanche, and how her lips moved as if in prayer; then he hurried out of the alley to catch up with Blanche. It was difficult; not that she was running so fast but something about the way she was moving, he thought, made the people in the street clear out of her way only to stop when she passed and stand there staring after her so that they impeded his progress.

Rose crossed herself. She did not recognize any of the people bowling, but Gino Ricciardi was sitting there on the bench, so she hurried to him. "Gino, you seen Eddie?"

He was watching the bowling and she was standing in his way. "Saddy night." He leaned sidewise to see better.

"You ain't seen Eddie since Saturday night, Gino? You're certain?"

"Saddy night."

Rose put her hand on the boy's shoulder. "Gino, that girl who just ran out of here, what was the matter with her, anyway?"

"She lost her kid, it seems. She asked everybody did they see her little girl?" He measured the little girl in the air. "She lost her little girl. She could be my little girl any time she says the word."

"What do you mean she lost her little girl, Gino?"

"Hey! Mrs. Negrito!" He pulled her hand off his shoulder. "She took her little girl to school this morning and the kid ran out after her and nobody can find her."

"Gino, do you think she went to the police, the cops?"

"How do I know? He had to lean so far to the left that he shoved the man next to him on the bench. "Excuse it," he said.

"Gino, you dead sure you didn't see Eddie since Saturday night? You can tell me. I'm Eddie's momma."

"Saddy night. I'm sure."

"Did any of the other boys see Eddie, Gino? You got to tell me. I got to find Eddie right away."

"Search me. That's a funny thing. You lost Eddie and she lost her little girl. You should get together with her, Mrs.

Negrito." He shoved back against the wall, the red coming into his face. For a minute there, he thought she was going to take a sock at him. "What's the matter with her?" he said, watching her run out of the place like a crazy woman. If he saw Eddie, he'd tell him his old lady was on the warpath. If he was Eddie, he'd keep out of the old lady's way, if he was Eddie.

She was talking to the policeman at the high desk by the time he caught up with her in the precinct station.

"That's right, off duty," the policeman said.

She was holding on to the high desk. He put his hand on her arm and she turned to him. Her eyes were so distended that he could see the shining whites of them, all around.

"He was in that bowling alley," she said. "The one I told you about, Klein. The nice one who cared. He's supposed to be looking for my baby and he's in a bowling alley!"

"Klein's off duty," the policeman behind the desk said to Dennis.

"They just *told* me he was out looking! Where is that lieutenant? In there?" She began to run in that same jerky way toward the wooden door to the right of the desk.

Dennis caught her arm. "You only saw the man for a — You can't be— Are you *sure?*" he asked weakly, because there was such scorn in the distended eyes.

"Yes, I'm sure." She knocked on the door and then flung it open. "I don't understand," she said to the man behind the desk. "Why did you lie to me? Why is that Klein bowling and not looking for Bunny?"

Dennis said, "I'm Dr. Newhouse. I spoke to you before, Lieutenant Duff." He said to her, "They did lie. A white lie, don't you see? It was obvious to Lieutenant Duff that you trusted Officer Klein so when you telephoned, Lieutenant Duff had them tell you he was out looking. Because you trusted him, to make it easier on you. Officer Klein, as you saw, is off duty. It is the Missing Persons who are looking for Bunny, isn't that right, Lieutenant Duff?"

"Yes, Doc, that's right."

"To be kind?" she whispered, leaning on the Lieutenant's desk.

Dennis could see the tear sliding down the curve of her cheek. "To be kind to you, that's all." He heard her low "Excuse me." The lieutenant made a helpless gesture, and then yanked at his belt.

"Why don't you give yourself a break, Mrs. Lake? Why don't you let us get your mother to you?" She shook her head. He yanked at his belt again. "See, it's we don't think you should be alone at a time like this. How about getting a friend to stay with you?"

"I have no friends. For heaven's sake," she said, "I've only been in the city three weeks. I have a job. I work very hard. It's very high pressure in New York, and when I get home I try to make it up to Bunny for not being with her. By the time I put my baby to bed I'm ready to crawl in next to her."

"How about one of the girls in the office?"

"No," she said. "I don't want anyone in the office to know about—this. It's important that they don't know. I *know* you're trying to be kind," she said, but her teeth clenched.

"Okay, listen, if you have no friends—New Yorkers aren't as hardhearted as they're cracked up to be—anyone in the house you live in would be glad to help out."

"No one in the apartment house. There's no one in the apartment house. I don't need anyone, really, I don't. I'll go," she said. "I won't bother you. Not you, either," she said to Dr. Newhouse. "Thank you, but I'd rather be alone now."

It was just more of the same, she thought. It was just like Officer Klein, kindness, that's all; it turned out to be kindness, that was all. It was only because she wanted each of the policemen in the outer office to be out looking for Bunny that she found something peculiar in the way they looked at her. She wanted the whole force to be turned into Missing Persons.

On the sidewalk, a young woman laughed up in a man's face. She wanted the whole world to be turned into a Missing Persons squad. Blanche moved up the street, trying in her mind to turn the clock back. It wasn't night at all. It was daylight. She saw Bunny coming out the front door of the school. (But how? Because now she could hear herself closing that heavy front door after herself.) She was Bunny trying to find Mommy. She had covered the houses in the direction which she had taken that morning from the school to the subway, forgetting that by the time Bunny had toiled down all those steps—two feet on each—deep sigh of achievement at each step—by the time Bunny reached the bottom of all those stairs and trotted through the blue hall and got the door open (somehow, obviously!)—she, Blanche, would have been out of sight. Bunny wouldn't have seen her to follow her, so she might have gone in the opposite direction.

As Blanche passed the school, she saw a light on the top floor, but she hurried on. If the director found Bunny, she would call the police, and so on— When she reached the first house that she hadn't covered previously, she could hardly breathe. On the ground floor, the people were very encouraging. They told Blanche that if Missing Persons was after Bunny, they'd find her. Once, they said, a relative had been lost and Missing Persons turned the neighborhood inside out. Upside down. They told Blanche that she didn't need to worry.

Instead of walking upstairs, Blanche went out of the house. The street was quiet. Why hadn't they told her that the neighborhood had already been turned upside down by Missing Persons? Why had nobody mentioned that they had already been questioned by them? Even the people who had been annoyed with her hadn't said that. Blanche looked up and down the block. The nearest drugstore was the one where the soda jerk had said Bunny might not be alone. She couldn't make herself go back into that drugstore and she walked in the opposite direction until she found another.

The telephone number for Missing Persons was Canal 6-2000. When the telephone was picked up, Blanche said, "Will you connect me with someone who can tell me—someone who has a list of lost persons. *Missing* persons.

"I want to know if someone has already been listed as missing, please. I think I saw—" She felt she had to give some explanation which would throw them off the track, and broke the sentence off, leaving it as vague as that. When the next voice came on she said, "Can you tell me whether a child of three—Bunny Lake—has been listed as missing?"

"When?" they asked. "Where? Address? Description?"

Blanche wondered if the voice was going down a list, running his finger down a list.

"No, ma'am, there is no Bunny Lake listed as missing. Do you wish to report it?"

"Are you quite sure? Are you absolutely sure?"

"Yes, ma'am, I'm sure. It's my business to be sure. Do you

want to report this person as missing? Who is this? What is your name?"

Blanche put the receiver down and walked out of the booth. There was no one at the soda fountain so she stood there staring at the list of prices. Hamburgs—35. Ham and eggs—65. They were not looking for Bunny. Ham and cheese—35. They had told her that they were looking for Bunny, but they were not. They had told her that Klein was looking for Bunny, but he was not.

"I'll be with you in a minute, Miss," the soda jerk said. "My God, the way some people won't wait a second!"

Blanche stood outside the drugstore. "I don't understand," she whispered. "I don't understand!" How could it be, she thought, and put her palms to her head because her head was going to burst open from the pressure inside it. You were brought up to fear policemen but to trust them. The law. The minions of the law. Guardians of the— "We're doing everything possible," the lieutenant had said. Everything she had been taught to believe was exploding inside her head like Roman candles.

If she went back to the precinct station on Sixty-seventh Street and told them that she simply did not understand—

But they had lied to her. They had lied to her. What would stop them from lying now?

She walked along the street, looking into faces. "Don't you have any friends?" the lieutenant had asked. "New Yorkers aren't as hardhearted as they're cracked up to be," he had said. But weren't they? She stared into the faces she passed. Maybe all policemen lied. Maybe no one in the world owed another the truth; maybe all kindness and charity was a lie. She looked at the lights in the building on the opposite side of the street and remembered the lights on the top floor of the school.

Maybe nothing was honored of what she had been taught, but money was honored, debts were. The school was where she should go since she had paid that woman $350 to take care of Bunny. That debt the director must honor. Blanche swerved out to avoid the man and woman coming by her and began to run toward the school.

Blanche went to the red door and found the bell and pressed it. After a little while, she heard a window being thrown open and moved out toward the edge of the sidewalk so that the director would be able to make out who it was, facing the building so that the director couldn't mistake her for someone who had no claim on her. She bumped into someone. "Excuse me," she said, and called up toward the open window, "It's me, Miss Benton. It's Blanche Lake."

"It's late, Mrs. Lake."

She frowned up at the dim face on the top floor, because any mention of time made her angry. "I must talk to you."

"I'm very sorry."

"Sorry isn't enough. I must talk to you. I don't understand what is happening." The window closed and Blanche ran back to the red door, putting her ear to it so that she would hear the sound of steps. She tried to wait patiently, reminding herself that there were three flights. Then she did hear steps, but behind her; she swung around to tell whoever it was to be quiet so that she could hear Miss Benton coming and it was Dr. Newhouse. She said, "Go away."

He said, "I wish I could, Miss Lake. I assure you I wish I could. I have a damned heavy schedule tomorrow, I—" Because he was annoyed, he pushed her aside rather brusquely and rang the bell, not once but four times, so that she peered into his face. He pressed the bell again in the same way, four times.

Blanche said, "She's not going to let me in!" She raised her fists to hammer on the door but he caught them.

"You'll only hurt your hands." He held both her hands with one of his, pressing them against his chest.

"Do you think I care?" It was intolerable, somehow, that his cashmere sweater should be so soft. She tried to pull her hands free.

"She'll let us in," he said. "Be patient. Be still." He held her hands quiet against his soft sweater. "She'll be down in a few minutes."

"Won't you come in?" Miss Benton said, holding the door open.

The genteel phrase, Miss Benton's voice, which was as soft as Dr. Newhouse's sweater, were equally intolerable. "Won't you come in?" As if she were inviting her to tea! Blanche pushed past Miss Benton into the hall with the blue paint and the wooden benches along the wall.

"Shall we go into the office, Dr. Newhouse?" Miss Benton opened the office door and put the light on in the room.

Dr. Newhouse looked from the wooden desk to the wooden chairs and back again to Blanche. "Upstairs. Maybe you can get Miss Lake to take something, Miss Benton. She's pretty much done in." He looked hard at Miss Benton, pressing his lips together, shaking his head.

"Of course," Miss Benton said. She led the way upstairs obediently.

Dr. Newhouse waited for Blanche to precede him.

Blanche saw that Miss Benton had changed her suit for narrow black trousers and a black sweater. She wore some bracelets which tinkled as she walked, and the sound of the bracelets, brassy and insouciant, grated on Blanche's ears, was magnified. Halfway up, Blanche stopped so short that she brushed against Dr. Newhouse behind her. "Of course I'm not going to 'have something'! How ridiculous! All I want is for you to tell me—you must know—you must have asked—why aren't the police looking for Bunny?"

"Let's go on up, shall we?"

"Let's not go on up, shall we? They're not looking for Bunny, do you hear? I telephoned Missing Persons and they're not! Why not?" Blanche pulled off Dr. Newhouse's arm, which was now supporting her.

"Upstairs," Dr. Newhouse said.

Blanche, glancing up, saw how Miss Benton silently questioned Dr. Newhouse. Miss Benton didn't want her upstairs; she was asking him if she had to have her upstairs. If Miss Benton didn't want her upstairs, Blanche would go up.

There was a small round table pulled up before the fireplace. A neat fire was burning in a black grate, dancing its shadows on a long circular cloth on the table, glinting off the china and silver. The door to the kitchenette was wide open and Blanche could smell dinner cooking and see the pots on the small range. The tiny plupping sound was coffee perking. She had been fixing dinner for someone. She had been expecting someone. She had a date, Blanche thought. It was intolerable that Miss Benton in neat narrow trousers and the black sweater and bracelets should have been expecting a date, should have softly set down the gleaming silver. "I want to know!" she shouted. She had frightened Miss Benton. She saw how Miss Benton was looking at this doctor for help.

"Haven't they found someone responsible for her?" Miss Benton was asking the doctor.

They wanted someone responsible. When they found someone responsible, they would tell. They would tell Mother and then Mother would tell her. Blanche threw up her hands and covered her face. "They did find Bunny! They don't have to look any more, that's it, isn't it? They have found Bunny!" He was pulling at her hands to make her see, but she would not see; she bent her head and dug her teeth into his hand. "Dead!" she screamed, but covering her face again because she had got rid of his hands. "They found her dead and they didn't dare tell me! Tell me," she said, and now removed her hands. "You tell me—tell *me!*" She pulled at his sleeve. Tell *me! I'm* her mother. No one else is her mother, I am. You tell *me!*"

He said, "No, they didn't find Bunny. No one found Bunny, Miss Lake. No one found Bunny dead. Get a glass of water," he said. He had his arms around her now. "Reach into my pocket, right side. There's a vial there. Now water." While Miss Benton hurried into the kitchenette, he said, "I want you to take one of these sedatives and I'm going to explain. Sedative and explain."

His voice was a sedative, she thought, shuddering. His soft sweater was a sedative.

"Miss Benton is going to explain. I promise. Thank you." He held the glass toward Blanche and gave her the pill, but when he saw her lips press together, he dropped the vial back into his pocket. "Just the water. Sip it while Miss Benton explains. Just the water, then." He tipped the glass to her lips. "Your child was not found dead. Drink the water, please."

He was waiting to see her make some movement. She swallowed a little of the water and then took the glass from him, but only to get it out of the way. "If Bunny isn't—if I'm wrong and they haven't—found her—then why aren't they looking for her?"

"Get her the book."

"Do you think we should, Dr. Newhouse?"

He kept his eyes on Blanche's face. "Yes, I do."

Miss Benton went to a small desk in the corner of the room and lifted a notebook off it. It had a stiff paper cover. She opened it and gave it to Dr. Newhouse, who looked around and laid it on the edge of a small table next to an easy chair. Blanche realized that she would see this notebook only if she first sat on the easy chair, so she sat.

"This is the list of parents in the Benton School, 1955 to 1956." He pointed to where the date was clearly printed, then ran his finger down the page on which there were names, addresses and telephone numbers.

"This is the Threes Group," he said. "This is where your name should be. Please read it." As Blanche read, he read off the names aloud. "Your name isn't there, is it?" He turned to the other lists, running his finger down them. "It isn't in any of the lists."

"What have lists got to do with finding Bunny?"

Miss Benton came around to where Blanche could see her. "When I returned from the agency this afternoon and heard what I thought was a burglar in the basement, I was so startled that it threw me off base. I wasn't quite myself, I suppose. And then when you said that one of the children had been locked in, all that mattered was finding her. I didn't stop to ask questions about the child. If the name meant nothing to me, well, the first day—and as I told you, I'm always bad at names, anyhow. Any child locked in—naturally!

"We rushed around to find her and when we didn't, we first assumed that she had gone out of the building, then you and that policeman went off to search for her and I called the staff to find out what they knew. They knew nothing. None of them had seen or heard of—her," she said. "Actually the reason I went to my registration book was to get your number and call you to get the thing clear in my mind." She pointed to the note-book. "You saw for yourself— And I had to wait to reach you until you called me back. Do you remember that I asked you for your telephone number? I said I had it down in the office and that I didn't want to go down, but it actually was because I don't have your telephone number."

Blanche looked from Miss Benton to the book on the table. She ran through the names again, then examined the book. A dime-store notebook, names, addresses, telephone numbers, written in ink. "I don't understand."

"Get the application blanks. Miss Benton will get the appli-cation blanks and show you that there isn't one there for Bunny."

"Of course there is an application blank for Bunny! Let me see them. I filled one out for Bunny and I also filled out a check for three hundred and fifty dollars. The tuition was seven hundred dollars, payable in advance, but I didn't have the whole amount, so—"

"In the back of that notebook you're holding are notations on tuition received. And here are the application blanks." She held up a thick file of them. "I brought them up from the office to make absolutely sure."

"Of course I filled out an application blank." Blanche held her hand out for the file.

"Do you have your cancelled check from the bank?"

"No, I don't. It hasn't been returned yet," she said. "It isn't time to get the cancelled checks yet."

Dr. Newhouse took the thick file from Miss Benton. "Show her where the dates of checks received are noted."

"They all had to be in by August fifteenth. I deposited them as they came in so you certainly should have had your can-celled check, shouldn't you?"

"My check was written on September twenty-first."

"All tuition checks had to be in by the end of August. I

couldn't operate if checks came in September, now could I? There is no school that I know of which doesn't—"

"But you took Bunny in because of the little girl who dropped out. I know your groups were all filled in June; you told me so." She saw Miss Benton raise her eyebrows at Dr. Newhouse.

"I told you so?"

"Stop shaking your head at him as if I were crazy. I don't mean you. I mean your teacher—your *representative*. I was so happy," she said, turning away from the raised eyebrows. "I was going to find a woman to take care of Bunny while I was at work, after Mother left New York, the way I'd done before, but that wouldn't have been half so good as a school where there were other children for Bunny, and Mother didn't approve of schools, but she kept telling me stories of women who took care of children and weren't trustworthy. She had this story about a nurse who doped two children with gas from the kitchen stove. And giving children beer to make them sleepy. So you can imagine how relieved I was when I got your letter saying you had been told by the registrar of the Stevenson Nursery School that I wanted to get Bunny in there, only they were all filled—"

"The Stevenson School on York?" Miss Benton was raising her eyebrow at Dr. Newhouse again.

"Yes, of course. When the registrar heard about this child dropping out of your school—" The eyebrow quirked. "As a friendly gesture! I thought it was so kind of her!"

"We had no vacancies in any of our groups this year, Miss Lake. They were completely filled by June and nobody dropped out."

Dr. Newhouse said, "Miss Lake, how could you come and pick Bunny up at five? Doesn't your job downtown keep you later than that?"

"Mother was going to while she was with me and the woman we were going to find to take care of Bunny—I mean

I was going to have to find a woman, but only part time. She would have had to take Bunny home from here at five and then get dinner and finish washing up. Part time. After Mother left New York, I'd need someone."

"Miss Lake, none of my teachers ever saw you before today. None of them knew your name."

Blanche noticed how first one of them asked a question and then the other did. "The one who interviewed Bunny saw us. Her name was Miss Ditmars." She closed her eyes because of the way the two of them looked at each other.

"Miss Ditmars. I see. Miss Lake, when did anyone interview Bunny?"

"The twenty-first. The day I wrote the check. I gave her the check. Miss Ditmars."

"On the twenty-first? The twenty-first was a *Sunday*, Miss Lake. Where?"

"Sunday because she wanted me to come with Bunny for the interview. She said you preferred to have the parent with the child and I have a job. So on Sunday. The interview was right here." She opened her eyes. "I don't mean here; downstairs. We went up to the room on the second floor and she watched Bunny playing with the toys. She wanted to see if Bunny was emotionally mature enough for the school."

"The school wasn't open then. It was closed for the summer recess."

"I know that. The school opened today. There was nobody here that day but Miss Ditmars."

"Who was in Chicago. Miss Lake—" She looked at Dr. Newhouse. "I was away at the Cape from the sixteenth to the thirtieth of September and the school was closed up tight. Dr. Newhouse, must we go on with this? This is so—*dreadful*—must we go on?"

"Miss Lake," Dr. Newhouse said gently, "perhaps I'm wrong to have gone into it this way. Miss Benton thinks so, but you do understand now, don't you, why they aren't searching for a little girl who disappeared from this school this morning? This school has no record of such a little girl. No application blank. No check. No teacher interviewed you, nobody who saw you before today has turned up."

"I have the stub," Blanche said, opening her purse. "I'll show you the stub."

Dr. Newhouse bent and put his hand over hers, pressing the clasp of the pocketbook closed. "Anyone can write a stub. Anyone can write anything on a stub."

"Your cancelled check is your receipt," Blanche said wildly. "I know that—but a school—I mean, you don't think of a school as being dishonest."

"Ask her if she's had any communication from me."

"The letter came. I told you about it. The registrar telling you—"

"Oh, yes. Signed by me?"

"Yes."

"Louise Benton? Where is this letter?"

"Bunny scribbled all over it. Mother told her she would have to learn to read and write in school and Bunny wanted to show Mother she could write, and she scribbled all over it. Children do scribble," she said. "Don't the children in your school scribble all over things ever?"

"But you threw out this letter?"

"It was all scribbled over, and torn. Anyhow, what did I need to keep it for? It wasn't so precious," she said. "I kept the brochure, though. I kept it to read to Bunny about how nice it was—and the pictures of the little sinks and the equipment—" She saw their faces. "I can get the brochure," she whispered, wanting to move, to run, to do anything but stay here with their faces looking that way.

Dr. Newhouse said to Miss Benton, "That is the way it's been all down the line."

"I know. The police told me so." Miss Benton sighed.

But she had to look at their faces. Blanche wet her lips. "You're saying that I didn't bring Bunny here at all? I didn't leave her here?" How could she have said that? She turned to Dr. Newhouse. "She is saying that I didn't—that her school didn't lose Bunny because they never had her? Then what did I do with Bunny? Why am I blaming it on her?"

"Where did you lose her, Miss Lake? We don't know what really happened."

She wanted to dig her nails into the evenness of his voice. "Because her name isn't in that book you made them stop looking for her? You told this—this bunch of hooey to the police and they stopped looking for her because of it?" She pulled herself out of her chair.

"Where will you go?"

"Get out of my way."

"Where will you go? I followed you. I saw how far you go. Where do you think you're going to get ringing doorbells? It's later now. It's not safe."

"And it's safe for Bunny? Get out of my way," she repeated. She saw Miss Benton's hand reach out and touch his sleeve softly, and then he stepped out of her way.

"I'm sure Miss Lake is just going to the police station and that is the best thing she can do. The police—"

"The police will attend to *you*," Blanche called back over her shoulder, hurrying down the stairs. "After they find Bunny, I'm going to the police about *you!*" The sound of the steps behind her made her go faster. When she reached the first floor he caught up with her, but he didn't stand between her and the door.

"May I come with you?" he asked. "Please?"

"Do you think I care?" she asked, and began to run.

"Don't you see?" she asked Lieutenant Duff when they let her go into his office. (They wouldn't at first; the one at the high desk wanted her to wait outside. He said the lieutenant was out, but the man, the psychiatrist, spoke to the policeman and then he went into the lieutenant's office and then they let her in.) "It's her school she's thinking about, don't you see? She's only scared that if the other parents find out that they lose children, they'll take their children away and demand their money back, don't you see?" She took a deep breath.

"She erased my name in that notebook she has. Or she bought a new notebook. You can get them anywhere. How long would it be to rewrite a list of names? She tore up my application blank." The lieutenant would not look at her. He kept his eyes on the doctor, who was standing beside her. "They're all hanging together, isn't that obvious? They're all protecting that school. It's their job!" She tried to force the lieutenant to look at her instead of at the doctor. One cheek was gray and the other a dark red where he had been rubbing at it. He had been rubbing at his face because he was sorry for her, but he didn't believe her. "All right," Blanche said, "don't believe I left Bunny there. Don't believe they're all in it together, if that's how you want it. All right! My little girl is lost in New York City and you've got to find her." The lieutenant began to rub his cheek again. His eye on that side of his face was half closed, as if he were hurting himself, rubbing so hard, but he just sat there. She began to pound on the desk. "Get up! Get moving! You're a New York City policeman, find Bunny!"

The lieutenant spoke to the doctor behind her. "I can't take much more of this, Doc. I'm not chicken, but this poor kid here—" His eye screwed up again as though her hands pounding on the desk top hurt his face. "We'd better take over. How're we going to wait until we can get her mother? We can step in all right, Doc, if you—"

"Find her, find her, find her!" she screamed. "How can you sit there and not find a little girl? Don't you have any heart? With nobody looking—can't you imagine what could be happening to her? Haven't you any heart at all?"

"Yes, I have a heart," he said. "Miss Lake. Miss Lake, if I had a kid who was lost and a big so-and-so of a cop didn't take the city apart to find her, I'd tear him apart with my bare hands!" He looked down at his hands. "I got a heart and so I can't take any more of this. You haven't got any kid so there isn't any kid lost, Miss Lake, and that's why we stopped looking. Okay," he said to the doctor. "Okay, I did it!"

She was still sitting in the chair but the room was—Someone lifted her head up from between her knees and a cool hand pressed her forehead. She opened her eyes and saw that it was the same office, the same desk; only the lieutenant wasn't there any longer and she was alone with the man, the doctor. He was kneeling on the floor in front of the chair and she looked straight into his eyes.

"Rest," he said. "You fainted."

He had told them that it wasn't that woman doing it to protect her school. He said that there wasn't any little girl lost. It wasn't his hand cool—a wet handkerchief. "You said there wasn't any Bunny." He moved the handkerchief to her cheek, but it was wrong to let it feel so good there. She moved her cheek away. *"Harvey,"* she said. "Imaginary rabbit! Imaginary Bunny, that's who you meant! I'm glad I slapped you!" She saw his Bunny-soft sweater. "I'm glad. My subconscious knew even if I didn't what you really meant. I wish I had slapped you harder. I wish I had— You spy!" Blanche said. "Poking around my apartment! You were poking around my apartment!" But that was silly to get angry with him; what did he matter? She tried to compose herself. "Let me explain to them."

"They understand already," he said, getting up, dusting off his trousers. "What good will any further—"

"Oh, you! *You'll* do me good, won't you?"

"Yes," he said, "I will if you'll let me. Let me help you, Miss Lake." He forgot to brush the dust off, but when she only glared at him, he moved out of her way and finished the dusting, tucked his scarf into the neck of his sweater more tidily.

The door was open and Blanche could see the lieutenant talking to a policeman in the outer room. She called out, "Lieutenant!" Since the doctor would not move away, and anyhow she was afraid she would fall if she tried to get up, she raised her voice. "Lieutenant!" What was his name? "Lieutenant Duff!" He was standing in the doorway.

"Is she okay, Doc? I just couldn't take it, her thinking we wouldn't be tearing the place apart!"

He was not looking at her or talking to her; as if she was imaginary, too. "I'm fine now. And think I know—I can explain. I want to explain. I haven't my own things here yet. There is no crib in my apartment because Mother is using the bedroom Bunny is going to have. When Mother leaves I'm going to buy a second-hand crib—Bunny's own one is in storage. She's been sleeping with me," Blanche said.

"No high chair—"

Bunny sitting on a year's copies of *House and Garden* topped by a big dictionary and covered with the old pink waterproof apron she used to wear when she bathed Bunny. She explained this. "No snapshot," the lieutenant was saying, "not a single person in the apartment house . . . The super— We figured that since she'd just moved in, there'd be something she'd 'a needed to see the super about. . . . One of those houses where they have carriage rooms . . . The super lifts the carriages up to a high shelf they have. . . ."

Blanche felt as if she were talking to herself. "Her stroller is back home with the rest of her things. *Listen!* The apartment is a sublet, furnished, and very reasonable. I was living in a hotel the first week looking for a place so Mother could come with Bunny. Mother kept Bunny in Chloe's house while I went to New York to find an apartment. This girl in the office heard that I needed a place and she had a friend who wanted to sublet, but this friend wouldn't have sublet it to me if she knew about Bunny. That happens all the time in New York, doesn't it? Doesn't it?" she asked the policeman again, although it didn't feel as if she were really asking him. "Don't people not want to sublet to anyone who has a young child?" She turned to Dr. Newhouse instead. "You *know* people won't! This girl in the office didn't know about Bunny because all of us there are supposed to be unmarried. I told you about that! I am unmarried so I wasn't lying when I said so to Personnel. That's why I didn't leave the school the telephone number of the office. I intended to explain to them first that if they had to call me they shouldn't say anything about having Bunny!"

The lieutenant said to Dr. Newhouse, "The elevator there's self-service, so that's no help. There's no doorman there, either, like in some of the big houses."

At home the milkman knew Bunny, Blanche thought, but here it is delivered before she gets up, and left outside the service door. And there's no postman here. Bunny used to wait for the postman back home; she can't even reach the mailbox down in the lobby here. This was no good. She said to the lieutenant, "Tell me the name of a detective! They look for people. I want you to tell me the name of the best detective you know. Private detective. This is a private matter, I mean. I could look one up in the Classified," she added, because he wouldn't look at her, was focusing on the doctor, who was brushing his hands together. *Wanted to brush her off?* she thought. *Go ahead, do,* she thought. "Lieutenant, I'm only asking you in order to save time, because you should know who is the best one." She saw the lieutenant was asking the doctor and that the doctor shrugged and agreed. "It can't do any harm," the shrug meant, but she didn't protest that because this, too, would waste time. She merely looked coldly at the doctor and saw how his thin cheeks turned red.

They allowed her to use the telephone right here, moving it close enough because she stumbled trying to get up.

The lieutenant and the doctor listened while she told the story to the detective.

"Have you notified Missing Persons, Mrs. Lake?"

"Yes, but I want you to look for her, too. No, I don't have any picture. No, the police haven't one, either." Now she remembered how oddly the policeman had looked at her when they couldn't find the picture. "I'll describe her for you." She saw how the doctor studied her as she described Bunny, thinking of *Harvey* the imaginary rabbit again, she supposed, and glared at him.

"Is there anyone who might want the child for any reason?"

Still glaring at the doctor, she told the detective about the boy in the fruit-and-vegetable store. The doctor, she noticed, wanted the lieutenant to listen to this. "I don't really think he took Bunny," she said, defying them. "I just thought I'd mention it." The detective kept saying he would find out what Missing Persons had turned up. "I want you to work independently," she kept telling him. "I want you to start now. This minute!" When she hung up the lieutenant asked the doctor about the boy in the fruit store. Blanche listened to the way Dr. Newhouse told the lieutenant about what Mrs. Negrito had said to her; he repeated what she had told him, he told the whole truth, but when he finished she saw how crazy it sounded. Keeping his voice even and expressionless that way, he had made it sound even more farfetched. Blanche told them to forget about the boy, Eddie. "Lieutenant Duff, I just thought— I mean, if I had *known* that you thought . . . Lieutenant, of course we can prove about Bunny! She has a birth certificate, you know! There are such things as records!"

"Sure there are, Miss Lake, sure there are. We're not for-getting that, believe me. Now you got to remember what time we got this, right? You got to remember record offices keep respectable hours even if we cops don't. Now, tomorrow morning, bright and early, believe me, we're going to . . . "

"Tomorrow! Tomorrow! You're going to wait until tomor-row!"

Lieutenant Duff said to Dr. Newhouse, "She talks as if we done nothing but sit around on our fat fannies! Come on, now, Miss Lake, we accomplished a lot in the couple hours we got this!"

"Tomorrow!" Blanche reminded herself of the detective she had hired. She would pay him, so he wouldn't just sit and wait. She pulled herself out of the chair and said to Lieutenant Duff, "If that detective comes here or calls here and you tell him that there is no Bunny so he won't even start looking for her . . . If you do that . . ." She pointed her finger at him. "I curse you," she said. "If you make him not look for Bunny, I curse you and your children and your children's children!"

Lieutenant Duff crossed himself, looked apologetically at Dr. Newhouse and said, "This I can't take!" He went to the door and opened it. "Gingrich! We come down to one thing. . . . You show me one thing we missed in your place to prove you ever had a child there. . . . Gingrich! When Klein went to your place he thought it was funny. Klein's got kids of his own, happens. Klein called us right away to ask what gives." Lieutenant Duff was talking to Dr. Newhouse, who nodded. "What gives, Klein wanted to know. By that time Miss Benton had phoned us, so we knew, but did we sit back on our fannies and take her word for it, or yours, Doc? We did not! Didn't we send a detail up on the double? Excuse me, Doc! No doc can come in here and say there's a screw loose and we take his word for it, what do you think? The detail went through your place with a fine-tooth comb, Miss Lake. If you had a kid there, where's her. . . ."

"I told you! I told you!"

". . . where's her clothes? Where's her nighties, where's her bathrobe, the little slippers to go to the john, nights, where's the *toidey-seat?* I have grandchildren," he said to Dr. Newhouse. "Doesn't she use a toothbrush, your little kid?" He waved at Blanche. "Well?"

She said, "There! Of course there!"

Lieutenant Duff said to Dr. Newhouse, "There! She says there!" He said to Blanche, "I say not there! Gingrich!"

Gingrich had been standing in the doorway for some minutes.

"Gingrich, you go with her. Miss Lake, you give me one shred of proof that there is such a child and I'll take this town down personally tonight, brick by brick. My children's children," he muttered, turning away and throwing down the papers on his desk.

Rose Negrito shoved hastily back into the doorway of the house opposite the police station and waited until the girl, the guy and the cop got into the cab together. But even when the cab moved off, she couldn't do like she planned and go into the station, just because the girl came out as she was about to cross the street and go in. What difference did it make that the girl came out of the police station? Just because she had seen the girl in the bowling alley looking for the kid by herself didn't mean she hadn't gone to the cops, anybody would know that! She had just had the hope. So she had just had the hope.

And if there was anything special about her going to the bowling alley where Eddie hung out, she would have asked for Eddie there. She didn't ask for Eddie there. She just asked did *anybody* see the kid.

Rose crossed the street in front of the police station.

The trouble was George. The stuff George had told her about when he lived in New Jersey and the Lindbergh baby being kidnapped. And about that friend of George who had seen Hauptmann. And his friend said such things. Also the other man, the customer in the store who came in every week and bought fruit to bring to his wife's son in jail. Probably that customer of George's had never laid eyes on the hot seat, probably just talked and George believed every word of it.

Would it make any difference that Eddie was just a kid himself? Would they take into account that Eddie didn't have no record? (Staying out of school didn't give you a record!) She tried to remember if she had told anyone about the kitten. Anyone. If she had told anyone about the kitten and then they turned up at the trial . . . (They would have a trial even if Eddie was a kid.)

Now that she thought about it, Rose thought, nothing happened to the Lindbergh baby right away. It was when Hauptmann became desperate that he killed the poor baby. She began to walk away from the police station. A baby wasn't a kitten. Cops were what drove them to it.

"Somebody talk!" Blanche said. "Somebody say something!" Silence in the cab. Someone walking on my grave.

"Here we are," Officer Gingrich said, opening the door.

"I'll get this."

Blanche did not wait for the doctor to pay the taxi but went into the house, hurrying to the elevator.

They followed her as she ran through the living room to the bedroom and pulled out the second drawer of the dresser, which they knew would be empty. Gingrich silently opened the closet and shoved the few clothes from one side of the rack to the other, to show her that all the things there were hers, adult. Dennis stood out of the way so that she could rush into the bathroom and look behind the door, where only her yellow toweling robe hung from the hook. Both men waited until she had looked for herself.

She pressed her hand over her lips to make them stop trembling and whispered, "Somebody took her things. Don't you see, somebody took her things, too!"

Gingrich cleared his throat. "Klein told the lieutenant a kid of three is all over everything, so we went over this place for fingerprints." He started to say it to Blanche, but then turned to Dr. Newhouse. "That was the clincher; no fingerprints where a kid could reach." If Blanche had tried to tell him that someone had wiped off the fingerprints, he could have called it a day, but she just stood there, just stood there, so he said, "Let's go through the house again. Maybe some of them who wasn't home when we asked . . . Let's go through the house again."

—————

Occasionally, the doctor thought, as, for example, it must have been with Keats, where the feverishness attendant on his T.B. added a special quality to his poetry, so with this girl; her delusion added to her piquancy. Her hysteria made her eyes notable and every motion of hers became exciting. When that died down, he told himself, she would resemble the others. It was that quality, he told himself, that made everyone they questioned unable to take his eyes off her, even though she didn't say a word. She let the policeman ask the questions, stepping forward after he had explained why he was going through this again, like a criminal in the line-up, letting herself be seen, stepping back.

No one in the house had seen Bunny. "New Yorkers see nothing, hear nothing, know everything," he said, miserably aware that she would not find the small joke amusing, but unable to resist trying to reach her. As if he could, he thought. No one could, he thought, not that way.

There was only one surprise. Only one man said to wait and came out with a boy of about eight. "You see what happens to kids that don't do what they're told?" He pulled the boy further toward them. "Take a good look at this one, Officer! One of these days you're going to be out looking for *him!*"

During the time the man had been gone, before she knew why he had brought the little boy out, she had hoped. "For the love of Mike!" Dr. Newhouse said, taking her arm, spitting fire at the father of the boy.

The man saw what he had done to her. "I figured . . . seeing Bovvy's always running off . . ."

"Everyone thinks of his own," Officer Gingrich said, motioning the man to take his boy and close his door. "You can't help thinking of your own!"

"Why don't you go to your place and rest and try to think?" Dr. Newhouse said. He could feel her arm shaking.

"You're just trying to make me stop. I won't stop."

"I'm not just trying to make you stop. I'm trying to make you think. Running around this way . . . Hold on, Miss Lake! Please, one minute before you go downstairs again!" She would not wait for the elevator. "Here's a thought." He told Officer Gingrich about the letter from her friend which she had given to Chrissie Robbins.

"I told you. I crossed the words out because it was personal."

"But wouldn't it be possible that we could make something of it? And if there was a mention of Bunny—from England—that might be the shred of proof that the lieutenant is waiting for!"

"I crossed everything out."

"You'd be surprised what a magnifying glass can do!"

"Of course," Dr. Newhouse said, "if you don't *want* to prove . . ."

Blanche began to run downstairs. "*You* don't," she said.

"Why Dr. Newhouse!" Mrs. Robbins called back into the apartment, "Here's Dr. Newhouse coming to see us! The mountain coming to Mohammed, in other words!" She was a sensitive woman and her light tone faltered when she noticed Blanche and the exhaustion on her face. "Come in, please. What is it?" When they told her, she looked at her husband. "Go on in and wake Chrissie, Bill."

Hurry," Blanche begged. She had warned herself to be quiet, but it seemed to her that everyone was moving in slow motion; a hiatus gaped between each of their words.

"Can't I get her a drink?" Mrs. Robbins asked. "Won't you take a drink? You could use one."

Blanche shook her head no, because she was willing the husband to hurry, the red-headed boy to wake up, the blue paper with Chloe's handwriting to appear. Under her breath she was saying, "Please. Please. Please."

When Mr. Robbins returned, he was holding the blue paper, but before he brought it to them he picked up the magazine he must have been reading when they came in, and put the paper on that; as soon as he got near enough Blanche could see why. Chloe's letter was dripping water.

"Chrissie was soaking the stamp off," Mr. Robbins said. "He told me about it. It turned out to be a duplicate so he intended to trade it to a fellow philatelist . . . a philatelist who, unfortunately, doesn't collect covers as Chrissie does, just stamps." Mr. Robbins shook his head. "So he was soaking the stamps off."

Blanche took the magazine with the blue sheet on it. You could see blue smudges that must have been words, but no magnifying glass would help.

"I'm sorry," Mr. Robbins said. His wife had moved close to him and her fingers were biting into his arm through his shirt sleeve. He pressed her hand once and then pried her fingers loose. She just stood there while the girl and the cop and Dr. Newhouse left; then she began to cry. He put his arm around her shoulder and tried to comfort her.

"You saw there was a letter," Blanche said, holding out the magazine as if she were offering them something to eat. She met the policeman's eye, then tore the paper across, dropped it and ran. The policeman bent to pick up the pieces and the doctor raced after her. She broke away from him and leaned against the wall and stood like that while they waited for the elevator.

He had a patient who did that. She would not use the couch or the chair; stood like that in the corner with her face pressed against the wall like a child who was being punished, and talked in that position. Except that Mrs. Dickenson was a middle-aged woman, except that her governess used to punish her by making her stand against the nursery wall, except that Miss Lake was far too young for such punishment to have been inflicted on her; it was the same. He wondered what it was that had been done to her by life. He would try to find out, he promised himself. He would try to help her, he told himself, in the only way it was possible to help her. Gingrich was trying to help her, too. She had made quite an impression on Gingrich.

"You say you've been in your place two weeks with the little girl. All right, so no one noticed her in the house in two weeks, that could happen, but didn't you take your little girl anywhere we could check?"

Blanche shook her head. She went downstairs and out with them.

"You were at your job all week, but how about the two weekends? Didn't you take her somewhere on the weekends?"

"I took Bunny to that school the first Sunday, for that interview. Only they say I didn't." She clenched her fists. "I'm sorry. Yes, and on Saturday, this past one, Bunny and I went to the Central Park Zoo. It was a beautiful day. We had lunch on that terrace."

"Did anyone—?"

"Did anyone! Did anyone! I told you it was a beautiful day. Do you think Bunny was the only little girl whose mother took her to the zoo?"

"Yeah. And Sunday it rained on and off, didn't it?"

Blanche looked up at the sky. "Yes," she said. "It rained on and off. I went out for a walk, but alone."

It was heartbreaking the way she looked up at the sky. They got a cab and took her back to her apartment house. There was nothing to do but leave her, but Gingrich was finding it hard to leave her.

"Miss Lake, you being at the job all week . . . Your mother took your little girl out, didn't she? Maybe your mother took her somewhere we could check?"

Blanche seemed to wake up. She suddenly pointed her arm to the left, down the block. "There's a lending library there!"

Its lights were visible. The lending library was on the ground floor of another of the big apartment houses.

"Mother went there. 'I won't go *there* again!'" Blanche turned back to the two men, chose between them, chose the policeman, going closer to him, touching his sleeve. "Why did Mother say, 'I won't go *there* again'? That way? Maybe she took Bunny in there." One morning on the way to work, Blanche thought she would borrow a book to read in the subway and she had tried that lending library, but it wasn't open. She had looked in through the window and could see that behind the library there was another back room. Mother had taken Bunny in with her. Mother at one of the bookshelves, skipping through a book to see whether she would enjoy it. (Mother had always done that.) Bunny becoming bored, going by herself into that back room, and someone in the back room

with little Bunny! Now she saw that horrible boy from the fruit
store with Bunny. Bunny crying out. What had the horrible
boy done to Bunny? (Why did it frighten her so abominably
now to realize that when she read about "sex crimes" in the
paper, she didn't actually know what had been done to the vic-
tim?) "Don't you see that that could have been because
Mother took Bunny to that lending library and something happened there?"

"We can ask." Gingrich hurried her down the street.

When the door of the lending library opened, a bell rang.
Dr. Newhouse held out his hand for Blanche because she was
shaking. When her hand touched his (as if this had impelled
the confidence) Blanche said, "That boy could have a job in
the lending library, couldn't he? Just because he was always in
his mother's store at six doesn't mean he was there all day?"
Blanche pulled her hand loose. "You go, too," she said.
"You're a doctor. Go."

Gingrich had gone into the lending library and the door
closed after him. When the doctor opened the door the bell
rang again. Blanche followed Dr. Newhouse inside. Gingrich
was standing with two middle-aged women.

"They run this place," Gingrich said to Blanche. "Sisters.
They never saw your little girl."

The younger of the two women went to a table near the
entrance and pulled out the drawer of a small filing cabinet.
"Name Lake?" she asked.

"Mrs. Daniel Lake." Blanche said to the other sister, "Do
you have a boy working for you in the daytime?"

"A boy? Haven't you heard of television? People don't read
any more. We can just make out without paying salaries to
boys."

Blanche studied the woman's face to see whether she could
be lying. (Perhaps everyone lied.) The other woman closed the
filing-cabinet drawer.

"We don't have a card on Mrs. Daniel Lake," she said to the policeman. "We have cards on all our members, naturally. No Mrs. Daniel Lake."

The doctor, gently taking her arm, led Blanche to the door. Gingrich opened the door. The bell rang.

The older sister said, "Alice!"

"Of course!" Alice said. "Lake!"

Blanche felt the doctor's hand tighten on her arm and he swung her around.

"We did have a card for Mrs. Lake. I'm sorry, we forgot for a moment. Mrs. Daniel Lake."

"She was—outraged—because we wouldn't let her take out a copy of *Marjorie Morningstar* she saw on the desk here."

"It was a reserve, naturally."

"No," the elder sister said, "I don't remember her coming in with any little girl, though. Do you, Alice?"

"She only came in a couple of times," Alice said. "No, as far as I can remember, there was no little girl."

The bell rang as the door closed.

Gingrich cleared his throat. "Well . . ."

He was going to go back to the police station. Blanche ran to him and touched his sleeve. "Please … please— *Anyhow,*" she said, "please! You can do it! Go back and tell him you saw something . . . or somebody said something, so that . . . Oh, please!" she begged. "Just tell him so he'll look for her." Gingrich kept his eyes on the doctor's face as if he didn't dare look at her. "Lie," she said. "Can't you lie to save my child?"

"I couldn't do that, Miss Lake. Miss Lake, look, you won't come to the station any more, will you? The lieutenant doesn't want you coming around again." He said to the doctor, "If she comes again, he said he's going to have to . . . You know."

"She won't," the doctor said. "Miss Lake understands that she mustn't go to the precinct station again."

"You tell her, won't you, Doc? She can understand, can't she? I mean, after all, it's not our place . . ."

"She can understand." He stood ready to hold her if she tried to follow the policeman Gingrich again. She wasn't going to go to Bellevue if he could help it.

As Gingrich strode away, she simply stood looking after him. He heard her deep, painful sigh. He wished he could make her know that he, at least, was aware that her agony over this lost child was no less because the child was imaginary. Her tired hand pushed at her strong hair. That was, he thought, how it seemed to him: strong hair, electric and resisting under the push of the tired hand. "Don't you think you could rest for a while?"

She said wearily, "Go away, please."

"I can't leave you alone this way. Please believe me. I want to be your friend."

"A friend would believe me. Go away."

He found, flushing, that he had raised his hand involuntarily as if to guard himself against a blow, and, of course, she might hit him. She was unpredictable, of course, he thought; it was impossible to count on her. But if she had meant to hit him (and something in her voice or in her body must have given him that idea) the impulse had been deflected. Her face cleared. She started to walk off. "Where are you going?"

"I have a friend," she said. "Yes, I do have a friend. I forgot."

"Let me take you to her, then I'll leave you."

"No, I'll go by myself. *Him*," she said.

He noticed that she smiled before she hurried off. She had said "him," and had actually smiled, was amused, realized perfectly then that he was drawn to her; knew that saying "him" would hurt! Dennis stayed where he was, watching the way she moved down the street. "Let *him* take care of you, then," Dennis said to her back. "Let's see what *he* can do for you!" She wasn't alone and she wasn't his patient. "You take care of yourself," he told himself. He thought again of the cast of the head of the girl drowned in the Seine. He remembered how he used to look at it when the other medical students went out and he stayed in his room and plugged. "Let her go," he told himself, and began moving in the opposite direction to the one she had taken. Then he heard himself whistling. *Let her go, let her go, God bless her . . . 'Twas down in St. James Infirmary . . . so cold, so white, so . . .* Marble. Lips meant for marble.

But it was Louise's dinner which would be so cold by now.

But not Louise, he thought. Never Louise. And now he heard himself sigh.

She hurried along York Avenue and turned up Eighty-sixth Street. The doorman of the big white building looked through the glass door and yawned as she passed by. It wasn't that late, not that late, Blanche thought; simply that the doorman was tired. She turned the corner and walked up the street about a fourth of the block, and then darted across.

Someone in one of the little houses in Henderson Place was playing the piano. Single notes, hunting, it seemed, for a tune. He could be a composer, she thought. Mr. Wilson had told her that many artists and musicians lived in the houses in the mews. Mr. Wilson's house was the third—fourth—house on the right. Third? Fourth? Fourth, she thought, telling herself that it really was the fourth, that she had not simply made it the fourth because there she could see a light while the third was completely darkened.

She hurried up the white stairs and found the doorbell and rang it, as commandingly as she dared, reminding herself that he had asked her to come inside, that he had been friendly. He had been inside his house on Sunday and had seen her looking at it and had come out and talked to her.

"Cute?" he had said. "Romantic, isn't it? Not many of these left in the city." Wouldn't she like to come in and see the inside, he had asked. "Oh, come on," he had said. "You may not get another chance. I'm temperamental because I'm a writer. Of course you haven't heard of me. Do you know how many books are published each year? Come on in," he had said. "It's broad daylight, isn't it?"

Broad daylight. Yesterday. Sunday. The sun had caught his bald head as it caught the panes of glass behind his head so that it glazed. If only she hadn't cared what Bunny might have said about Mr. Wilson's bald head then he would have met Bunny. She pulled down her jacket and took her finger off the bell, then nervously pressed it again. He had been kind. He could not help the way he looked with that shiny head and his pink face coming out of a black turtle-necked sweater and one eye smaller than the other. He must be a kind man, he must be, she thought, hearing the steps inside. She licked her lips as if she were posing for a glamour photograph.

"Yes?" he said, because she just stood there, licking her lips.

His voice was gruff and impatient. This time his mouth looked twisted up toward the smaller eye, which was set higher in his face than the other eye. He was wearing the same black turtle-neck sweater with a tweed jacket over it. "It's me, Mr. Wilson. Blanche Lake."

"Blanche?" He pronounced the name in the French way. "Oh, Blanche!"

"Mr. Wilson, I came to you because you're the only one in the whole city who was friendly to me." He pursed his lips and was, she saw, about to say that he couldn't believe that. "Something terrible has happened," she added quickly. "I'm in terrible trouble, Mr. Wilson."

"You don't know what trouble is, Mademoiselle Blanche; you're not a writer. Sic—sic writer! Sick writer!"

"Please help me, Mr. Wilson! Mr. Wilson . . ." Talking rapidly, she explained about Bunny. When she finished, he merely bunched his lips again.

"Now, Mademoiselle Blanche, you just go to the police, that's what they're for. Excuse me."

He had shut the door. It was of a piece with the rest of what was happening. This was only one more door shut in her face, but it was one door too many; she began hammering on it.

"Now, lookey here, kid!"

"I told you. The police won't believe me about Bunny. They're going to shut me up in an insane asylum if I keep bothering them."

"Why should I believe you?"

"Because you're different."

"A writer, you mean?"

"You told me you knew everything and everybody in Yorkville. Please help me."

"I did at that. Come on in, then. Turn left."

She was in a small room with a fireplace on the far wall and a huge unframed cubistic canvas hanging above it. The brilliant colors of the picture made Blanche blink. The fireplace had no logs in it but there were rows of glasses, some empty and some with cigarette butts disintegrating in amber liquid.

He saw her looking at the glasses. "That's my housekeeping system while the wife's away. When the fireplace is full of dead soldiers I know it's time to have the char in."

There was a red velvet chair to the right of the fireplace. A big doll, with a crown askew on her head, sat on the velvet chair.

Mr. Wilson said, "That's my chaperone, Mademoiselle Blanche. No really, can't you see it?"

Blanche, trembling, was pointing at the doll. "Mr. Wilson, you have a little girl of your own, Mr. Wilson! Oh, if you have a little girl of your own!"

"I have two big girls of my own, Mademoiselle. They're with their mother in Wellfleet. Didn't you know that, Mademoiselle Blanche?"

"You didn't tell me yesterday. You didn't mention . . ." She stared at the doll hungrily.

"Yesterday," Mr. Wilson said. "Yesterday I was under the impression that you had just dropped into Henderson Place out of the wild blue yonder for my . . . edification . . . so I didn't mention that I was the father of two great lumps of daughters. You see? Of course you see. Sit down. Let me get you a drink."

"No, thank you."

"Come on, now," he said, taking her hand and leading her to a chair. "Sit down. Stop making like Pearl White!" He pushed her into the chair, resting his palms on the arms of it, looking into her face with his head cocked.

Couldn't he see out of the smaller eye? "I can't waste time, Mr. Wilson." It seemed to Blanche that she had to talk against the strong current of his smell, made up of liquor, stale air, tobacco, tweed and black wool, but after she began about the boy in the fruit-and-vegetable store, he moved away, pulling a pipe out of his jacket and lighting it.

"And the police don't think you have enough to go on? They don't think that the young men would be driven to such desperate measures by your *beaux yeux?* How ungallant, the Finest!"

"They just think I'm crazy. This psychiatrist told them I'm crazy."

"Psychiatrist?"

"His name is Dr. Newhouse. He's a psychiatrist."

"Newhouse, yet! Newhouse thinks you're crazy but me, being a writer myself, you come to me? I'm supposed to have more imagination, is that it? I hobnob with queer ducks and queerer drakes?"

"Please, please," she said. He had put the pipe back into his pocket; now he clamped his palm against it hard, as if his pocket were on fire.

"I could tell you where to look? I could help you find her, is that the idea?"

"You do believe me!"

"Of course I believe you! Nobody else would, but I do! If the rest of them won't, it's because they don't know that truth is stranger than any tired fiction." He came and bent over her and kissed her cheek lightly.

She did not dare remind him to hurry; he was being so kind.

"So you thought of me right away?" He walked up and down the small room with his hand clapped to his pocket as if he were stanching a wound there, then went to the fireplace and, looking them over first, chose two of the cleaner glasses.

"Please, there isn't time to drink."

"Dutch courage? You may need it."

"I don't. Really, I don't."

He shrugged and put the glasses back in the fireplace. "Come on, then. I'll tell you where to look."

The way he opened the door and the way he looked up and down the alley before putting his hand on her shoulder and pushing her outside made it seem darker and colder than it was. He even turned up the collar of his jacket.

"Now, Mademoiselle, you go straight down to the corner. Cross the street. Got it? Walk through the park and up the steps to the embankment walk there. You'll find the river straight ahead of you."

Blanche said, "The river?" He gave her a little push and stepped back into the doorway.

"Yes," he said, "there's always the river, isn't there?"

The sound of the door slamming shut was the most terrible sound that she had ever heard. "Mr. Wilson! Mr. Wilson!"

But he didn't answer. He wouldn't answer.

Because she had been told to go straight down to the corner, she began to move in that direction, but when she came out of Henderson Place she stopped, shuddering. She turned her face away from the park and the embankment and the river. She thought, "The doll! Bunny's doll!" and began to run up Eighty-sixth Street toward York Avenue.

That couldn't be gone with the rest of Bunny's things because she had brought it to the Doll Hospital on Friday. "They couldn't have got that," she thought. She swerved to the edge of the sidewalk and stood there for a moment, considering. Should she call the police and tell them to come with her? Should she telephone them to go and get Bunny's doll? The one thing! The proof! (*"Miss Lake, you give me one shred of proof that there is such a child and I'll take this town down personally tonight, brick by brick!"*)

She began to walk again, keeping to the edge of the curb in case a taxi came. She would say to Lieutenant Duff, "Here's your proof, Lieutenant Duff! Now do you think I'm crazy? That's *paper* dolls, Lieutenant Duff!" This one was one of those realistic baby dolls, life-size, almost as big as Bunny, so that it had been like having two children on her hands getting Bunny to the apartment from the station, because Bunny was so particular that the doll be treated like a real baby. Bunny had adored that baby doll Chloe and Gavin had given her so much that she hadn't even considered leaving it behind in storage. It was as much a necessity as Bunny's toidey-seat.

And then on Friday when she came home from work, Bunny was crying because her baby's eyes wouldn't close. The minute Blanche had come in, Bunny rushed her into the bedroom to show her, even before Blanche had her hat off, so Blanche hadn't taken her hat off. She had lifted Bunny's baby doll off the big bed and promised Bunny to take her right to the doctor and get her well again.

Mother had been so annoyed. "But you just this minute got

in, Blanche. You look so tired, Blanche."

She had told Mother that if she didn't have the doll fixed, if Bunny had to keep trying to close its eyes, she was certain Bunny wouldn't go to sleep either, and then she'd really be tired.

"You spoil her, Blanche," Mother had said.

Blanche remembered how she had carried the doll out of the apartment, with Bunny watching, as if it were a real baby. It was because her arms ached to carry a child now, to carry it into the police station, to show them *("There! There!")* that she started running toward the Doll Hospital. It was so near here. It would take her so much less time than the police would need to get there. She would get Bunny's doll and then get a taxi and go to the police station.

"There!" she would say. "You wanted proof, Lieutenant Duff? There!"

The Doll Hospital was on the ground floor of a small corner house on Eighty-third Street. It had a big painted sign, red on a white background, with a red cross at either end. Blanche pressed her finger against the bell.

She could see inside the window when the light went on. She saw a man's legs stuffing themselves into trousers; then the door was opened.

"Yes, ma'am?" He hooked a pair of glasses over his ears.

He had thin blond-white hair and a long face. His ears were very big and looked waxen in the dim light; he put his glasses on as if his ears were tender.

"I'm sorry to bother you. I wanted the doll I left here to be fixed."

"The doll? You want a doll *now?* Ma'am, do you know what time it is? Come back tomorrow, ma'am."

"Please, I have to have it now. I must have it now!"

He pulled tenderly at his big right ear. "Matter of life and death? Not that you're the first. You're not the first came here in the middle of the night. Had a lady last month who came here like you, said her little girl wouldn't take her penicillin without her dolly, can you beat it? Like a real hospital, this is!" He stepped backward, nodding to Blanche. "Believe me, a real hospital! When they're in trouble they come here and price is no object! But when you got the patient cured up—then you're charging too much! Come on in." He closed the door after Blanche. "You see how many patients I got on hand?" He waved at the shelves built around the room. "Which one is yours?"

"She had to have her eyes fixed."

"Yes. What's your trouble, won't your little girl take her penicillin without she has her doll? Is that why you woke me out of a sound sleep?"

There was a row of doll's legs neatly laid out on one of the shelves. Some of the feet had shoes on them and some were bare. "No, I need to bring her doll to the police."

"What's that you say?" He had been turned toward the shelves where the dolls were; now he swung around.

"My little girl is missing. I have to take her doll to the police for proof . . . Oh," Blanche said, "never mind. Please, where is Bunny's doll?"

He said. "The police. The police."

"Where is Bunny's doll, please?"

Keeping his eye on Blanche, the man swung an arm toward the shelves. "You got a receipt for her?"

"For the doll?"

He watched her shaking her head. "You don't have no

receipt?" He went to the door and opened it. "Ma'am, do you know how many dolls I get in here? I can't go through all of them this hour of night. You go back and get your receipt."

"But you didn't give me any receipt." He blinked at her behind his glasses. "You didn't say I needed any receipt." He pressed his lips together. "If you think, you'll remember. Please. This was on Friday, in the evening, after work. Please think. It was about seven o'clock on Friday, you can't have forgotten. Don't you remember, while you were trying to find the eyes, you asked me about Bunny? I told you about how beautiful Bunny was, what an angel, and how we had just moved to New York?

"How Bunny had never even ridden in an elevator before. Oh, try to think! You must remember me. I told you I had a job and couldn't be with Bunny and how Bunny was going to go to the Benton School. . . ."

He shook his head.

"You knew the school. You told me. I told you that I wanted to have the doll fixed before Monday . . . today . . . so Bunny could take it to the first day of school with her, something from home. I told you. Why, of course you must remember; why, you said you knew just how I felt about wanting her to have the doll to take with her and you asked for my address so if you could get hold of a pair of eyes the right size before Monday from the wholesale place, you'd bring it over so Bunny would have her in time for school. If you could get them."

"If you had a receipt . . ."

"You took the address and you said you'd bring the doll over yourself if you could get the eyes fixed before Monday!"

"I don't remember a thing, ma'am. I'm going to ask you to go. I don't remember a thing and I'm asking you to go. You got no receipt and if you don't go I'll call the cops!"

But she heard how softly he closed the door after her, as if the last thing he wanted was to call attention to himself. Even when he had said he would call the cops, he had kept his voice soft.

He put out the light in the Doll Hospital but she believed that he was still there in the dark, watching her. Blanche walked away, turned the corner. How could he not remember Friday when she brought Bunny's doll in? She had brought Bunny's doll there.

He had said, "Yes, ma'am?" He had hooked the glasses over his big waxen ears. "T-t-t," he had said. He had tilted Bunny's doll back and forth several times. He had looked at Bunny's doll, shaken his head and then, holding out his right hand with the pinky finger stiffly extended, had put his index finger into the doll's eye. When she had gasped—because it had looked *awful*—he had smiled at her. "Broke," he had told her.

Then he had seated himself and, holding the doll's body between his knees, he had grabbed the wig and pulled. When the wig came off, he had flung it onto the table behind him.

She remembered the hollow sound the eyes had made falling into the cavity of the head. She remembered the blind eye sockets, the scalped head with the dried glue on it like a scrubby rash. She remembered that he had asked her to sit down but she had not been able to sit comfortably with the mutilated bodies all around, the severed heads . . . as if heads could be put back. . . .

She remembered how he had thrust his hand into the head and fished the eyes out.

He had held the eyes in the palm of his hand, studying them; then he had put the doll on the work table, horribly settling the skirts as if they must be made decent. His hand had many small cuts on it which, catching in the soft material of the baby doll's dress, had rasped. "It's the size worries me." He had taken several small boxes from a shelf, then had reached up and taken down a cracked saucer. "Maybe here. These are odds and ends, all mixed up." He shook the saucer, she remembered. "I'll go through the regular boxes and you can see if you can find . . ."

She had felt so uncomfortable, swallowing hard as he fished around among the eyes and then held the cracked saucer toward her. He had noticed how uncomfortable he made her.

"Bothers you, don't it? Like fish eyes. They tell me the Chinese eat fish eyes; you think that could be so? They eat rotten eggs; heard that, too. Bury them and dig them up ten years later and eat them. Takes all kinds, don't it?"

Now it seemed to her that he had enjoyed her discomfort, that when he had picked up the doll again, he had liked looking at the empty eye sockets, the scalped head with that dried glue like a rash.

As she stood there, around the corner of the house, Blanche saw a light go on in the basement underneath the Doll Hospital. She crouched down so that she could stare into the small barred window.

She saw what he was carrying. She saw where he put it.

She heard herself telling him that he knew the school, that he knew her address, knew where she and Bunny lived.

The light in the cellar went out.

She ran around the house to the door of the Doll Hospital and began to bang on it and he came almost immediately and opened it. One side of his pajama top had come out of his trousers. From carrying, from lifting, from raising his arms. Blanche said, "I called the police! I just called the police!"

"Let them come then. Let them come one and all!" He took off his glasses and began to polish them on the pajama top that hung over his trousers. He said, "I got nothing to hide," and held his glasses out, then breathed on them.

Blanche saw that a door in the back of the shop which must

lead to that cellar was open. She made a wild snatch at the glasses, got them and threw them as hard as she could into the corner, and ran for the open door. Her hand searched frantically along the wall for the light switch and she felt the knife . . . the splinter . . . the *what* . . . tear through her hand, the back of it, but did not stop feeling for the switch, and when she found it and put it on the first thing she saw was the mean sullen mouth of the cut, welling blood. Then she saw the pink breathing furnace on the right of the cellar and the pile of trunks up which he had climbed on the left.

Blanche pressed the back of her hand to her lips and tasted the blood there. She sobbed and clattered down the stairs, hearing him moving clumsily around in the room behind her.

On top of the pile of trunks was a box, a crate, with a wire front, a traveling box for some animal, Blanche thought. That was where. She moaned. She could see, pressed against the coarse wire grating, an arm . . . a leg? She clambered up until, by reaching out, she could easily touch it through the grating, but she could not.

She closed her eyes and with her left hand pushed her second and third fingers through the wire. Cold. Smooth. Soft. Giving. Gasping, Blanche pulled the lid up with her right hand, seeing the bright smear of blood. The crate opened and she thrust her left hand in and pulled by the clothes, by the yellow dress with the appliquéd bunnies.

She heard him coming down the stairs, but she could not move. She was so nauseated that she could only stay where she was; the sour saliva filled her mouth. He had another pair of glasses on, silver-rimmed. He came slowly toward her, and when he reached her she was able to talk. She said, "Where is she? Where is she?"

He said, "You got her!"

"Not Bunny's doll, not Bunny's doll! Where is Bunny?"

"You see?" he said to no one, to the doll which he pulled

from Blanche. "You see, you see?" He ran crookedly across the cellar and pulled open the furnace door. "Give a dog a bad name," he said, "you see?" He held the baby doll's body in one hand and pulled at the crooked, dimpled right leg with the other. There was a rending sound.

"No!" Blanche screamed, and frantically climbed down. "You mustn't! No, I've got to take it to the police!"

First he tore off the other leg and then the body fitted easily into the furnace and then he said, "You got to take *what* to the police?"

Although she tried to explain to him how much it meant, what it would mean if he didn't come to the police with her and tell them about Bunny's doll, he would not go. She followed him up the stairs begging, but he would not go.

She better go, he said. She better get out of there and go. He had the street door open for her. "You're not going to get me into more trouble, ma'am; you go. It's just your word against mine. You can go if you want to!

"Your hand is bleeding, ma'am," he said.

Wilson said, "I've been trying to find you!" She was standing in front of, leaning against, face pressed against the big window of the delicatessen store on Lexington and Eighty-fourth Street. The *Muenchner Wurstgescheft*, the gilt sign read. "Please forgive me, Mademoiselle Blanche. After you left, I called my wife in Wellfleet. I thought she'd put you up to it, you see. I thought you and Marta were in cahoots." She wasn't listening to him. "What are you staring at in there?"

He touched her arm but she didn't stir. "Come on back with me now and I'll try to help you find your little girl." She was staring at the sausages—fat sausages, thin ones, huge ones, wrinkled sausages, pink, yellowish, dark red sausages. To get through to her, to get closer, he pressed his own face against the glass. "Blood sausage," he said, pointing, "head cheese. *Head* cheese, isn't that . . .? When I was a little lad . . ." He had her now; he could sense that she was attending now. "When I was a broth of a boy, I thought head cheese was made of *heads!* All those stories of cannibals I fed on, of course." She had begun to shiver violently. Wilson said, "Now that I'm grown up, I know of course that it's only gelatin and bits of . . . stuff . . . but it takes a certain amount of callousness to be able to wolf down *head* cheese, don't you think?" She was glued to that window. "Come on, Mademoiselle, you don't expect to find Bunny in there, do you?" Now she was pressing both hands across her abdomen.

"My dear," Wilson said, holding her, catching a glimpse of her face, "what is it? What did I say?" (*"You don't expect to find Bunny in there, do you?"* he had said. *". . . thought head cheese was made of heads,"* he had told her.) He pressed her tighter and began to shake her. "Darling! Sweetie! That's Poe, darling, that's Evelyn Waugh or whoever the hell it was who wrote that gem about the man who ate— You can't think anyone would . . . You can't think . . . Come on, sweetie."

She knew that this was Mr. Wilson's bed she was in because it smelled of him. This was Mr. Wilson's bed in Mr. Wilson's bedroom, but how had she got there? Blanche sat up and, raising her right hand to push her hair out of her eyes, discovered a handkerchief tied around it. It must be Mr. Wilson's handkerchief. Blanche was grateful for it because she always felt sickened at the sight of blood. She shivered, remembering the thin spiteful mouth of the long cut, welling blood. She called, "Mr. Wilson! Mr. Wilson!" and pulled herself out of the bed.

After a little while she could stand upright without the room going away from her and then rushing at her. After a bit, the big chest in the corner of the room ceased from toppling toward her, stood steady. She must have fainted, she told herself. She must have fainted and been brought here. "Mr. Wilson!" she called, and when there was no answer told herself that perhaps because she had fainted he had gone out to look by himself, so as not to waste any time.

She pulled her hand free of the footrail of the bed and walked shakily to the door. Mr. Wilson would have left a message telling her where he was and what she must do when she came to. "There must be something I can do," she said, pulling at the doorknob because it would not turn, banging on the door because pulling wouldn't open it. Then she stood there and the room began to dance again, the bed backward and forward, the chest of drawers backward and toward her like a fantastic square dance. ("I'll help you find Bunny," Mr. Wilson had said.)

Blanche stumbled toward an open door and found that it was a bathroom and went in, turning the cold-water tap on full, dashing water at her face until she could look into the mirror and see herself and not the window with the hundreds of sausages, not the arm pressed against the wire of the crate, so soft and cold and small. Blanche closed the tap and, dripping, went to the rack for a towel, but there was only a used one. She took that but could not make herself touch it to her face, it smelled so of him. (Or fish? The man with the hand fishing in the saucer full of eyes?) Her gorge rose at the smell and she could not spend time vomiting. She pulled her skirt up and tried to dry her face on the slip, but it was nylon and wouldn't absorb the water.

"A closet," Blanche thought, but there was no linen in it, just two of Mr. Wilson's suits which, she found, hastily closing the door, also smelled of him.

She went to the chest of drawers because it might contain towels but though she looked carefully in each drawer there was no towel so she eventually used a laundered shirt. (I will send it to our laundry tomorrow, together with our things, Bunny's and Mother's and mine. Tomorrow.) But since it must not be tomorrow until Bunny was found, Blanche hurried to the door again, banged again, turned the knob, pulled at the knob and then, because now she heard someone, began to call, "Mr. Wilson! I'm up! Mr. Wilson!"

"That's fine, sweetie. Look, will you stop that damn banging? I'm trying to get Dennis."

"Who?" She stopped hammering on the door and heard what sounded like dialing. When he finished she called, "Mr. Wilson, *who?*"

"Dennis. Do you happen to know where he is at the moment?"

"Mr. Wilson!" After a few minutes she heard the phone banged down and then his steps.

"You can't tell me where Dennis is?"

"*Who* he is! I don't know who he is! Mr. Wilson!"

"*Oh, poor Ophelia!*" thought Mr. Wilson. "Never mind,

Mademoiselle Blanche, never mind. You just rest a while like a good girl."

"Mr. Wilson, I don't want to . . . This door is locked, Mr. Wilson. Let me out, please."

"You just lie down and close your eyes and rest a while. You've had a tough night of it."

As the footsteps became fainter again, Blanche began to bang on the door frantically.

"Sweetie! Take it easy, will you? Take it easy."

"But we have to look for Bunny! You said you'd help me look for Bunny! Aren't we going to look for Bunny?"

"Not just now, sweetie. We're going to stay just where we are for a while."

He wasn't going to help her look for Bunny. "Then let me out."

"Uh uh. I'm not letting you out a second time."

"Mr. Wilson! Let me out. Let me out! Mr. Wilson, you said now you believed me. You said you'd help."

"And I intend to help in the best possible way."

"You don't believe me? Is that what you're saying? There isn't any Bunny, you think?"

"Oh, now, really, Mademoiselle!"

He didn't believe about Bunny. He had never believed about Bunny being lost. "I will kill him," she decided quite calmly, and was able, at the first try, to remember exactly where she had seen the revolver. It had been in the second drawer. It had been hidden under the jacket of a Paisley-print pair of pajamas. Blanche slid the drawer open quietly, so that he wouldn't hear, and removed the revolver, made sure that it was loaded and then shoved the drawer back in without a bump. Quietly, Blanche went back to the door.

How to get him to open the door? She was a pretty good shot. (He hadn't bothered to ask about that, had he? He had let her talk about her private affairs and not believed her for a minute, but about guns he hadn't asked!)

She couldn't be sure unless he opened the door for her. Blanche looked down at the gun, shivering, because if she killed him they would lock her up. They wouldn't let her look for Bunny since they didn't believe, either. She was the only one.

Well, after she found Bunny she would kill him, she thought, because he deserved to die for what he had done to her. She saw her purse lying on the bed and squeezed the revolver into it. Because she was so tired, she sat on the bed, smelling his smell again, which came, she decided, from the sheets.

Blanche ran to the bathroom and, stepping into the tub, shoved the window open, then, perching on the rim of the tub, looked out. Yes, this house must be like the ones which backed on her house; that darker shadow below must be the first-floor extension. (She *still* smelled his smell. He had tied his handkerchief around her hand where the cut was, that was it.) She ran back to the bed, ripped off the sheets, tied them together and then knotted them at intervals and shoved the sheets out of the window. She pulled in her breath and stuffed her purse with the gun in it into her waistband because she needed it to kill him with later. He would die for all of them who had refused to believe that Bunny was lost, and he *should* be the one because he had lied to her the worst and locked her in.

She climbed up on the window sill, first taking off the clumsy bandage. She was going to throw it on the floor but when she saw that the cut was bleeding again she stuffed it into her pocket. Turning awkwardly, so as to face the wall of the house, Blanche let herself out. With one hand on the sill, she tested the sheet. It gave a sickening lurch and then held. She yanked her skirt up and twisted her legs around the sheet.

There was only one fence to climb because the next three houses in the mews had made a community garden out of their back yards. Although she found a neat little gate that led through the side alley of one of the houses on East End Avenue to the street, so that this was easy also, her hands, she discovered when she shoved her hair back from her face, were both bleeding and splintered. A man was walking along East End Avenue. If he caught sight of the blood, she thought, he might become curious about her. She was able to rip Mr. Wilson's handkerchief into two and bound her hands, then, with her purse stuck under her arm and both hands thrust into her pockets, she began to walk.

First she would stop in the all-night drugstore there and telephone the police station. She had not called for hours. She opened her purse but then when she thrust her hand into the pocket where she had put the change for calls, there was no change. She could not ask the druggist for change to call. "Ask nobody for anything," she told herself. She would have to go to the police station.

Blanche had the money to get to Sixty-seventh Street; it wasn't that; it was that it wasn't safe to go. She turned instead toward her apartment house. Safer to telephone from the apartment. They could not do anything to her if she just telephoned from the apartment. There could be news and if there wasn't she could sit down while she thought what to do next. (Of course she could think what to do next!) "Mommy's coming," her steps said. "Coming, Bunny. Mommy's coming, Bunny." Exhausted as she was, she broke into a trot to change that rhythm.

He was sitting in front of her door with his knees pulled up and his face resting on them in the pose called "siesta," seen on thousands of ashtrays and plates and other souvenirs from Mexico. After blinking down at him for a long moment, Blanche recognized him. Because he was barring her door and the telephone, she hated him. ("We have found Bunny for you," the policeman would tell her the moment she called the precinct station.) But then, as she stood there, he stirred and opened his eyes and she stopped hating him.

"Miss Lake! I thought you would never get back. I should never have let you go by yourself, no matter what you said!" He saw the streaks of blood on her forehead and her hands bound up in blood-stained rags. "What's happened to you?"

"It doesn't matter. I want to get inside my apartment, please."

"Let me see your hands. Have you hurt yourself? Please, let me help you."

"You can't help me. No one can help me unless they believe in Bunny."

Dennis thought of *Peter Pan* and Tinker Bell asking, "Do you believe in fairies?" But he was a man of thirty-two and a psychiatrist. He wasn't a child. He could believe neither in fairies nor in Bunny but he could help her, he told himself, just because he was what he was and not a credulous child. Because he was a psychiatrist and not credulous he was the only hope.

"I must call the police station." Just in time she remembered to turn away so that he could not see into her purse while she was clumsily finding her key. When she tried to open the door, he took the key from her and did it. "Thank you." He was coming in. Let him come in. While she dialed the precinct station, she saw how he was brushing himself off.

He always was brushing himself off, she thought. She tucked the telephone receiver under her chin and, as if taking gloves off, pulled off first one and then the other half of Mr. Wilson's handkerchief and revealed the small cuts and the long thin, angry one.

He said, "What happened to you?"

She shook her head at him because the phone was being answered. ("We have found Bunny for you.") She told the policeman who she was. "Nothing? Nothing at all? Please, you will let me know if . . . After all, she may be brought in there any moment, so please let me know." She put the telephone in its cradle and when the bloody handkerchief halves fell on the floor from her lap, she kicked at them.

Dr. Newhouse pointed to her hands. "What happened to you? Please tell me, won't you?"

She ignored this. "What shall I do now? What time is it now? She pulled up her sleeve and he saw the smudge of dried blood on the watch band.

"Tell me about it, won't you?" He seated himself and smiled at her quietly. In his practice he said this innumerable times every day and they always told him. She told him.

"—and it was Bunny's doll, of course. I needed it but when I touched it, it . . . Is it rubber? The skin felt . . . It's supposed to feel that way, of course, but when I *touched* it . . ."

"And then, you say, he tore it limb from limb and burned it in the furnace? That's a pity, isn't it?"

"Pity! It would have been *proof! Pity!*"

"That's what I said. Go on. And then what happened?"

Perhaps it was his air of authority, his calm expectation that if she did tell him he could help, perhaps her fury against Wilson was so great that she had to talk, perhaps it was only because she did not know what to do next and had to do something, but Blanche told him.

"Who did this? Who said that about the head cheese? Your

friend, you mean? The man you went to?"

"Mr. Wilson, yes."

"Iss Wilson? Does he live on Henderson Place? In that mews on Eighty-sixth Street?" She was nodding that it was Iss Wilson.

"He locked me in his bedroom," she said. "I had to climb out of the window!"

"Iss? Mr. Wilson locked you in his bedroom?" What she wanted from him was an echo of the anger she was feeling but this, or course, was the last thing to give her. Dennis, not smiling now, rather expressionless, did not comment. Iss Wilson was a friend of his. Her delusions, Dennis thought, were spreading rapidly, alarmingly broadening in scope, covering more and more territory. Now she was waiting for him, Dennis saw. He would have to give her something or her fury might be directed against him. "Iss Wilson is a friend of mine, too. Where did you meet him?"

"I passed his house. I was looking at it and he began to talk to me. On Sunday." It would never have occurred to her to say "yesterday"; how could it have been yesterday?

"You weren't working yesterday. Sunday. Was Bunny with you since it was Sunday?"

"She was home."

He did not want to point out that here was still another opportunity for someone to have seen the child, which, for still another good reason—and he saw the reason coming to her lips and being pressed back—had been missed, too. It would be one more plausible or implausible explanation added to the weary list of them. There were more than enough of these already. He could see that she realized that. "Miss Lake, as I said, Iss Wilson is a friend of mine, and although I grant you he looks the part, why would he be so cruel to you, and why should he have locked you in his bedroom? Can you tell me why?"

Her hand rose and fell helplessly. "I don't know."

Seeing the dingy blood-stained handkerchief, Dennis told himself that there were any number of ways in which she could have gotten that cut on her hand.

She said, catching the implication from the way he was staring at the handkerchief, "You don't believe this, either? You don't believe Mr. Wilson lied to me? You don't believe that he said those things and that he took me to his house and locked me into his bedroom and wouldn't let me come out?"

"Now," Dennis said, "now! I wish you could tell me why you think Wilson would behave that way." If she had met Iss while sightseeing in Henderson Place yesterday, just as described, could she have used him to fasten the fantasy on because of that twisted mouth, the uneven eyes, the sinister bald head, because of his appearance? "Can you give me any reason for Wilson's behavior?"

She stood up, "No, I can't and I don't have to. Stop talking to me as if I were your patient. I'm not your patient, you know. I don't have to be if I don't want to be. I would like you to go away, please." He didn't move. He was, she saw, particularly quiet, showing that he wouldn't leave, would sit there patiently, no matter what she said to him, discount, she saw, any insults; but it didn't matter, really. She had to go out and look for Bunny, anyhow, so he could stay if he wanted to. Blanche picked up her pocketbook and walked out of the apartment.

He heard the door close after her and, shortly after that, the protest of the ascending elevator. He wondered whether she was not forcing him to call the police in. Looking for the telephone, he noticed the handkerchief on the floor and picked up the first piece, but not, he acknowledged, from curiosity or tidiness but simply because of a desire to touch something that had touched her. Wasn't there an Elizabethan poem about wanting to be her kerchief? "I would I were the kerchief . . ." Or was it the poet wishing he were the rose at her breast? "I wish I were the strait jacket . . ." Dennis said, and then he saw the monogram on the piece of the handkerchief.

So she had seen Wilson tonight! She had gone to Wilson tonight. Dennis stuffed the bloody handkerchief into his pocket and rushed out of the apartment.

The reason she was getting nowhere fast, Rose thought, was because she hadn't asked Georgie to help her. When you're a widow like she had been, you got to learn to do everything on your own; a married woman, now, she got to depend on the hubby. Five years married and she had to have Georgie help her find her own son, Eddie. She had gone back to the house, right in front of her own door she stood, but the trouble was if she went to Georgie with this, he'd make her go to the cops. Other things, yes. Georgie shot off his mouth at Eddie, sure; he had stood for a lot Eddie did, but this, no. Only a blood father would go to bat for a kid on this. (And maybe not then, Rose told herself. Maybe even Emilio would have gone to the cops on this. Maybe only a mother wouldn't. And the girl was a mother, too. She could imagine what the girl would do to Eddie if she laid hands on him!)

Where next? She had already asked everybody she knew who would lift a finger for Eddie or lend him a buck. You couldn't get in a flea circus in this town without a buck. And you couldn't get out of this town without a buck, either. He would stick in the old neighborhood. Eddie didn't feel right out of the old neighborhood. Had he stayed in that camp, for instance? The other kids, they took their two free weeks, and thanks, but Eddie got homesick the first night and got himself shipped back home. Eddie didn't feel safe nowhere else but around here.

And it had to be where no one would notice when the kid began crying. (If the kid couldn't cry any more then she didn't want to find Eddie because then it was too late.) By the river? But since that time the guys threw Eddie in the river, he wouldn't go down there on a bet. He would go, she figured, if all he could think of was that was the place to get rid of the body, in the river, but if that's what it was, it was too late, also.

She was on Third Avenue now, Eddie's old hangout. Now it came to her why the street seemed so peculiar tonight, not because of Eddie and being out so late, looking, no! Now that she was here where they'd left the steps and the old station and part of the platform, she could tell it was because, dope that she was, she had been thinking the El should still be up, and of course it wasn't. The Third Avenue El. The times, she thought, she had chased Eddie up those steps to catch him and make him go on home to bed. She used to almost bust her lungs running up those stairs because Eddie would be under the turnstile in a minute and she'd have to pay to get out to the platform after him. The times he got up there first and out on the platform with the man from the little making-change room chasing out after Eddie, cursing.

Then her heart started pounding as if she had already run up the iron-rimmed steps because wouldn't Eddie be up there now? With nobody up there, with no lights on? Eddie knew it like a cat in the dark! Wouldn't that be where he could take the kid so if she cried nobody would be around to ask questions, and if she cried a lot, the people on one side of the street would suppose it was a child crying on the other side, and vice versa?

She moved away from the steps, back toward the houses, craning her neck to see if there was anyone up there on the jagged bit of platform, but, of course, with no light on, she couldn't make out a thing. She began climbing the old stairs, and, setting her hand on the rail, prayed, because she was scared to death of heights. When people used the El if you kept away from the edge of the tracks you were all right, but now? Now she didn't know what was left of it. Now if she took one step too many, she'd be down in the gutter mashed like potatoes. She thought of the way Eddie stood in the store eyeing that girl; what he said when Georgie needled him with that kidding . . . and the kitten. She hurried up the old steps of the El.

The steps were okay. Of course the steps were okay, those she had seen. She cursed herself because she didn't pay more attention to what they'd torn down because exactly how much of the platform was left, she didn't know. (She could see Eddie with the kid in his arms, moving away the closer she got . . . and then?)

The door to the room you waited in when it was cold or raining was still there.

To the left, the change booth was still there.

The thing you put your nickel in was gone. What would they want that for? It took nickels, not tokens. But they could fix that easy, she thought. Of course they could fix that up, hadn't they fixed the subway ones from a nickel to a dime and then to tokens?

She was scared to go out on the platform. The platform was what scared her stiff. It seemed to Rose that she heard a stirring behind her in the waiting room and she realized that it could be from the steps she was hearing the noise. Somebody, she realized, could have seen her going up the stairs and had called the cops, and that could be a cop coming to find out what she was doing up here. She found the courage to go through the doors to the platform because no one was going to find her until she got to Eddie.

She felt the guard rail to hold on to. If they had taken that away, she would crawl on her hands and knees, but it was there. All she had to do was take one step at a time, holding with everything she had to the guard rail, and feel with her foot ahead of her. Even if one foot stepped into air, she could pull herself back if she held on. She took a step and called, "Eddie!"

If the kid was sleeping and her voice calling woke it, just because it didn't cry could just as well mean that Eddie had his hand over the baby's mouth and not hurt it. (Not to hurt it. You could put your hand over a kid's mouth and not hurt it!) "It's me, Eddie." She took another step and then another and then another. "Where are you, Eddie?" Another step. "I don't want to yell out, Eddie. There's people down in that street and if I yell out they'll hear me and then even if the kid is okay it will be too late for you. You did it, then, you see what I mean, Eddie? I mean I won't be able to talk her out of it. If I bring the kid back now, Eddie, I'm sure I can talk her out of it. Eddie!"

She could not take another step. "I get dizzy, Eddie. You know that's the truth, Eddie, you want to murder your own momma?" She squatted down and felt with her hands along the wooden floor boards. She couldn't go any further. "Eddie," she said, a little more loudly this time so that he couldn't miss this, because if Eddie was here and she said "in the name of your dead father, Eddie!" . . . She said, "Eddie, in the name of your dead father!"

Rose waited for what seemed a long time squatting like that, with one arm aching from holding it pulled back so she could grasp the guard rail; then she pulled herself up and started back along the platform to the waiting room.

When she was inside, when she was just standing there; she heard the tap, tap. It was coming from the little place the station man who gave out the change stayed in. It had been like a little room, she remembered. She heard the tap again, distinctly, and, as she was moving toward it in the dark, Rose was already explaining to the girl that Eddie had been careful of the baby, had taken her to this little room, just kept her there.

"I'm coming," she whispered. As she approached it, she could make out the door of the change booth opening.

Rose was so sure it was Eddie down there on the floor that she merely reached down when she felt his hand on her leg, but then, of course, she knew that it couldn't be Eddie and grabbed frantically for the hand. She had time enough to realize that once she yelled, the cops would be in on it, but she couldn't help yelling as she fought the hands off. Any decent woman had to yell.

———————

Wilson was up. Dennis could see him pacing up and down in his living room. He pressed the bell and remembered her description of Wilson shutting the door on her, telling her there was always the river. (He told himself that what he was feeling was relief at being able to project his monumental anger at a human being instead of whatever combination of genes and life situations that had done this to her.) Wilson came to the door immediately, tilting his head to make out who his visitor was.

"Newhouse! Am I glad to see you!"

"I'll bet you are!" He brushed by Wilson and got into the house before pulling the bloody handkerchief out of his pocket. "I would like an explanation of this!"

"That means you've found her! Thank God!"

"I would like an explanation of this," Dennis repeated. "Why lock her up? Why didn't you get me?"

"I tried hard enough! Where were you? Didn't she tell you I was trying to get you?"

"She did not. You tell me, Wilson. You explain."

"The explanation would seem to be more in your line than in mine. You're the psychiatrist."

"I'm the psychiatrist, yes, and what kind of a son of a bitch are you?"

Wilson chose a glass from the rows of them in the fireplace and poured gin into it and then shook bitters over the gin. Both men silently watched the pink appear in the colorless fluid. "Dennis, I could use your services. I don't think I'm ever going to be the same after tonight."

"If what I heard has any truth in it, I would agree with you." He watched Wilson gulp the gin. "You mean it is literally true? She was telling me what actually happened?"

Wilson nodded grimly.

"You threw her out when she came to you? A blind man could have seen her . . . condition . . . no less a sensitive soul like you, but first you told her to go drag the river. . . . No thanks to you they're not dragging it for her! And after what she went through . . . or thought she went through with the guy in the Doll Hospital to cheer her up with head cheese and cannibalism."

Wilson set his glass down. "What do you mean 'guy in the Doll Hospital'?"

"Where she went . . . or thinks she went . . . after you were so hospitable! Didn't she tell you about that?" Then he told Wilson, who groaned, filled his glass again and then stared at it as if it disgusted him. "What the hell kind of a sewer do you live in? What kind of a bastard are you, anyway, Wilson? Put that glass down," Dennis said. "Put it down! I don't want to cut out your good eye. I just want to knock you for a loop!"

Wilson reached into his pocket for his glasses and shoved them up on his nose.

"I'm not joking, Iss! Leave the glasses on, if you prefer. I find I do want to cut your eye out, after all!"

"Cut the comedy! Cut the comedy, will you? How do you

think I feel? I agree with you. I'm supposed to be sensitive. I should have seen immediately that she really believed she lost a child."

"She believes it!"

"She mentioned you, of course. She said that you thought she was crazy, but I just figured that was putting a little english on the story. I didn't believe for a minute that she was a patient of yours. Damn it, Dennis, if only you'd told me about her before tonight! If you guys weren't so stodgy about professional ethics!"

"I couldn't have told you in any case. I never saw her before tonight."

"You never saw her before tonight? Never? Oh. Then she mightn't know your first name was Dennis. I thought it was another evidence of insanity when she said she didn't know who Dennis was after she talked about you. Man! When I discovered she was gone! You don't have to cut my heart out, Dennis; I could do it myself, man!" His hand began to tremble so that he had to set the glass down. Trying to put it back into the fireplace, he hit it against the next glass and knocked that one over. This acted like a signal, a starting bell to Newhouse, because the next thing Wilson felt was the thud of his shoulder hitting the mantelpiece. He shook his head clear and grabbed Dennis, holding him in a bear hug. "My God," he said, "you don't know why, do you?"

Wilson was much heavier than he was and more accustomed to brawls. By a tremendous effort Dennis could get himself free of the bear hug but that was about all. He stood a way off, pulling his sweater straight. "No, I don't know why and there is no reason on earth I can think of to excuse—"

". . . think she just walked in here, told me the story and *cold* I just kicked her out into the cold night? Listen, you don't walk in on anybody cold! As a psychiatrist you know that better than anyone else. You walk in on a ready-made situation and this one was a lulu. Two weeks ago, tomorrow, maybe, no go; if she walked in here tomorrow it would be a different story, but get a certain concatenation of events, one following the other, and . . . the works, man! What else do you think makes history?

"For god's sake, Dennis, you know me, Al! Last week I sent Marta my latest manuscript. Today I had a letter from her. For Christ's sake, sit down and have a drink. Marta says what I'm writing isn't realism. She says, for Christ's sake, it's only in my book that nothing happens. She says, read the papers, turn on the radio. She says, by God, she'd *make* something happen if I didn't. I'll show you her letter if you don't believe me. . . . '*Make* something happen if you don't.' Oh, hell, Dennis, call Marta! She's in Wellfleet with the kids, you know that!

"I assure you that when this kid appeared on the doorstep after fifteen minutes of conversation together yesterday when I found her rubbernecking into my parlor window, when she comes to me as her only friend and tells me this Gothic tale, it never occurred to me that this wasn't Marta's childish notion of . . .

"Marta is my wife and I suppose she's entitled to goose me occasionally, particularly when, if my manuscript is as dull as she thinks, the kids are apt to go hungry, but I didn't see why this girl should get into the act gratuitously! I'd been nice to her yesterday, and that made me feel foolish, too. I didn't see why this kid should get away with it, so I pretended to believe her and then kicked her out and told her to go drag the river.

"All I could think of was that Marta had insulted my intelligence. Maybe Marta doesn't think I can write, I thought, but she should certainly know I can read. It was an insult to my intelligence to expect me to fall for that story. I didn't give the girl another thought after I kicked her out. I just called Marta up in Wellfleet to give her hell, but when she convinced me that she'd never heard of the girl—and it took some convincing—man, I was out of the house like a bat out of hell to find her!

"I locked her in the room so I could get hold of you. Where the hell were you? And then, when I found she'd climbed out the bathroom window using my bed sheets . . . knotted sheets, yet! She could have killed herself! I haven't had your experience with lunatics, Dennis. I thought she'd stay put in there until I could get her psychiatrist to her . . . meaning you. Where is she now, Dennis? I've got to try to make it up to her somehow."

"I don't know where she is. Oh, where do you think she is?" He made a face. "She's out looking for the lost Annabel Lee!"

"She isn't with you? You don't . . . ?"

"I couldn't. She reminded me that she's no patient of mine. She would have none of me because—" he remembered Tinker Bell—"because I couldn't believe in fairies."

"Couldn't believe in fairies . . . And you're not her psychiatrist, and you never laid eyes on her before tonight?"

"That's right. After what you did to raise men in her estimation, she would have none of me. Damn it, Wilson, how could you go off half-cocked like that?"

"I told you how." Wilson chose another glass and poured some gin into it. "For that matter," he said thoughtfully, "how could you?"

"Me?" Dennis bent to take a glass, grimaced at them and took the bottle from Wilson.

"You're usually an awfully thorough guy, Dennis. You usually do a lot of investigation before you call someone insane, don't you? When you first walked in, I was under the impression that you'd had lots of time to study this case, but if tonight is the first time you saw her . . ."

"Come on, Wilson! Really!" Dennis drank from the bottle of gin.

"This is the second time I've seen her, remember. She certainly didn't seem insane to me yesterday."

"She didn't get on Bunny yesterday, did she?"

"Just on the one subject of the child, you mean?"

"Unfortunately, no. What did you think of the tale she told about the Italian boy in the fruit store?"

"A bit farfetched, I thought."

"Believe me, Iss, there are precedents for imaginary children."

"Couldn't have a child, you mean? Sandy didn't come along for three years and Marta certainly was a wild woman. With Mademoiselle Blanche, it wouldn't be for lack of co-operation, I wouldn't think."

"She had co-operation."

"Oh?"

"The one reality situation in my opinion is that she does feel guilt because of an affair she appears to have had, that seems documented. She certainly thinks she's the scarlet woman. She said she worshiped some young squirt because he was willing to forgive her sin."

Wilson noticed how Dennis took another pull at the bottle. "You don't like that?"

"Do you?" And he didn't like the way Iss was smiling, either. He said gravely, "I'm trying to make up my mind whether I'm justified in going to the police right now and telling them they better not wait until they can find this damned mother of hers!"

"You don't like her mother, either? You said it the way I talk about my mother-in-law."

"Iss . . . this girl's insane. If she'd go far enough to take the chance of breaking her neck climbing out of your window she's apt to do anything." He set the bottle down and headed for the door.

"The butterfly net? Bellevue?"

"No, a private hospital. I'll look after her myself." Wilson caught him just as he was opening the door.

"Wait a minute, Dennis. What I said before . . . You're being most uncharacteristically quick on the draw here. I don't think you have any right to get out the wagon for her."

"Every right. I'm a psychiatrist."

"You're not acting like one. Wait a minute," Wilson said, puffing.

"I didn't, but I am now." Dennis spoke as he walked, heading south. "I didn't act like a psychiatrist when I accepted her dictum about not wanting to be my patient. I had no right to accept that." Better walk toward First where he would be more apt to find a cab.

"You're going to wait a minute." Wilson got in between Dennis and the door of the taxi and pounded his chest to show Dennis he would have to catch his breath first. "A couple more minutes isn't going to matter one way or the other. Listen: when you heard her saga about me, you assumed it was a fantasy. So would I. Do I have to hold on to you or will you wait?"

"If you're brief." He told the cabby to pull down his flag.

"I'll be brief. You assumed that story was the product of a disordered mind just as you assumed that what she told you about the child was fantasy."

"That's right. Until I found your handkerchief."

"Othello."

"What's the connection? Othello?"

"Othello wouldn't have believed in Desdemona's infidelity without that fatal handkerchief. Oh, don't make a big deal of that; I just said it." Because Dennis was staring at him intently and rubbing at the top of his nose.

Dennis was remembering how he had let her go to Wilson in the first place because she had told him that her "friend" was a "he." Othello for jealousy. He had been jealous. "Nobody just *says* anything. Iss, you're right. I am intensely attracted to her. I'm going to do everything I can for her and that means not letting her wander around by herself!"

"Maybe doing all you can includes assuming that her story is true and trying to work it out from there before you get out the butterfly net?"

"Assume what?"

"I say assume, just assume. Find her because she shouldn't be allowed loose, but at least *assume* she's telling the truth."

"The police went along on that assumption, I assure you. At least they didn't assume I was the final authority. They couldn't find anything." He reached out and opened the door of the cab. "Don't be a damn fool, Iss. How can I possibly *assume* such an incredible . . . Get out of my way, Iss, will you?"

"Look who's talking! Man, come off it, you're a psychiatrist, aren't you? You've had more practice than anyone else. Let me tell you, to assume that Mademoiselle Blanche's little tale is true should be nothing to a guy who assumes that what Sigmund Freud says is true!"

"Look, Iss, some other time, I'll be happy to . . ."

"How about the Oedipus complex, for the love of Mike!"

"Some other time!"

Wilson watched the cab move off and then went and sat on the steps of the nearest house. He kept seeing the poor kid with her face pressed against the window of the *Muenchner Wurstgescheft*, and her head full of her latest fantasies about the guy at the Doll Hospital. Wilson straightened his back so suddenly that he gave it a whack against the cement step. He had warned Dennis about assumptions and here he was assuming himself. What was all that stuff one heard about sadists becoming surgeons or butchers, depending on their opportunities and their I.Q.'s? The idea was that in these two trades they could successfully sublimate their sadistic desires. Suppose the creep in the Doll Hospital wasn't cut out for a butcher . . . *cut out* wasn't bad, Wilson thought. Suppose this creep in the Doll Hospital didn't have the opportunity to get as far as drooling over his frog in elementary biology . . . why not a Doll Hospital? And, what was more to the point, wouldn't a Doll Hospital with all the little girls flocking around to bring in their busted dollies be a bright idea for a creep like that? Wouldn't that kind of creep be snug as a bug in a rug in a Doll Hospital?

"Now, wait a minute," Wilson told himself. "If so . . ." If the Doll Hospital guy was that kind of creep, might he not have had a spot of trouble with the cops already? Might not one of the little girls . . . or a little girl (Don't lay it on too thick!) have snitched to Momma, gone crying to Momma, and might not Momma have gone to the cops? And if she did, if she had, wouldn't that perfectly explain the creep's behavior? What would seem to be something out of a nightmare with another man would be perfectly explicable in the Doll Hospital man! And if there had been a doll, if Mademoiselle had left her doll with the Doll Hospital creep, if it was proof, if the only reason she had no proof was because the creep had burned it up, shouldn't he, Wilson, go straight to the cops and tell them?

Shouldn't he get the cops up and at the creep? Couldn't they make the creep admit that he had had such a doll? Third-degree him into talking? Beat it out of him? Even as Wilson had the thought, he realized that his use of such terminology, thinking "third degree" and "beat it out," both of which he knew to be obsolete in police procedure, indicated how forlorn such an idea was. If the creep, *particularly* if the creep had these tendencies, he wouldn't admit that there had been any doll. If he had been in trouble with the police before, he would deny Bunny's doll to his dying breath. He'd know what would happen to his business if such an accusation got around. If it was true, he'd got rid of the proof and there was nothing to tie him to Mademoiselle except her accusation, the accusation of Mademoiselle-without-all-her-marbles, and Iss Wilson who would then also be accused of not being all there.

Even Mademoiselle had known better than to go to the police with no doll, no proof. He'd better follow her example.

There was an electric light over the door in a round glass globe. Inside the globe Wilson could see insects crawling up the side. As if they could get out that way, he thought. God knows how they got in there, but they're not going to manage to get out that way. He wondered how Mademoiselle Blanche was going to get out. "There's always the river," he had told her. "Go down to the river and look," he had said, and, he thought, standing and pulling up the turtle neck of his black sweater, he would bet that she was ready to consider the river as the way out by now. With what she believed must be happening to her child and the whole world against her, she must certainly be ready for the river by now. She would certainly think that it was all that was left to do by now.

Surely she would be reduced to that, he thought, walking rapidly toward the East River Drive; to staring down into the black water, straining her eyes for any suspicious object down there . . . and if she saw something? Anything, half floating, half submerged, might she not? Oh, might she not! Wilson thought and broke into a lope.

He turned the corner quickly, going toward Eighty-second Street, where there was another entrance, because the promenade dipped lowest there and she would certainly go where it was lowest in order to get closer to the river. He pulled at his turtle-neck sweater because running, and imagining her climbing the railing, going in, committing suicide, had made him sweat.

He did not notice her and wouldn't have if she hadn't started to run. "Blanche, this is Wilson! Is that you, Blanche?" It had to be her, anyone else would have stopped running when he announced it was Iss Wilson. Nobody but that poor creature was scared enough of I. Wilson to run from him. "I won't fol-

low you, just listen. Listen, I'm not following you!" Her footsteps slowed down. "I guessed you'd be down here and I came
to stop you. Don't do it, Blanche! Don't do it. I want to help
you." He heard her voice. "What did you say?"

"Again?"

"Not again. I want to help you. Now. If you don't want the
police to put you away, although it probably is the safest thing,
I'll see they don't get you. I owe it to you after what I did."

She said, "No, just leave me alone."

"The police won't let you alone. They'll certainly think of
the river. It's a cliché, the river. They'll detail men to find you
and they'll find you sure." He saw how she moved off, too
tired to run, he thought, just moving. He stayed where he was
and raised his voice. "I'll take you to a place right near here
where you can lie low while they're searching down here."
Her steps were slowing down. "Trust me. It's where my Sandy
once hid in the playground on Eighty-fourth Street. Blanche,
may my Sandy disappear if I mean anything but what I say."
She stopped walking.

"Tell me where."

"In the playground on Eighty-fourth Street where that
pavilion is, with a john on one side and an office where they
keep play equipment on the other, but I can't tell you where
Sandy hid, I'll have to show you. Do you want to walk ahead?
You know where the playground is, don't you?"

"No. That proves I have no child, doesn't it? No, I don't."

"Shall I walk ahead of you and show you? If I'm ahead of
you I can't grab you, can I?"

"Yes. All right. Go ahead of me."

He started off. "I'm glad after what I did that you trust me
enough for this."

She smiled because she did not trust him. "This I trust," she
thought. "In gun I trust." She held her purse open against her
with her left hand so that her right hand could be on the

revolver, but he couldn't see that, of course, and he wouldn't. Because if this was another trick, he wasn't going to see the gun or the bullet that killed him, either.

"Blanche, can I try to excuse myself while we're getting there? I was sure my wife had put you up to this, that she had lifted your story from the Paris Exposition one. You know the one. Where the girl arrives with her sick mother in a Paris hotel at night and is sent on an errand . . . faked . . . so that when she returns, her mother is gone and she can't get a soul to admit to having seen her mother . . . or herself, for that matter."

"I know the story," Blanche said. "I do know the story."

"Then, Blanche, don't you see? Don't you see the similarity?" Wilson heard the earnestness in his own voice. He was talking to her as if she were sane. He hoped it wasn't dangerous to talk this way, to bring this up. Maybe Dennis would tell him this was the worst thing he could do to her, and it was an awkward way to talk to someone, behind you this way so you couldn't see the other person's face. Perhaps if he could see her face, he would stop talking this way.

And he was listening to her, Wilson thought, with his third ear. That was Theodor Reik's expression, "the third ear," without which, Reik said, no psychiatrist was worth his salt, since this was the ear which heard what was not said, the ear which, hearing the unsaid, the unsayable, imparted its secret facts to the mind, which then made the leap to knowledge. He was listening with his third ear for the discordance of insanity in her, and he could not hear it, and because he could not hear it, he was talking to her as if she were quite sane.

"Everyone knows I believe I have a baby girl, but they don't believe in Bunny. I left her at that school and everybody says I couldn't have."

"Exactly like the girl in that Paris story."

"They ask me if I think anybody would have kidnapped

Bunny and I tell them about that Italian boy, but they only ask me to find out what else I believe."

"But the boy only looked at you. Blanche, I want you to forget about the boy now. While we're walking will you tell me a couple of things in detail? I didn't care to go into detail earlier; why should I? But now . . . will you?"

"Why?"

"Because of that Paris story. Because once the motive was uncovered there it becomes perfectly understandable, if highly dramatic, that a respectable hotel would spirit a woman away and deny that she existed. We're going to leave the Italian boy out of our calculations for the moment and see if there could be any reason why, if you brought your child to school, they tell you you didn't."

"But I can't think why. Don't you think I've tried to think why?"

"Then we're back on how. How could it have happened as you say it did?" He remembered what he had said to Dennis about assumptions. Nobody had assumed she could be telling the simple truth. "Will you answer some questions? Can you?"

"I can answer questions," she said. "I can do anything but think about what may be happening to my baby. If he is hurting her . . . if now, this *minute* . . ."

"He" was her King Charles's head popping up, and the character with the King Charles's head affliction was mad as a hatter. "Can't I walk along with you?"

"No."

"This is an awkward way of talking, but all right. Assuming that you left Bunny in school this morning, how could she not be there at five? Start with nobody seeing you bring Bunny into the school this morning, how could that be?"

"I don't know how they didn't. I only know what I did."

"Tell me what you did this morning, then. Give me the

details about this morning and let me see if I can see how you and Bunny could have been invisible in the school. My kids went there, you know, so I know the ropes." She didn't speak. He stopped walking and turned and faced her. "For God's sake," he said, "make me believe you! What else can you do besides jump in the river?" That suggested something. "Blanche," he said softly. "I believe, Lord, help Thou my disbelief!"

"Tell you about this morning?"

"This morning." He turned and walked on.

"Everything went wrong," she said. "Every single thing. It was one of those mornings like a dream where you can't go forward. What I mean . . . Mother is supposed to dress Bunny while I shower and dress for work. We had that all figured out so that I could manage to take her to school, but then Mother made up her mind about her house. I was showering when she told me. She'd had this letter on Saturday, she said, saying if she wanted to clinch the sale she could. On Saturday Mother wasn't going to let these people buy it, but now she was. She'd never be able to hold her head up at home, anyhow. You know. Mother had to catch a train, so she couldn't help with Bunny. Then she took up a lot of time, too. She couldn't find her overnight bag, and what should she take? When I finally got Bunny dressed, I had to help Mother find the overnight bag and I'd borrowed the mirror out of it and I couldn't find that. I finally remembered I had taken it to the office to keep in my desk." She sighed. "Things like that. Then while I was busy looking for the bag for Mother, Bunny wetted. She was excited, too, her first day in school!"

"Don't cry," Wilson said. "Go on talking. Do you see the pavilion to your right there? Go to the open part of it."

"I had to change all of Bunny's clothes, top to bottom, and then it turned out that Mother had forgotten to do Bunny's things in the machine in the basement, and that started another fuss because there were no clean blue jeans for Bunny. You see, I'd told Bunny that you wore blue jeans and T shirts to school. She had that in her head and I had a terrible time persuading her into a dress-up dress which was all that was clean."

He could see how eagerly she was throwing herself under the spell of these details, what a respite it was being for her to think of wetted panties and no clean clothes as troubles. Good, he thought.

"And then Mother chose this morning to lecture me on the importance of good breakfasts for little children. You can imagine that . . . a *crime* to send Bunny off without a good breakfast and wouldn't that keep happening with the rush we'd be in? I could only stop her by warning her she would miss her train. And then, because her feelings were hurt, I had to go downstairs with her, waving her off when she did get a cab. That's when I saw that boy outside the house."

"Uh huh," Wilson said.

She drew a long shaky sigh. "Well, when I went upstairs, on account of Mother . . . I suppose it's childish to think Mother knows best, but, anyhow, I just couldn't get Bunny off without a good breakfast, and the only thing to do was to read to her from *The Little Engine That Could.* She loves that book. Well, then she did eat and then I had the telephone call from the school."

"Who called you from the school?"

"Miss Ditmars, the same teacher, but now they tell me she never called me. She's the one who interviewed me but now that director says she didn't."

"Go on. Don't get sidetracked. You'll just be going over the same ground if you do."

"She asked whether Bunny was ill, checking up because it was so late by then. I said, no, just late. I told her about Mother leaving and so on. I was very apologetic because she was a teacher. *Tardiness!"*

Wilson said, "Remarkable how it lingers, isn't it?" Not so remarkable in her case, of course. "We all have these hang-overs from school days." Her school days must have been very recent, poor kid, so young, so lovely and so lost. He reminded himself that he was assuming this was the truth and not fantasy. (Because of the documentation it had the ring of truth.)

"She said perhaps Bunny better not come today because she would disrupt her group coming in when the other little ones were just settling down without their mothers. I told her Bunny had to come. I mean, Mother wasn't here and I couldn't appear at my job, they wouldn't like it, so she said I better wait until ten thirty when the children had their juice. She told me Bunny's room number and said I should just leave Bunny there. The others were doing without their mothers, see, and she didn't want me coming in and maybe starting the rest of them wanting their mothers again. After all, they're just babies, really."

"Don't, please, Blanche dear. And that's what you did?"

"Yes. I called the office and told them I'd be late and I tidied up a little at home."

"That shows why none of the parents saw you, but how about the teacher in the room?"

"There was no teacher there."

"They don't leave children alone in nursery school, Blanche."

"There was no teacher there. I can't help it. Maybe she was in the washroom; she wasn't there. Just the children were there, about four children."

"We can't exactly use them as witnesses, can we?"

"Wait," she said, "but at ten thirty in the morning don't they get their orange juice and crackers? That's why she told me to bring Bunny then, because of that!"

But she never called you, never saw you. "Go on."

"I was there only long enough to put Bunny in the room. I did what she told me to."

The comfort of it had faded, Wilson knew, because the strain was back in her voice.

"There were some big blocks on the floor. I had told Bunny there would be these big blocks to play with, so I took her to them. I picked one up and put it in front of her so she could look at it while I was taking off her sweater. I didn't know where her things were supposed to be put, so I left it next to her. I thought when the teacher came she— That's gone, too, Mr. Wilson! Every single thing of Bunny's is gone! I—I could tell from her expression that Bunny would get busy with those blocks as soon as I went away, so I went away. She didn't cry or anything, not once. She didn't say anything. It was all so quick. I expected to hear Bunny howling any moment, so I went downstairs as quickly as I could so I wouldn't hear if she did."

They had been standing at the gates of the playground for some time now. "Here we are," Wilson said. "Walk to your right. Up to the first pillar." He waited. "Got it? Now walk through toward the back of the pavilion, counting the pillars. We want the third one from the back. Are you there? It's hollow, feel it. Sometime I'm going to ask Robert Moses why it is. Broom closet? I should imagine that you fit in there as neatly as Sandy did; push back and anyone would have a hell of a time finding you . . . I know, and Sandy hid there in broad daylight. I only found her because she giggled." Where he had been able to see an outline of her against the apartment house in the back, there was nothing. She was in the pillar. "I know you won't giggle, but don't despair. I have an idea, Blanche."

She stepped out of the hollow pillar. "What?"

"Just an idea. I'm not going to tell you. I tell you, while you're waiting there . . . and I think I hear a police car now . . . while you're waiting for the police to cover the waterfront, you think over what we talked about; maybe you'll come up with the same idea. So long, Blanche," he called, and waited a moment before he walked off. He could not hope to hear her say thank you, he told himself. If anyone had put him through what he'd put her through, thank you would be the last thing he'd want to say! "No, that's an ambulance," he called out, pulled his turtle-neck up and walked off.

Blanche's trigger finger ached and she shoved the revolver back into her purse and flexed her fingers, but she kept the purse open, taking no chances. She found that she could sit on the stone floor of the pavilion with her back against the pillar and her knees drawn up and still be hidden, and that was lucky because she wouldn't have been able to stand very much longer. The scream of the ambulance (or police car) faded away and she heard nothing but the river behind her and the sluggish noises of traffic on East End Avenue. She could not see the sky from where she sat, but in the big apartment house in front of her on Sutton Place there were lights on the two top floors and she was glad that the whole of this terrible city never slept; always on every street some-one was awake and could see and hear. Her eyelids began to droop and it required tremendous effort to keep her head from falling forward on her raised knees. She would think over what Mr. Wilson had talked about and try to discover what his idea was. Was it about the Italian boy? Mr. Wilson (and everybody else) dismissed him because they did not think he'd take Bunny just because he had looked at her that way, but perhaps he was being paid for Bunny? Couldn't there be some woman who had money and no child? A woman who could not, for some reason, adopt a child? Blanche remembered how particular the adoption woman in the hospital said they were, saying Blanche wouldn't have to worry about the kind of parents Bunny would have. *Parents,* the adoption woman had said, making it plural, meaning that a child needed two parents. "If I find Bunny now, I promise

I'll give her for adoption because I'm not fit to have her." She was promising this to the adoption woman (to God?) but because she did not trust that promise even as she made it, Blanche took it back. Give Bunny up once she held her in her arms again? Never let her go. Never let her go, she thought, never leave her for an instant!

"This woman who wants a little girl is rich," she reminded herself, desperately. "Why is it so impossible that somehow she knows the Italian boy and told him how much money she will pay him? Why couldn't that be the reason he looked at me that way, because he was trying to make up his mind? He must have seen me with Bunny. He was trying to make up his mind. His mother and his father could think it was because of me; he wouldn't tell them. They wouldn't let him do such a thing if they knew about it." She tried to think that this was Mr. Wilson's idea, and that he had gone to the police with it and that they would begin looking for the Italian boy and they would find him, and . . .

Blanche did not think that she had fallen asleep but the step across the cement of the playground startled her. It was one pair of feet and not searching, not tentative; there was no flashlight. The footsteps, she realized with fury, were coming straight across the playground to the pavilion. Whoever that was knew about the hollow pillar. She pulled herself to her feet and held the gun in her right hand, because he had betrayed her again. He had left her here where she would be easily found and gone straight to them and told them. She could not have been asleep—how could she sleep?—so she would have heard other footsteps if there had been any, surrounding her, so that when this one came close enough so that she couldn't miss, she would shoot and then run out the back of the pavilion and get away in time.

"Miss Lake?"

She recognized the voice; the other one, the doctor. He

shared Mr. Wilson's betraying, she thought, curling her finger around the trigger. He was a part of it. Wilson put her there and he came to get her. He was coming closer. When he spoke again, when the next betraying, rotten, lying word came out of his mouth . . . He would say, "I want to help you." As they all did. And she would shoot. It would be easy, she thought. They had made it easy, she thought. She wasn't the girl who closed her eyes when there was going to be killing (even in Westerns); she *was* a Western now; her trigger finger itched; it *did*. She waited almost impatiently for this final betrayal.

"Miss Lake," Dennis said. "Miss Lake, I love you!"

"Keep away," Blanche said, because how could she shoot? *Miss Lake, I love you!* "Please keep away," she said again, and how could she add, "or I'll shoot"? *Miss Lake, I love you!* "Don't come any nearer." He didn't come any nearer. He just stood where he was.

Dennis felt his face burning. *Miss Lake, I love you!* He heard it ringing out into the darkness. *Miss Lake, I* . . . that was it—the Miss Lake, the incongruity, he thought. It had been the contrast between the formal address . . . *Miss Lake* . . . and the tumult and tumbling inside himself which had produced that. It was the tension and trembling of his voice as he had said the formal "Miss" that had undone him. Undone. Yes. Precisely, the Victorian word was precise. The thing had been pure Victoriana: Miss Lake, may I ask you for the honor of your hand in marriage? The formal address spoken into the soft night in a voice which had trembled appropriately had led to the "I love you," which was, when you understood it, perfectly rational.

"He told me I would be safe here and then he went straight to you."

"No, he went to the police and I was there."

"He told the police!"

"He told me. I went to the police station because I was afraid for you, what would happen. I intended to ask them to find you." (What is happening to me, he wondered, remembering the change of heart as he had walked toward the desk there, remembering, "Miss Lake, I love you.") "I didn't ask them to find you. I simply asked whether they had any news. They had none," he added hastily, feeling how the hope must have leaped in her. "They had another piece of evidence against the possibility that your child slipped out of school after you. . . ."

"I don't want to hear it!" Blanche said. (I want to hear, "Miss Lake, I love you.")

"All right. I came here to persuade you to give the police your mother's address. I'm sure you're past caring whether she'll blame you now. And once they get your mother and she puts an end to the doubts in their minds . . ." He heard the snap of her pocketbook clasp. (It must be. Getting a handkerchief out, no doubt.) "Don't cry, or do cry, but first give them the address."

She came out of the pillar and moved toward him. He put his arm around her and she did not mind it or, this time, the softness of his sweater.

"My place is right here. The quickest thing to do will be to call from there." She did not agree but she was silent and that, he knew from his experience with his other patients, was permissive. "I'll call the police and get them started and you rest a bit." She did not say no. Her exhaustion was so distinct that he could feel it through her body. "Ah," he whispered, "poor . . ." and stopped short, avoiding the word "child"; the word, he reminded himself, which one might never be able to say to her. And how little "Miss Lake, I love you" meant when one could never say "child" to one's girl! But this was no time for words, Dennis told himself. Words would come later; later he would help her with words, but now (he could feel this too, where his arm touched her shoulder) wordlessness and the comfort of touch.

In the elevator she allowed him to put his arm around her again. He could see the blue veins in her white eyelids and how they trembled, although her face was set and she was biting her lower lip.

Dennis had given his apartment a good deal of thought. There was no room in such a small place for mistakes, and he didn't have the money (or the time) for mistakes, and mistakes, you could say, were his business all day long, so he made sure there were none here. Dennis had a feeling for design and balance, and each piece of furniture was exactly where it should be (in his opinion, of course) to make the room the kind of picture he desired. He knew the effect of certain colors on himself and had been careful to avoid those which unsettled him. (Unsettled people were his business all day long, of course.) He was sensually responsive to textures and here he could indulge his sensuality. (Although not, of course, during the day.) Tidiness here was a restful contrast to the untidiness of neurosis and it was natural, he felt, that nothing should be out of place here.

She was out of place here.

Her tension, her misery, the color spectrum of her insanity did not belong here. After tonight, Dennis told himself, he would see her in his office, where she did belong. Just tonight.

He led her to the yellow-green, raw-silk-covered chair and motioned for her to sit. The telephone pad was where it should be and, while he dialed the precinct number, Dennis wrote down her mother's address and telephone number. "They'll get her." He saw that she was sitting on the edge of the chair, but he didn't have to see to know. He was as conscious of every movement she made as if her body were an extension of his own, which was, of course, traditional to the state, always this magnified consciousness of the other. "I want you to rest now." She could not lean her filthy jacket against the raw silk; he knew that and knelt in front of her, tugging at the sleeve of her jacket. "You must rest now." She allowed him to get the sleeve off, then the other sleeve and then the jacket. "Now, lean back and put your feet up." She frowned because, he understood, she was fastidious, too, about soiled shoes against fine fabrics. He squatted back and, lifting her foot, pulled off her right shoe and began to massage her foot, not speaking, just massaging and looking up at her. He felt that he could not have enough of looking into her face, or thinking of touching or kissing it. What was it in her face, the oval shape of it, its coloring, the fine pale oval in that dark setting of her hair, in the texture of the skin? In the dark eyes, was it, their shape, their position in that face, or was it the blue veins he had noticed on her eyelids in the elevator? "It," he told himself, smiling at the word; was "it" the precise scale of her voice, was it that her mouth was made for marble, was it that rather dirty hand, was it the way her body moved, or smelled? Because "it," he knew perfectly well . . . who better? . . . was something as preposterous as that most of the time, something in the eye of the beholder much of the time. He remembered Mrs. McKenna, from eleven-o-five to eleven-fifty-five that morning. Mrs. McKenna had been telling him of how she had fallen in love at first sight. "He was standing there talking to Madge Caspary. Madge was doing her best. He wasn't even looking her in the face while she talked, looking down his nose at Madge and the rest of us at the party. I was with Bill. He was looking us over," she said, "giving us the once-over! I know what I thought, Dr. Newhouse. I thought that man doesn't think we're good enough for him. I like that, I thought, who does he think he is? To hell with him! And then he looked straight at me over Madge's head and I was in love with him. You can laugh," Mrs. McKenna said.

He hadn't, of course, laughed. Mrs. McKenna falling in love at first sight because a man didn't think she was good enough for him was a perfect fit for her pattern, but it wasn't so easy to understand why Blanche fitted his. He remembered that Freud had been quoted as saying that in the choice of a mate one should always be governed by these "yes sir, that's my baby" decisions coming from the deep needs of the unconscious. And he would heed the master, Dennis thought, if only she weren't insane. As it was . . .

He had pulled off her other moccasin and was holding both her feet in his hands, not massaging them, just holding them, and that, he saw, looking at her relaxed face, must have been the right thing to do. For the first time since he had met her, her face looked as it would if she were . . . herself. Dennis could not help himself; he bent and kissed her feet, first one and then the other.

"Don't," she whispered.

He set her feet on the floor gently and started to pull himself off the floor. With his hand on the arm of her chair, he was very close to her; he heard her rapid breathing and saw how the white eyelids fluttered, and he put his two hands on her face and kissed her. Because response leaped in her lips as in his body, he released her. With Blanche what she was, the Oath of Hippocrates had better be the oath of chastity. He must be careful not to do her harm by adding to her guilt and self-hate because she was capable of response to him.

It was the smell of this man which made Blanche think of the other. It was because she enjoyed his smell, because her nostrils sought it out, drew it in, that she remembered what Mr. Wilson had told her to think about. "I want to talk," she said. Mr. Wilson had asked her if she could think why the director of the nursery school would have done it. Before she spoke out, she tried to be just and called up the image of the girl in the narrow black pants and the black sweater and the bracelet, but wearing all of these as if they were a gift to someone, as if her choice would be something different, something more modest, something more Boston. (To go with her voice, Blanche decided.) She thought of the modest way in which the director had deferred to Dr. Newhouse; not genuine deference, that is. She thought that anyone who could run a nursery school like that, and cook the dinner Blanche had smelled, and set the table that way would not really defer to anybody. Yes, Blanche thought, I think she is capable of doing it. She told herself that the dislike she felt for Miss Benton and the conviction that she was a hypocrite were intuitive. It must be intuition, she thought. Mr. Wilson had mentioned this story in which the hoax had been con-cocted because the mother had died of the Plague and all the money spent on the exposition would be wasted if word of this got around Paris. Why would the nursery-school director tear up the application she must have received, and the check? Why would she get the teachers to lie? Why would she—like the people in the story—just say there was no Bunny? Blanche moaned and jumped out of the yellow-green chair, beginning to pace the room.

"What is it?" Dennis asked. "What do you want to talk about?"

She stayed at the far end of the room so that he could not touch her and quieten her again. "In the park, Mr. Wilson told me what happened about Bunny was just like a certain story. . . ."

"Wilson! Wilson and his stories! He's a writer. Let's forget Wilson and his stories, Blanche." This was the first time he had used her Christian name. It made him feel more like a psy-chiatrist than "Miss Lake."

"You must know it! The Paris Exposition story where they tell the girl she didn't leave her mother in the hotel. Mr. Wilson said if I could think up the reason *why* she would do this!"

"She who, Blanche?"

"Miss Benton. She is the only one," she said, stamping her

bare foot and looking down with surprise to see her shoes off.

"Ridiculous."

"Miss Benton! Miss Benton! Don't shake your head. Mr. Wilson said he had an idea . . . he must have figured out why she did it!" She stamped her foot again. "Don't shake your head at me! 'Ridiculous' is that boy stealing Bunny! Why should he? I thought perhaps some rich woman hired him to steal Bunny, but that's ridiculous, not this!"

"Ah, Blanche!"

"Don't touch me. She'd read the story, don't you see? Everyone has. And then when this happened, it was all ready in her mind to use." Now she ran to him. "Bunny couldn't have the Plague? You're a doctor!"

He must touch her; his touch would help but his words wouldn't. He must wash the grime and dirt and blood smears off her face, bandage that cut on her poor hand.

Blanche pulled away. "No, no, not any sickness! I would have known that this morning. No sickness. And that wouldn't be Miss Benton's fault, anyhow, if Bunny was sick, but Bunny ran down after me. Maybe she fell down . . . fell down. . . ." She threw her hands across her face as though she could see the little girl who, in her hurry to get to her retreating mother, did not go down the laborious two-feet-on-each-step way she had to with her short, plump legs, who had not clutched as far up the guard rails as she could reach for support, who had not paused at each step or sighed her little sigh of congratulation because it was still so difficult for her. "Bunny was killed," Blanche said. "She fell down those stairs there. She killed herself and that would ruin a school . . . a thing like that! Would anybody send her child to a school where a little girl was killed like that? It was to save her school! She did it to save her school like the French hotel man did it for the Exposition . . . said Bunny had never been there, tore up the check and the registration, that's why!"

He picked her up, pressing her close to him. "That wasn't what Wilson meant." He kicked his bedroom door open, put her on his bed and lay next to her. "Lie still, lie close to me and still. I know Miss Benton well enough to be sure. I know what her school means to her and what she would and wouldn't do. She would not do it, Blanche. It isn't in her." He held her with one hand and smoothed her dark, soft hair with the other. "No sane person would, Blanche." (With a kind of terror, he heard himself using the word "sane" to her.) "And that brings me to what Wilson's idea really was."

The minute Wilson had come into the police station, Dennis had told him about the witness they had found, this night watchman who made a habit of sitting at his window during the morning and early afternoon. Some of the residents of the neighborhood had told the police about the old man and they had gone to his place of employment. He lived on the top story of the tenement opposite the school. This witness testified that he had seen Blanche leaving the building that morning at the time she had said she had left and that she was alone. He testified that he hadn't seen a child following her, he was certain of it. He took a great interest in the comings and goings of the nursery school and swore that he would not have missed a child leaving alone. Children did not leave the nursery school unaccompanied and he would certainly have noticed it. He would, he said, have even gone to the school and told them, because little children weren't safe alone on the streets. Wilson had looked at Dennis very curiously while he relayed his information, and, when Dennis finished, had shaken his head as if he couldn't believe his ears.

"I would have sworn you'd have taken Psychology. One, Dennis! That's all I ever took, but I know about what happens between the eye and the memory in regard to accustomed sights. Your reliable witness saw *la belle* Blanche. She was new and worth noting, but, Dennis, this old codger sits at the window every morning, you say, knows the routine of the school, you say. Every day . . . I know the routine, too, Dennis. Every day that it doesn't rain or snow, he sees the teachers taking the kids out to Carl Schurtz Park. Every day, barring bad weather, out come the orange smock and the little darlings. Teacher equals orange smock, Dennis. Kid accompanied by orange smock means watched-over kid. Little girl, coming out of the school door . . . and it needn't been right after Mademoiselle . . . little girl coming out the school door some minutes later accompanied by orange smock means little girl safe, so he says, 'No, officer, I can swear on the Bible no little girl ran out after her mother this morning!'"

Even while he had been asking Iss what that proved, since no orange smock had taken the child out of the school building, reminding him that Miss Orange Smock Ditmars who Blanche said had interviewed her had never seen or heard of Blanche, he had known what particular orange smock Dennis meant. Wilson, whose older girl had been in her group, knew all about Ada Ford.

Wilson had grinned at him. "Yes, Dennis, Ada Ford. Ada would fit the bill perfectly."

He had explained Ada to the police.

Wilson had said, "You know, Dennis, what I can't make out is why you didn't think of Ada immediately."

He had told Iss that he had thought of Ada, thought of her and dismissed her because it was impossible that Ada should have had anything to do with this. Ada, he had reminded Iss, had been gone for a year. ("Gone *and* forgotten," Iss had said, shaking his head, wondering.) Wilson had got him sore and he had told him off.

"Did you check, Dennis?" Wilson had asked. "I want to know, did you check before you dismissed Ada as an impossibility?"

He had said, "I'll check now." He had called Louise from

the police station. (Now he pressed his hot cheek against Blanche's soft hair, remembering the conversation with Louise.)

"Darling," she had said, "I've been waiting for you!"

He had been afraid that someone in the station might be listening on another wire and so he had been (understandably) stiff with Louise. "I'd like some information."

"Of course, Dennis. But do you need to sound so curt?"

"I'm calling from the police station." He had hoped that would cover it. (He had been resentful of the possessiveness of Louise's "Darling! I've been waiting for you!" and why shouldn't he have resented it, since it wasn't in the cards? Not "in the bond"? This was being quite a night for Shakespeare; first Othello and now Shylock! Dennis told him that whenever the big uncontrollable emotions popped up, up popped Shakespeare, who dealt in them. Shakespeare and the big uncontrollable emotions were inextricably caught in the dark net of the soft hair brushing his cheek.) "There is something I must ask you, Louise."

But he had not "asked" Louise; he had fired questions about Ada Ford at her: As far as Louise knew was Ford still in that old house in Brooklyn Heights? Had Ada been seen again? Had she approached Louise and begged to be allowed to work in the school? Had Louise, after everything he had explained about Ada's state, permitted Ada to come back into the school in any capacity whatsoever?

"This is incredible, Dennis!" Louise had said.

"There is no possibility that she could have sent Miss Lake the registration blank and interviewed her while you were in Wellfleet? Iss Wilson is here. He suggested that if Ada was around the school, then the whole picture changes. I want to know if, after everything you were told about Ada Ford, she did turn up and you did use her in any capacity whatsoever."

Louise had said, "How dare you!"

He had been so angry that he had simply shoved the telephone toward the policeman and walked away from the desk. (The tension had, of course, produced its usual effect and the pain behind his forehead had been almost intolerable. He had had to go into the next room where there was a water cooler so that he could take two of the Miltown pills he always kept in his pocket.) When he returned to the inner office, the lieutenant had been waiting for him with such an odd expression on his face that he was sure Wilson had said something outrageous to him. The lieutenant's expression, that is, Dennis had told himself, striving as usual for precision, had been an extension of, if not a duplicate of, the curious look which Iss Wilson had bent on him.

But according to the lieutenant, who relayed what Louise had said to him, Louise had simply not known what he was *"raving"* about. Louise had denied his accusations *"categorically."* She had not seen or heard from anyone who had seen Ada Ford. She could be in the house her mother had left her in Brooklyn Heights or she could be in Siam. Ada had not written again after the letter last year begging to be allowed to work in the school again, and if she had Louise would certainly not have permitted it. Louise had told the lieutenant that Dennis couldn't be more mistaken. She had followed the advice he had given her when the Ada Ford thing came up, to the letter, and simply could not understand him.

He, of course, could understand himself. His behavior had been standard for a man who wanted to be shed of a girl: find something to blame her for, blame her for it and get her off your conscience. He had used Ada Ford, that was all; had accused Louise of flirting with her after he had warned her off, just as other men used rivals, real or as here, as imaginary as Ada Ford.

Dennis held Blanche close to him with one arm, and stroked her cheek and caressed her soft dark hair with the other and told her what Wilson's idea had really been. "Iss is a very acute person, Blanche. He would certainly pick up the resemblance between this" (this what?) "and that story; he might tell you to see if you could work out a motive for Miss Benton's having lifted that French hotel story and using it for her own purposes. . . but, believe me, Blanche, he said it because he thought it would keep you occupied in the dark there, and not because he thought there was any truth in it."

Blanche stirred in his arms and spoke. "What?" Dennis asked. He had not switched the light on so he could not see how her lips moved as she spoke, but he could visualize them perfectly. "What did you say, darling?"

"It was occupational therapy, you mean?"

"That's right, busy work. Iss Wilson knows that fiction is fiction and fact is fact. Iss is a damn smart guy." She stirred again, but only to lie more comfortably. "Rest," Dennis said, "just rest. Trust me."

Iss was smart enough. And what, Dennis wondered, remembering the expression on Iss' face and its extension on the face of the police lieutenant, had smart Iss Wilson said about him? But then Dennis forgot about Wilson and the police lieutenant because Blanche moved again, because the quality of her breathing changed. (Became an extension, a copy, of his breathing, which had also changed?) He did not need to hold her any longer. She was not more relaxed, but he did not need to hold her. The texture and temperature of her skin had changed. Dennis said to himself, "And who do you think you're fooling with this clinical observation you're doing?" Humans, like animals, did take comfort from another body near them, and his body had leeched the hysteria and tension from hers, and that was therapeutic, but a little more of this, enough of this to make it unmistakable, and he might do her a great deal of harm. He took her hand, turned up the palm of it and kissed it, then laid it down. "Blanche, I have to go out for a while. Will you trust me and stay where you are?"

"But Bunny . . ."

"There is nothing you can do now. Let me go out and you stay where you are." She pulled herself up on one elbow as he got off the bed. He understood that she believed he was going out on behalf of her child, but he did not correct the impression. He leaned over her and gently pressed her down again and kissed her forehead lightly.

As he went into the other room, he saw that she had stayed where he left her. He thought, taking one last look at her, that she might even sleep, and if she did, it would be the best thing she could do.

The cops said, all right so she was a decent woman the way she said, all right, she was no floosie. The guy they *did* know all about. He was a drunk they picked up regularly, but, they said, attempted rape was out of his line. That he should have taken a bottle of belly wash up there was to be expected—with the El empty and comfortable as it was, why shouldn't a bum without the price of a bed hide up there?—but if she was a decent woman the way she said, what was she doing up there?

She kept telling them that she had yelled, hadn't she; she had yelled, hadn't she? Yes, the cops said, she had yelled, all right, but what had she gone up there for in the first place?

The trouble was that they saw Rose was scared to talk. If the cops saw you were scared to talk, they wanted to make you talk. They wouldn't let her go home. They took her in.

The cops did their best to make her talk, but they couldn't

make her talk, not when it might mean the hot seat for Eddie if she told them.

They could book her for soliciting and could lock her up, but they couldn't make her talk.

It was a different story when they brought George to the Sixty-seventh Street police station. George was a different story from the police. The cops, naturally, they were nosy, but George was her husband and that was a different story. When they told George about the drunk and her being up there in the El station and he asked her what she was doing up there, she had to tell him. "I was looking for Eddie," she said.

George had shoved his pants on and shoes without socks and a topcoat, but naturally he hadn't combed his hair. George had this thick black hair and he used Bryl-creem on it, but sleeping that way, a tuft of his hair stuck out and it bothered Rose. Without thinking, she reached out to smooth it back into place, the way she did a thousand times mornings, in bed, but when she touched George's hair with her hand, that made him see red. (Maybe it made him think she had touched the drunk's hair that way, loved the drunk up, too.) She could tell then that she would have to admit the true reason why she would go up to the El like that or George would be through with her. It was either Eddie, then, or George, so she asked could she speak to George alone without cops around, and the cops left them alone.

She told George why it was so important to her to find Eddie that she would take a chance like that with herself. She told him about Eddie knowing where the girl lived, and about

Eddie and the kitten and how when she found out in the bowling alley that the girl's baby was lost, she knew!

"Go wan!" George said. "Just because I kidded him a little?"

She told George about Eddie and the kitten again. She didn't know how to say it the way it had been. If Georgie could have seen with his own eyes, the way she had seen with hers, he wouldn't say nuts!

"Your really *mean* it, Rose?"

She got down on her knees in front of George and begged he should get her out of here and go with her to find Eddie and not tell the cops. When she saw the way George was looking down at her, Rose grabbed his legs. "That's why I wouldn't go wake you," she shouted. "That's why I was scared to wake you, George!"

George said, "You should'a, Rose. You wasted a hell of a lot of time." He pulled himself free of his wife's arms and went out where the cops were.

She did sleep. She had not meant to sleep, just to lie there and be able to rest, to breathe without it hurting when she breathed, to feel the buoyancy of a mattress, the smoothness of the bed cover, the coolness of the pillowcase, and under the coolness the softness of the goose down in the pillow. She had meant to just lie there waiting. Men must work and women must wait. To lie there thinking that a man was working for Bunny and all she had to do now was wait. To lie there thinking, for the first time since she had known that Bunny was missing, that she was not alone with everyone in the whole world against her.

It was her body which had taken advantage of her and put her to sleep, so deeply that she did not know what had awakened her, and it took what seemed a long time for her to place the noise and the ringing and ascribe the ringing to the telephone. Then she realized that it must be he calling . . . because he had news for her! And she ran, ran, ran until she located the telephone and snatched it up. It was because she was so breathless with anticipation that she didn't say hello.

"Darling," the woman's voice said. "I've been waiting for you, Dennis. I've been keeping dinner, darling! It will be breakfast soon!"

His name was Dennis. Dennis. He hadn't come to dinner. Blanche put the telephone back into its cradle.

"Darling, I've been waiting for you," the woman had said. Darling, for men must work and women must wait. *Dennis.* Her body knew its treachery before her sleepy mind did and expressed its loathing primitively. Her mind only caught up with her body after she had vomited, and the sour smell of the vomit, the feeling of being torn apart inside were perfectly symbolic.

Blanche knelt over the toilet bowl until the retching stopped, then pulled herself up and staggered out of the bathroom. She stood in the living room, staring at the yellow-green chair in which she had sat, where he had kissed her. Her torn and soiled jacket lay on the floor where he had thrown it. Blanche walked over to it and stood looking down at the soiled, flung thing, then turned and found her pocketbook.

It was impossible, she thought, to go on in a soiled world which had no Bunny, only people like those two, the two of them. She thought of the two of them together in the school director's apartment seated across from each other at the small table covered with the long white *unsoiled* cloth. He would be telling her not to worry, that he had fixed it for her. He would be telling her that Miss Lake (*Miss Lake, I love you*) had finally realized what it was all about, but he had fixed that. How he had fixed that, Blanche thought, remembering that she had kissed him as much as he had her, that she had lain on his bed pressed close to him. She would not live, she thought, in a soiled body which had done that, and she took her gun out of her pocketbook.

Looking into the grey-black mouth, she began to retch again, but was that worse than seeing herself as the hypnotized guinea pig in the biology lab, when the teacher had stroked its soft belly and it lay tranced on its back with its legs in the air?

He had put his hands on her and had stroked her and that was how she had lain on his bed, like the guinea pig. And she had wanted him to. He had made her lie there. She sobbed and released the safety catch and put the gun to her forehead, shivering with nausea.

"*Darling,*" the school director had said, "*I've been waiting for you.*"

Blanche put the safety catch back on and thrust the revolver back into the purse, grabbed up her blue jacket again, thrust her arms into it, and then went to the chair where he had kissed her. "Yes, that chair," she said to herself. "Sit right there!" Because she had been the guinea pig, but that didn't mean she had to die a guinea pig. Blanche bent and picked up the shoes he had shaken off. She pulled the moccasins on over her ripped stockings, gritting her teeth because her hands were so clumsy and she wanted to hurry.

He wasn't there yet or else she wouldn't have said, "*Darling, I've been waiting.*" If she could get her moccasins on and get there and hide in the shadows under the stairs, he would come, and when he did . . . Before he was safely inside with her, to report, gloating, to give an imitation of her, of himself humbly on his knees before this chair while he efficiently made a tranced guinea pig out of her, to report mission accomplished, guinea pig hypnotized, kill him!

She would kill him. She would make sure that he didn't go up there with her. (*"Miss Benton, I love you,"* he would say.) "Trust me," he would say to her. "I handled it fine. The little fool finally caught on, but I managed her all right. Trust me and she won't make any trouble for you."

But he wasn't going to gloat because she would kill him. And then herself. And if that woman went unpunished . . . How could she go unpunished? She would be losing him!

Blanche stood up, stamping her feet into the moccasins. "She'll suffer, all right. She'll suffer. She'll pay!"

As always, when she hadn't eaten, she felt the cold, and now, as she stood propped against the rough brick of the school building, her teeth were chattering so badly that she was afraid that when he came he would hear them and be warned. If only she could get inside the building, if she could only hide somewhere inside and wait there until he was with her, until the two of them were together. Two birds with one stone, two of them with one bullet. That was silly. Two bullets; she could shoot quickly enough for two bullets, and it would be the two of them together because she did not know which one she hated the most. No, she thought, rubbing her right wrist to supple it; it was the two of them together that she hated most.

But if, as the policeman had done this afternoon, she went to the house next door and woke them up and asked to be let through to the back yard and climbed into the school building that way, the people next door might guess. They would see that the director's light was on and ask why she didn't ring the bell and be let in that way, and then they would telephone the director, who would then warn him.

"Darling," she would say, "she isn't as stupid as you thought. The hypnotism didn't last as long as you thought it would. She came to," she would say (darling), "and realized that you and I are in this together. She realized that you helped me work this out from the beginning. Tell the police that she is crazy and have her locked up and then you and I will have the rest of our lives together."

And now she was warm, hot, searing all through her. Her teeth had stopped chattering. (Her teeth gritted.) She could wait.

Blanche listened impatiently for his steps, but the street was quiet, and then she remembered how he had come up behind her when she tried to get in here earlier and how his arm had reached out and how he had rung a special ring. She threw her left arm over her face and made it dark inside her eyes to bring it back. Dum-dum-dum-di! The Fifth Symphony. Oh, yes, she thought, that's it! If it had not been the Fifth and familiar to her, the rhythm wouldn't have registered; it would just have been many rings.

Blanche slipped her gun back into her purse and rubbed her fingers together briskly in a pianist's way, as if she were going to play the Beethoven, and walked quickly up the stone steps. When her fingers felt elastic enough, she pressed the bell, firmly, dum-dum-dum-di, doing it staccato, with assurance, and then stepped into the shadow in case, even with the signal, Miss Benton should want to make sure, but immediately she heard the ticking, and, biting her lip, because this showed how hard she was waiting for him, Blanche opened the door and stepped inside.

"Oh, Dennis!" the ladylike Boston voice said in a fervent Bostonian. "Oh, darling, I'm so glad you've come!"

So that she need not answer, Blanche slammed the door as

hard as she could. She stayed on the right-hand side of the stairs where the shadows were deepest.

"You are still angry! If you won't *talk* to me, Dennis!"

————————

They found Eddie in the storage room in the back of the store. He was stretched out on two sacks of potatoes and when George saw how many bananas he had eaten, he forgot for a minute why they were there and began to give Eddie hell about the bananas.

The cops didn't forget. They went on out in back and they turned the storeroom inside out. Even though George said Eddie couldn't have moved the hundred-pound sacks out of the way to open the cellar door, the cop and George got the door open. "You'd be surprised what a person can do when they feel the rope around their neck," the fat cop said. Then they went down in the cellar.

Eddie asked what they were looking for.

Eddie said they were out of their mind. He hadn't kidnapped no little girl. What would he want to do a thing like that for?

Rose said, "*Her* little girl, Eddie." Even with the light so bad, you could see how Eddie turned red. George noticed it, too, and he shoved Rose aside from where she was standing in between him and Eddie, and grabbed Eddie by the neck. All George was thinking about was to choke where he had put the little girl out of Eddie, and because Eddie couldn't get loose from George, he didn't watch him. It was Rose who pulled the knife out of Eddie's hand before he cold get the blade out.

When she held the knife in front of George so he could see it, he let go of Eddie. Rose said, crying, "You see?"

Two cops grabbed Eddie and held him.

"I'll kill him!" Eddie said.

"Never mind about killing him. What about the little girl?"

Eddie said he never touched the little girl. Eddie said he never had nothing to do with a little girl. Sure, he said, he had been around the chick's house in the morning. "There's no law against that, is there?" Eddie said he didn't know what he was hanging around the house for. He didn't know what he had in mind, he only knew what he did. He was there and he saw the chick come out with this old lady, carrying her suitcase. He had looked at her. "And there's no law against that that I know of, either." He hadn't done anything or said anything, just stood there and watched until the old lady got a cab and gave the address and went away. He never kidnapped any little girl. "What the hell for?" He didn't know until they told him that she had any little girl. The chick didn't wear any wedding ring and he didn't know she was married, even.

The cops started looking at each other and asking Eddie questions; didn't he really see the little girl, didn't he really know she had a little girl? Rose could tell there was something funny the way they kept asking didn't Eddie never see any little girl and then looking at each other.

Of course they weren't going to let Eddie go on his say-so or because the little girl wasn't here. Eddie could have dumped her somewhere else. It was no good Rose begging them to let her take Eddie back home; they began hauling him off. Rose forgot all about the girl and the little girl, but one thing she would never forget to her dying day, she thought, was the look Eddie gave her when they began hauling him off and she stayed in the store with George to help him clean up so they could open for business in the morning.

Wilson wondered whether it was smarter to stay right where he was, nursing the hot feeling behind his eyes and the tendency of his thoughts to shift from sense to nonsense, which indicated sleepiness, or to take the chance of losing it by trotting himself up to the bedroom and having to start the whole process over again. He groaned and pushed up out of the chair because even that much indecision had completely roused him. He decided to go up to the bedroom so that if Morpheus beckoned again there would be no question of moving in order to embrace him.

He had tucked the bed sheets Blanche had climbed down on behind the post at the foot of the stairs and, as he moved wearily past, he grabbed them to take them up with him and stick them into the hamper. There was no question, no uncertainty about whether he would make up the bed. Marta wasn't around to be scandalized, so he would just lie on the bare mattress. He thrust the sheets under his arm and began to climb the stairs.

If the sheets, dragging behind him, had not caught on the nail at the head of the stairs, left there and overlooked when he had removed the gate they had put when the kids were young enough to tumble downstairs, he would not have remembered the gun, but the ripping sound the sheets made cracked like a pistol shot. "Oh, Jesus!" Wilson said because now he recalled his clean shirt that had been hanging over the bed rail when he had unlocked the bedroom to let her out, and fitting the shirt into its proper place, which was in his chest of drawers, knowing that it had been she who had taken it (although he did not know why), it had occurred to Wilson that it was more than possible that she had discovered the revolver. . . . And if she had . . .

He dropped the sheets and ran toward his room. If she

had . . .

What had been keeping him awake down there was the attempt to convince himself that Blanche must be, as Dennis insisted, insane. Dennis was a competent man, a careful man (too careful!), and if Dennis said she didn't have all her marbles, then she didn't have. No matter how she seemed to him, she didn't have. It was important to convince himself because if she wasn't insane then it was just too bloody awful. She had to be insane. Dennis was a competent man. That was how it had gone, round and round, and each time the uncertainty, no, the stubborn refusal to believe it, hit him in the guts. He pulled the second drawer of his chest of drawers open and felt in the Paisley pajamas. Once he had discovered that it was not a trick Mademoiselle Blanche and Marta had decided to play on him, he had been sick, gutsick, realizing (sane or insane) that she had come to him as her only friend in the city and he had thrown her out on her ear. She could have killed herself for all the friend he had been. He would never forget, Wilson thought, her face pressed against the window of the *Wurstgescheft*. He threw the Paisley pajamas on the floor and then, one by one, the other things in the drawers and then the things in the rest of the drawer because he could have been wrong about just where he had tucked the revolver, because, he told himself, knowing now that the nightmare she had been put through, fantasy or no, was real enough to her, if she had his gun, wouldn't she use it?

The gun was gone.

Wilson sat on the bed and tried to remember whether he knew where she lived. He closed his eyes and banged his fist down on his knees, rocking back and forward while he banged, a mnemonic habit of his, but nothing came. That it was close to Henderson Place, yes, in the neighborhood, of course; not a small *romantic* house like this; an apartment, she had said, but that was reasoning and not remembering and he couldn't reason his route to her that way. Wilson sat banging his knees and then jumped up. Dennis would know. (Wilson just saved himself from being entangled in the clothes he had dropped on the floor. "With her luck," he thought, "I should have tripped and been knocked unconscious until it was too late.") He could see her dead with a neat hole in the front of her head and a not so neat one to mark the egress. He could see only her dead face and not the preposterously small print of the telephone directory. Newhouse A . . . Newhouse C . . .

As Wilson dialed, he counted long enough, he thought, to wake the dead in case that damned unimaginative fool of a psychiatrist had been able to sleep, but there was no answer. ("And the dead don't wake," he told himself, seeing her dead face again.) If he didn't get to her, there wouldn't be any waking her. This time she had pointed the thirty-two to where she believed her heart was and the blood, dyed purple-black by the time he reached her, made a macabre cummerbund under her young breasts. He had always been curious about suicides ("Morbid," Marta said. "All the world loves a lover, not a suicide."), always wondering what could be decisive enough to make them do it, because low as he could sink (a nothing since not good writer; a nothing because surely not a good man), he couldn't do it. But this time, he thought, she needn't write an explanatory note. This time he knew why.

This time he could write the note himself because he understood, this time, for surely no one could ever have felt more brutally used than that poor girl. If she shot him, Wilson thought, he couldn't blame her.

If she shot . . . Suppose not herself, not only herself, but Louise Benton first? If she shot Benton, Wilson thought, finding the Manhattan Directory again, it would be his doing. He had put the Paris Exposition story into Mademoiselle's poor head. Why would Benton have pretended she had never seen Bunny, he had asked. Think about that, he had advised!

Had he known about the gun, he might have been more careful with his advice, but as it was he had given her Benton to chew on with about as much thought as when he gave Sandy a picture puzzle to do on a rainy afternoon. He tried to tell himself, his hand trembling as he leafed the Directory, that Mademoiselle Blanche was incapable of thinking that straight, but it didn't go down. She was quite capable of it. She had invented the Italian boy, which was more difficult surely. . . . All she had to do here was substitute. Her child had died like the mother in the story, somehow her child had died (or been killed) and for the French hotel manager, there was Louise Benton all set up to be used. To save *her* investment, Benton had played the same ghastly game with Mademoiselle Blanche, using her child as a pawn. Wilson found the Benton school.

If Mademoiselle had substituted along those lines, if she had come up with the substitute villain . . . since she had his gun . . . He dialed the number.

"Don't answer that," Blanche said. "Stay exactly where you are. Let it ring!"

It was time to wake her up, Dennis thought. He had every reason now to go back and wake her up. He frowned into the yawning face of the cab driver as he paid him because he had to recognize how happy he was to have sound reasons so that he might indulge his desire to hurry back to his apartment, to tiptoe into his bedroom, to bend over her on his bed. (Because he was so all-fired anxious to get back to her on his bed, he over-tipped the driver. Very well. He was aware of it. All right!)

The two good reasons for waking her, Dennis thought, returning to them (to reason!) with relief, were that if she slept too long she would feel too much guilt, and that it was necessary to question her about her mother. He told the police lieutenant that he would ask her whether she could explain why, as far as the local police could ascertain by questioning neighbors, her mother had not appeared in Providence at all. The local police had questioned the real-estate people who handled her mother's house, and they stated that they had not written to her mother that they had a firm offer. What he had to find out from Blanche, if he could, was whether she thought she was telling the truth about her mother's trip back home. If Blanche believed her mother had gone home, then was it a fantastic belief, or had her mother told her she was returning to Providence? If her mother told her she was going to Providence, then why wasn't she there? The police apparently thought the mother business required immediate investigation. ("It smells," was the way Lieutenant Duff had put it.) It was only after solemn professional warning from him of the damage they might do if they went over and questioned Blanche themselves that he had been able to convince them to stay out of it and let him talk to her. He couldn't go along with the police that the mother business was of any great importance, but then he wasn't a detective. "Psychiatrist, stick to your last," Dennis thought, but felt rather more adequate when he reminded himself that it was a psychiatrist and not a policeman that Blanche really needed. Whatever she thought! He would use his training and his time, everything he had, to help her, and perhaps he could. "Eventually," Dennis thought. "Someday. Darling, darling Blanche," he thought. "White. *Blanche*. Her white skin," he thought, "the dark net of her hair," he thought, and pushed the elevator button hard.

When he discovered that he had forgotten his key— although he couldn't help knowing that this had significance, great significance since he so rarely did forget anything, probably symbolizing his natural desire to take this new and infinitely disturbing emotion Blanche had aroused in him and lock it away—he could have kicked himself because it meant that he had to ring the doorbell and awaken her that way. When she did not answer the doorbell, Dennis thought of her white eyelids with the blue veins stubbornly closed in sleep and wasn't alarmed, but it meant going down and getting the passkey from the super. The super's surprise at being knocked-up by Dr. Newhouse pointed up how rarely he did forget anything. He gave the super a five-dollar bill for his trouble and calmed him down and hurried back upstairs with the passkey.

Although it was foolish, since she hadn't heard him ringing the bell, he removed his shoes in the living room. When he left he must have forgotten to put the light out—another indication of his state, since Dennis usually was meticulous about such things. (He enjoyed spending but not wasting his money.) When he set his shoes down he saw, in a double take, that her shoes, which he had left in front of the yellow-green chair, were missing. He tiptoed into the bedroom, which was dark, and stood in the doorway holding his breath to hear her breathing, acknowledging to himself how much he wanted her to be asleep so that he could kiss her awake. Standing there, not hearing her breathing, he did another double take and remembered that her blue jacket should have been on the living-room floor, too. Cursing, he switched the light on, although he knew without looking that she was gone.

Dennis ran out of his apartment and was waiting for the elevator to come up before the cold of the floor, penetrating his socks, reminded him that he had not put his shoes back on. "What's come over me?" he wondered miserably, knowing perfectly well. And, of course, he had locked himself out. The super's passkey lay on the table where he had put it down to take his shoes off and he hadn't the faintest idea where his own key was!

Dennis opened the elevator door, walked into the cage and pressed the B button. Surely, he thought, the super would have another passkey? Surely, it would take less time to get him up again (another five bucks!) and to explain what had happened. . . . A patient sleeping in there. I thought I didn't want to awaken her. When found her gone so worried because she is in a pretty bad state. . . . "I'm sorry about this," was all he would have to say. "I'm afraid I was so worried about my patient, Mike, that I left your passkey on the table and forgot the latch was on."

He could see the expression on the super's face and this was enough to make Dennis push the M button. When the elevator stopped at the main floor, Dennis hurried out. Better to go in his stockinged feet than to see the expression on Mike's face: "Why, Doc? Why Doc! WHY, DOC!"

Wilson put off going to the police until there was nothing else to do because once he did that, reported his gun missing, got them out after her, she would be a goner. Once the police got wind of this aspect of the case, she would be their baby. He had marked the school's telephone number on the wall near the phone. He would try that again first. Warn Louise Benton first, if he could.

"Let it ring," Blanche said, "and don't talk any more unless you're going to tell me where you put her. I must know," she said. "I can't stand this much longer, not knowing!" Her voice did break but the revolver was steady in her hand.

"I never saw her. I never saw her."

"If you say that again, I'll kill you now."

It was the peculiar sensation of feeling pavement through his socks that was making him feel so insecure and helpless. "Barefoot boy with cheek of tan"! Dennis was an adult. He was an adult in his stocking feet and not a barefoot boy. He had made a mistake in leaving her but he would find her again. Dennis stepped into something wet and felt his stomach muscles tighten in distaste. "Stop being such a damned old maid," he said to himself. So he didn't approve of himself right now. Granted. Wilson, rushing around the corner, almost knocked him over.

"So you're not asleep!" Wilson said.

"Asleep!"

"Out of the question, is it? And you the guy who doesn't take his troubles to bed with him?" Wilson, who was a head taller than Dennis, looked down at him, cocking his head. "And you the guy who doesn't take his troubles to bed with him," he repeated, and then, in one of those flashes of comprehension, even while he was asking Dennis where Blanche was, he had the answer to what had been puzzling him. Dennis had been in character, the guy who didn't take his troubles (Blanche) to bed with him. Dennis had the third ear, all right, but because he was afraid of what the siren (Blanche) would do to his Odyssey, to the long journey he had to take before he could afford Blanche, he had, like Odysseus, carefully stuffed cotton in his third ear so that he hadn't been able to hear her song and to know that it was a song of sanity.

"She was up in my place but she's gone." He did not like the way Wilson said "Blanche." "Why?"

"Because I've got to get hold of her before something happens."

He did not like the way Wilson pronounced her name or his wanting to "get hold of her." Jealousy again. Othello again. "Before what happens? I don't understand you."

"You will, Oscar, you will! When I locked her in my bedroom she found the gun I keep in my chest of drawers. Loaded."

"Oh, my God!"

"Where do you think she could be, Dennis?" No time for cowardice. Hit it. "Dennis, I was a damn fool. I'll tell you about it later. In the meantime, would she have had the time, since you left her, to go to the school, use the gun and get out again?"

"Plenty of time, but . . ."

"Come on then." Wilson started toward the nursery school. "I told her to think over the Paris Exposition story and I think it's a dead certainty that she'll have decided that Louise Benton is the villain in the case and go for her."

"She did, Iss. I mean she did accuse Louise of having lifted the plot of that story; there is what would be a remarkable similarity to the two plots, except, of course, it was Blanche who did the lifting!" He was out of breath. "Anyhow, I convinced her that it was foolishness. I told her that you didn't believe in it for a minute. I convinced her that Louise had nothing to do with it."

"Maybe she didn't stay convinced, Dennis! I tried to get Louise several times at the school and there no answer. I rang the doorbell and got nowhere. I leave it to you, should we go to the police?" Dennis shook his head and began to run. Dennis was the faster and Wilson, pounding away in back of him, caught a glimpse of his feet and it seemed to him that Dennis had no shoes on. Why no shoes, for the love of Mike?

———————

"No," Blanche said. "I won't let you go. Even if you do tell me, I won't. Tell me," she whispered, "tell me."

"Why won't you believe me? I have told you. I told you. I

told you."

Blanche rubbed along her right hand to keep her fingers limbered and ready. "I will never believe anyone again. What happened to Bunny? Where did you put her? How did she die?"

"What's the good of this? Get it over, then. Why don't you use that gun and get it over with?"

"I told you that. Because when I shoot you someone will hear and then *he* would be saved and it must be both of you because you are in this together." The word "together" acted like an electric shock which she could feel in the hand she was rubbing, which made the hackles of her hatred stand on end.

"But he won't come here."

"Of course he will. Of course he's coming here, don't you realize that I know that? For his reward, of course!" Miss Benton was in a nightgown and robe now; the severe, chic trousers and sweater were put away; what she was wearing now was supposed to be seductive. When Boston tries to be seductive it goes too far, Blanche thought, her lip curling.

"Dr. Newhouse is angry with me. He called me from the police station and accused me of doing the most . . ." And then Louise remembered what she had *not* done and saw what it might mean. Dennis had been so curt, she thought, so hard and rapping. He had made those staccato accusations, one after the other, and she had denied them the same way, all her energy employed in denial and all her imagination busy trying to understand why Dennis should have turned against her, should seem to hate her. She had *not* seen Ada again. Ada had *not* approached her or begged to work for her without pay. This was what Dennis had implied, of course, that she was so . . . *saving* that she would have been tempted to make use of Ada because it would save money. And couldn't it have been her . . . savingness . . . which had betrayed her, after all? Now that she had time to think, now that she was not so humiliated and confused hearing Dennis talking to her that way after the week in Wellfleet, she could remember the one small thing she had *not* done. Dennis had thrown that one off so airily, just because one of the mothers *thought* she had seen Ada in the supermarket! "It might be a good idea to have all the locks changed just in case Ada has a key," as if Dennis didn't know how much that would have to run to, as if he didn't know how close their margin was! But she hadn't had the locks changed, and if Ada could have got into the building while they were in Wellfleet, she could have interviewed Miss Lake here on the twenty-first as Miss Lake said. Since she and Dennis had been in Wellfleet from the sixteenth to the thirtieth, Ada could have sent the application and removed any letters she wanted to from the mails, could have let herself in this morning and could have abducted the child. Ada knew that she always took a vacation two weeks before the school year began. Louise said, "Miss Lake . . ." She closed her eyes for a moment, because might not this confusion make the girl . . .? "Miss Lake, I know how all this could have happened. It just came to me now. I just now saw . . . Miss Lake, won't you put that gun away and listen to me?"

"I'll listen to you. You can talk."

"We had a teacher here. I became concerned with her . . . Certain things happened. I received reports from the parents of the children in her group. I called in Dr. Newhouse to see her because I was definitely concerned. Dr. Newhouse saw her several times and told me that I must get rid of her because she had become unbalanced; he called it menopausal psychosis. Ada was forty-eight and when menopause came and she had to face the fact, which she had apparently been evading, that she would never be able to have a child of her own, well, she couldn't face it. Dr. Newhouse thought that she had probably gone into teaching for the wrong reasons. He doesn't believe that a teacher should want to be a mother to the children. She should want to be their teacher."

"Don't you be a teacher, please. I don't want to be taught. Stop it. Dr. Newhouse already told me about this teacher, so don't you try that on me, Miss Benton!"

"Yes, but there's something Dr. Newhouse doesn't know. Miss Lake, don't you see that it must have been Ada Ford who wrote you that letter saying that there was a place here for your little girl because someone dropped out? It was Ada who interviewed you here while I was away. I was away in Wellfleet." She blushed. "Ada must have planned all this to kidnap your child today."

"It's so funny how a gun pointing at you makes your imagination work."

"It isn't imagination. I told you. I just realized how she could have gotten into the building while I was in Wellfleet. Why won't you believe me? I just realized that I didn't change the locks, which was the one thing Dr. Newhouse advised me to do that I neglected to do. If he'd questioned me about it specifically when he called from the police station, I would have remembered before, but he didn't mention the locks and I didn't remember until just now."

"Yes. Just now!"

"Just now. I didn't change all the locks because the idea of Ada breaking in here . . . Why would she, don't you see? It seemed ridiculous, pointless, so I didn't. But now it became clear to me. Now. This minute! So, please, let me call the police, Miss Lake. I'll tell them how the whole thing must have happened. It would have been so easy for Ada to get into the school this morning without being seen. She knows exactly when and where we are every minute of the school day and she could choose the precise time. It would be easy not to be seen. She would know just when she could get . . . Bunny . . . out without anybody noticing her. And then, with all the other unfortunate coincidences . . ."

"Unfortunate coincidences! Coincidences!"

"Let me call the police and tell them about the locks not being changed. That is something so definite. Then they will take this seriously."

"Will they? I don't," Blanche said. "I don't take it seriously. What kind of idiot do you two think I am, anyway? How many times do you think you can fool me? Clever as you two are! Oh, you're very clever. This mysterious teacher who suddenly appears!"

"Not suddenly, no, I told you! Dr. Newhouse called me from the police station about her, so he thought of her before this, don't you see? Mr. Wilson, too, Mr. Wilson, too! Don't you understand that when I denied that it was possible for her to get in here, they dropped her as a possibility, but they thought of her before! Miss Lake, both Mr. Wilson and Dr. Newhouse . . ."

"Why don't you call him 'Dennis'? 'Dennis, darling' . . . You know you do!"

"Please, Miss Lake!"

"How did this crazy, convenient, mysterious teacher find out about Bunny in the first place? Why would the registrar of the Stevenson School tell this crazy, mysterious teacher that I had applied there? Why would that school give her Bunny's name and address so she could write me that convenient letter saying there was an empty place in your school? Who told this crazy teacher about me?"

"Miss Lake, I— She must have seen your daughter and— Why, with your mother, Miss Lake! When your mother— she—"

"My mother! Now my poor mother!"

"But why not, Miss Lake? Ada couldn't have done it alone, you're right about that. She would have to know about you in the first place, of course, that goes without saying, and she'd have to have quite a few facts. But couldn't your mother have met Ada when she was out with your little girl? Couldn't your mother have talked to Ada—in the park, say, when she was there with Bunny, while you were working?" If she dared to come closer to the girl. If she could touch her. (If she could only touch her!) "You said that your mother was terribly ashamed because your child was illegitimate. You said that she wanted you to give your child away for adoption."

"Because mother didn't feel I was able to take care of Bunny by myself. For Bunny's good."

"But that's just it, Miss Lake. Don't you see how Ada fits into place? Your mother doesn't feel that it is good for the child . . . or for you. She thinks your situation is bad for both of you. Now, if she told this to Ada, who believes that she would be the best possible mother a child could have, and that it is a sin that she has no child . . . Dr. Newhouse believes—"

"Dennis! Dennis!"

"Dennis believes that Ada has a messianic belief in her capacity to mother a child. She would feel that she was appointed to take care of this unfortunate baby, why can't you see that?"

"I can't see, no, but I can see where you got all this, Dr. Newhouse had no right to tell you all this. I told him about Bunny and Mother in confidence; he had no right to tell you!"

"Of course he had a right to . . ." It seemed to Louise that she saw Miss Lake's finger tighten on the trigger; she continued hastily, "Can't you see now how Ada got into this? How she found out about you and then convinced your mother . . . who was convinced to start with, anyway, that your child would be better off with her? That you would be better off without Bunny? It seems so clear to me that Ada and your mother arranged this. Your mother to go away today so that she couldn't testify to there being a child, Ada to take the child . . ."

"My mother did this terrible thing to me? My mother had Bunny stolen and walked out and left me? Do you think I would believe for one single moment that my mother would

do such a thing to me? She loves me! She may think that
Bunny . . . But she loves me and she loves Bunny and she
wouldn't do a thing like this in a million years!"

"It's the only answer! It's the only answer!"

"It's the only answer you can find. To save yourself. It isn't
going to work, Miss Benton! When he comes," she said, "I'm
going to lock you in that kitchenette so you can't warn him."
She watched Miss Benton crying, with curiosity, as if weeping
were something she did not understand. She stared at the tears
now running down Miss Benton's face as if she did not know
what tears were. Except to rub her right hand with her left, she
hardly moved at all.

Dennis rang the bell. Dum-dum-dum-di. He heard Wilson
puffing up the stairs behind him and rang again. Dum-dum-
dum-di.

Wilson said, puffing, "Why didn't Louise give you a key?
Discretion? No, you preferred it, didn't you? No keys, no
locks and no keys for you." No "ball and chain" was what he
really meant. "Let you in or not let you in just as she chooses;
her pigeon. Maybe she doesn't choose just now or maybe it's
too late for choice in anything but funeral decorations!"

Dennis said, "Don't be ridiculous. She wouldn't shoot."

"Why do you think she took my gun?"

"She wouldn't shoot."

"Wouldn't you call that wishful thinking, psychiatrist?"
Wishful thinking all along the line, Wilson thought.

"I can understand Blanche wanting to shoot, but she wouldn't." His hand was on the knob waiting for the click.

"Maybe I better get the cops, eh?" He saw Dennis shake his head. "Dennis, I know, but maybe we better."

The mechanism clicked and the knob seemed to jump in Dennis' hand like a live thing, as if the desire in the pressing finger on the release button up there was so powerful, so overwhelming that it made the dead metal live. Dennis turned the knob as quickly as possible, grimacing.

Wilson whispered, "What's the matter?"

"Nothing," Dennis said. He walked through the hall and started up the stairs, first one step at a time and then, when he could hear the frantic but muffled banging overhead, two at a time, leaping. "Louise!" he called. "Louise!"

There was no answer, only the repeated pounding.

Dennis was almost at the top of the second flight of stairs and then, although she couldn't see him yet, he could see her with the gun in her hand, framed in the doorway to Louise's place. He said, "Blanche! It's me!"

"I know that. I know it's you."

"Then why are you pointing that gun at me?"

"Because I'm going to kill you," she said, as if he should have known.

"Why, Blanche?"

She said, "Because."

Like a child. *Why? Because.* He heard himself, in something between a sob and a laugh, saying, "Oh, Blanche! Because!"

"I stayed there in your bed. I believed you. I trusted you. I let you . . ."

"You can trust me," he said. "I swear you can trust me, Blanche!"

She said, "Really?"

"I swear it. Where is Louise?"

"*Louise* is locked in her kitchen. There's no window there."

Dennis said, "I'm coming up, Blanche." He took a step toward her, walking as heavily as he could in his damp stockinged feet. "You see, I know you won't shoot me."

Blanche snickered audibly. "You're coming up because she's locked in the kitchen, that's why. To save her. She's the one you want to save. She and her school! *Louise!*"

"Blanche . . ."

"You know I'm going to kill her first if you don't come up. Because you and she . . . Oh, you'll come up!" she said. "Come up and then I'll kill you!"

"Let me talk to you, Blanche!"

"I don't want to hear you. I'm waiting and I won't wait too long."

"Dennis," Wilson whispered.

"Shut up."

Blanche said, "Hurry. I told you. I won't wait."

"Let me talk to you."

"I know how to shoot. You didn't know that, did you? I'm a hick from Providence, Rhode Island, but in Providence, Rhode Island, I used to go duck shooting in the fall."

"I'm coming up to talk to you."

Wilson whispered, "Coming up talking, is it? Coming up talking, psychiatrist?"

"Blanche . . . you found out about Louise and me. . . ."

"Louise and you! If you don't come up here now I'm going to shoot through the door!"

"Blanche," he said. "Don't Blanche! I love you."

"Louise and me!"

Dennis felt Wilson's hand on his arm, restraining him. He whispered, "She's bluffing. I'm going up."

"She's going to shoot," Wilson said. Action, he thought. I learned that tonight, he thought, and, as Dennis began walking up, he suddenly shoved Dennis aside and ran up ahead of him.

Dennis heard the shot and saw Wilson lurch and grab his shoulder. He heard himself say in an amazed way, "You shot Wilson!" and when he looked up she was pointing the gun at him. "You shot Wilson," he repeated, unable to get it through his head.

"Winged me," he heard Wilson say. "What do you know? Winged me!" Wilson was clutching at his shoulder. "I'm glad you did, Mademoiselle Blanche! In a nice primitive way, I'm glad you did. An eye for an eye. We're quits now," he said.

Blanche kept her gun on Dennis and her eyes on him while she spoke to Wilson. "You shouldn't have interfered!"

She didn't mind having shot Wilson.

"Somebody must have heard that shot. Come on and lock the door after you."

She was finished with Wilson. She meant *him*. "But he's losing blood, Blanche, don't you think I better . . ."

"You better come up!"

"Blanche, I'm no surgeon and even if I were I couldn't get that bullet out without a probe. . .."

Wilson said, "And anesthesia. You're no surgeon and I'm no two-time hero." He reached out to hold Dennis. "And don't you be, either!"

"I'm going to count," Blanche said. "One. Two."

Dennis pulled himself free of Wilson's restraining hand. "She won't shoot me."

"If you don't get up here by the time I count ten and come in and lock this door after you, I'm going to shoot her first. Three . . . Four . . ."

The bullet was in his shoulder and not his leg so he could get down the stairs, all right, and since he wasn't the one who was walking up to meet his executioner at the top (because surely Dennis must have worn through his wishful thinking by now?) he was down the three flights in the time it was taking Dennis to do half of one flight, although it wasn't easy. But Wilson was pretty sure that right after the shot he had heard a car pull up in the street. He was feeling pretty rocky by the time he got to the front door and if the car had been a mirage, or if somebody hadn't heard the shot and gone for help, he'd never be able to make it himself.

Even though it was, thank God, a cop for whom he yanked the heavy front door open, it was drawing it pretty close because he had heard the door to Louise's place slam and now he heard the lock turn.

". . . a shot," the cop said.

Wilson leaned against the wall. "Quick. Gun. Up!" But it was too late now. The cop wouldn't make it, Wilson thought, groggily receiving the sleeping child the cop thrust into his arms. He'd never make it with that door locked up there.

"Hold it up there!" the cop shouted, but she'd never hold it. She would know that it was The Law and get it over with. Bang. Bang.

Wilson certainly didn't have the time to remember consciously that Marta had always been able to pick out her own kids' crying voices anywhere, any time; his good hand, of its own accord, reached for the plump little leg and pinched it cruelly.

"Like a living doll," Wilson thought hazily, when he heard the lock up there click, and the door up there being thrown open. "Like a living doll!" "You should be thankful your chil-

dren have healthy lungs," Marta used to say when he had com-
plained about the volume of sound their two could produce.
Well, he did thank God. "Thank God," Wilson said, listening
to the lusty shrieks the little girl was now producing. Then he
heard Mademoiselle Blanche.

"Bunny! It's Bunny!"

Wilson closed his eyes because he felt less dizzy that way
and heard Mademoiselle Blanche come clattering down, just
the way Marta always did when one of theirs bawled for her.
Wings on her feet, Wilson thought.

He felt the child being taken from him and gave the leg he
had pinched a little pat of farewell. That was the cop taking the
child. The cop, Wilson saw, having opened his eyes again, was
holding her up in his arms for Mademoiselle Blanche to identify, because he was scared she would break her neck in her
headlong hurry to get to the baby.

Would do anything to get to her baby, Wilson thought. Sure
would. *Mothers*, he thought.

Now Blanche sat on the steps cradling her baby tenderly in
her arms and crooning softly over it. Wilson looked at that
angelic bent face, seeing the ineffably tender curve of her lips,
the pure way her soft dark hair fell forward, the exquisite line
of her white eyelids, which half hid her eyes.

Now Dennis came down, not quite so fast, rather shakily, Wilson thought, and after him, in a rather floosie robe
and nightdress, Louise Benton. Wilson dreamily observed
the tableau, the cop in the foreground, the mother-and-
child and, above them, first Dennis and close to him,
Louise. "All over," he thought, "but the shooting." But
"shouting," wasn't it? All over but the shouting, wasn't it?
But for the shouting, you might say, it would have been all
over.

The cop was talking now.

"So we go to look for this Negrito kid and we find him

cuddled up in the back of his old man's store. He denies the whole thing. His old man had kidded him about Mrs. Lake and he couldn't take it so he ran out on his folks and hung around all day, but he didn't know anything about the little girl. By that time we didn't know whether we was standing on our head or our feet. When Mrs. Lake's mother wasn't in Providence, we began to think there was something in it, after all. Why wasn't she where she said she was to you, see, Mrs. Lake? What was going on with Mrs. Lake's mother that she wasn't where she was supposed to be? But then when the Negrito kid says he didn't take the little girl and there's not a single thing we can find which says he's a liar . . . when he says he thought you was a single girl and he didn't know there was any little kid . . . Well, the lieutenant says we should have listened to the doc here because he knows about such things. I tell you, we didn't know were we on our heads or on our feet!

"Then, the next thing is, that while he's giving his statement, the way Negrito tells us is that you were inside the door, Mrs. Lake, and then your mother gives the address to the cabby. First you went away from the door and *then* your mother gives the address. And that's why it stuck in Eddie's mind, because of the way it seemed to him that your mother was waiting until you were out of the way. So it stuck in his mind. What was the big secret where your mother was going?"

Blanche rubbed her cheek against Bunny's hair. "She went home to Providence."

"She did not! She was right in the Hotel Statler the whole time. Hotel Statler, Manhattan. Eddie give us that. Funny how things work out, isn't it? If it wasn't for this crazy notion Mrs. Negrito got in her head that Eddie had kidnapped the little girl, we wouldn't have got to Eddie, and if Eddie hadn't give us the Statler, we'd still be looking for your mother, and then we wouldn't have got hold of this Miss Ford in Brooklyn, and your little kid would be there yet. Not that she hurt the little girl any. She was sleeping peaceful as an angel when we found her. You don't need to worry about that."

Louise Benton put her hand on Dennis' shoulder. "It *was* your mother, Miss Lake, exactly as I told you!"

The policeman looked shocked. "If you mean did the old lady know that the Ford woman was going to snatch the kid, she did not! Don't you go thinking a thing like that for a minute, Mrs. Lake! No grandmother's going to do a thing like that!

"Your mother told us what happened, Mrs. Lake. She's not here now because she collapsed the minute we found your little girl safe and sound, and we put her in New York Hospital, here on Sixty-eighth Street. She'll be okay there. But what she told us, she met this here teacher in the park the first day she took your little kid there. I think the seventeenth, she said. Your mother didn't know Ford was a teacher. Got her name first time they talked, but after that Ford didn't talk about herself at all. She didn't know much about her and that's a fact, but that never stopped any lady I know of from spilling anything she's got on her chest!

"What the old lady had on her chest was about how she had just got to New York City and this apartment you'd sublet, Mrs. Lake, was no place for a kid. How the baby had to sleep in one bed with you, and all."

Blanche, Wilson noted hazily, did not appear to have any need to say "I told you so." Admirable Mademoiselle! Just sat cuddling the child.

"You know how dames get to talking. She went on about how you was going to send a little kid like that to school. It wasn't thanks to you she wasn't in school this minute. You'd gone to this school, to that school, whatever school you knew about, I guess. No room!"

No room at the inn, Wilson thought. Mademoiselle did look

like the Madonna sitting there with the Babe.

"The teacher said your mother was right. She got herself in right with your mother. You know, whatever your mother said was okay by her in spades. The next day she was right there in the park when your mother showed. Your old lady was all up in the air. You'd got a letter, after all, saying your kid could go to this kindergarten here." The policeman waved. "You were going to send her, your old lady said, nothing she could say could stop you. So that was when the teacher says, why don't your mother make it hard for you instead of helping out, see? All your mother knew, Mrs. Lake, take my word for it, was she was going to make it hard for you instead of helping out. The first day of kindergarten she was going to make it just as hard as she could, so maybe you'd see it wouldn't work out once she was gone. You'd have to get the little girl ready and then get to your job, see? You'd have to give them some excuse on the job so you could go pick up the little girl, leave early and all.

"That was the whole thing, see? The teacher put her up to it: say she got a letter and had to go home. It was your mother told about selling her home, of course, but your mother didn't mean no harm, she didn't know that was just up the teacher's alley. Your mother just went to the Statler, and she was supposed to waltz in tomorrow after a good night's sleep when you'd learned your lesson. She was supposed to say emergencies like that could happen every day the kid had to go to school, and believe me," the policeman said, grinning, "they do!"

Wilson wanted to ask about the baby's belongings—no crib, all right, no stroller, okay, but . . . He thought back to when Sandy was there. (You got more stuff with the first child, but even with Betty when they weren't such suckers for each and every Lilliputian Bazaar ad!) The place had positively been lousy with kid things; what about the rest of Bunny's appurtenances? It seemed as if the policeman could read his thoughts. (Or had he spoken? He was becoming a bit vague around the edges.)

"Your mother said you'd remember the day she lost her key, Mrs. Lake."

"Yes," Blanche said. "I remember."

"Only she didn't. The teacher took it. Your mother doesn't know how but it doesn't seem hard to me. Your little kid gets into a rhubarb with another kid in the park, or she faws down and goes boom. Grandma runs to pick her up and leaves her pocketbook on the bench with her friend. See what I mean? The teacher gave it back the next day. 'Your key must have dropped out of your pocketbook.' Did your mother tell you someone found it the next day?" When Blanche nodded, the policeman nodded, too.

Wilson thought that the old lady shouldn't have done that, should have said she'd misplaced it. Blanche might have remembered, when she discovered tonight that the apartment was emptied of all of Bunny's things, including fingerprints, that the someone who had found her mother's key could have had a duplicate made of it and gone there today and taken every hide and every hair of little Bunny. Only she hadn't remembered about the key.

"I don't think this teacher knew what we'd think when we couldn't even find fingerprints. What I think is she didn't want there to be any prints handy to identify the kid, see? The lieutenant thinks so, too," the policeman said modestly. "I told him and he thinks so, too. The lieutenant says he bets tomorrow we'll turn up a witness who saw Ford walk in your apartment, or maybe saw her walking out, loaded with your little kid's stuff. We found a cute little blue bathrobe. . . ." He measured his hands in the air to show how small. "She had it in the bathroom, with the little toothbrush, and all.

"You see," he said to Blanche, "this all happened too quick.

For us, for we cops, I don't mean for you. I can imagine it didn't seem so quick for you, Mrs. Lake. Why, tomorrow we could have got the facts out of you straight and contacted where you lived with the kid. . . ." He was getting out of breath. "And all," he said. "Well, to make a long story short, your mother didn't know a thing about the kidnaping. When we told her, she went to pieces. You know, crying and screaming. But she'll be all right in a couple days."

Mademoiselle Blanche, Wilson saw, was smiling down at Bunny. "Yes," she said.

Louise Benton said, "I'm sure she will be, just shock."

But Dennis, the talking psychiatrist, said nothing. Tar Baby said nothing! Dennis just stood there staring at Mademoiselle Blanche. Then Wilson heard the revived Boston in Louise Benton's voice. Boston Renaissance.

"You see, Miss Lake? Just as I said. However, that's water under the bridge and this really is no time for further explanations or recriminations or anything but thankfulness that it wasn't much worse. I do really think now, Miss Lake, that Bunny ought to be taken home to bed."

"She's right, lady, that little kid should be in bed." The policeman bent toward Blanche to help her up.

All over but the shouting, Wilson thought. I can let go now, it's all over but the shouting. But something was still happening, so he held on. Mademoiselle Blanche, ignoring the policeman, was looking up at Dennis. Asking Dennis to go with her, Wilson decided. And Louise, he thought, seeing her fingers on Dennis' shoulder, was asking him to stay with her. Dennis, the ci-devant talking psychiatrist, now Tar Baby, was saying nothing and staring at Mademoiselle Blanche.

And who could blame him, Wilson wondered. He blinked his eyes so that he could study the expression on Dennis' face, noticing that it was complex. Attraction, repulsion? Fear and desire? Then he traced Dennis' glance and found that he was

not looking at that delicious face of Mademoiselle's, or at the
child, either. Dennis' eyes, Wilson now discovered, were glued
to what was in Mademoiselle's hand at the end of the firm,
fondling arm which so tenderly clasped her child. The
revolver, Wilson saw was what was in that hand and the
revolver had Dennis hypnotized!

Would she have? Wouldn't she have? That was what the
staring Dennis was wondering. Would she have . . . *accurately*,
trying for the heart, the bull's eye, and not just down a dark
stairway? Not to discharge the accumulated effects of the day
and night she had had, but locked in the room up there, with
the accumulation already discharged, would she have shot if
he, Wilson, hadn't pinched the baby? Would she have, would-
n't she have, Dennis was pondering. She loves me not!

Oh, she loves him, Wilson thought, because now she was
giving Dennis such a look! And he loves her. He said he loved
her, but Dennis had billed the two of them as star-crossed
lovers from the moment he had seen how that girl could knock
his carefully laid plans into a cocked hat. From the first
Dennis had decided that it could not be, which was easier,
Wilson decided, than it must not be.

So what now?

The policeman helped Blanche to her feet. "You coming
with us, Doc?" He explained, "Look her over, maybe? See if
she's fit to stay without her mother in her place tonight?"

"Dr. Newhouse is a psychiatrist, officer. You better take
Miss Lake and Bunny home and then she should see a medical man. It's quite clear now," Louise said, smiling at Dennis,
"that Miss Lake doesn't require Dr. Newhouse's services!"

Now it was a tug of war between the two girls. Definitely,
Wilson thought: Go with Blanche, stay with Louise. Go out
into the night with the unknown or go up those stairs to the
known. The lady directress he can count on, or Blanche who
he can never be sure wouldn't have shot him! If he goes with

Mademoiselle Blanche, it's for keeps now, not just for psychi-
atry.

Wilson pressed his hand against his throbbing shoulder and
gritted his teeth. Waiting, he fought off the swirling black, the
dark unconsciousness.

"Hurry up," he said, "make up your mind, Dennis! Come
on, Dennis . . . the lady or the tiger?"

In 1957, the year four-year-old Bunny (real name Felicia) Lake is reported missing in the novel that bears her name, Albert Camus was awarded the Nobel prize, popular tastes were slaked by James Gould Cozzens's *By Love Possessed* and William Inge's *The Dark at the Top of the Stairs*, Henry James's psychological thriller found strange new tones in Benjamin Britten's opera *Turn of the Screw,* Eugene O'Neill was posthumously awarded the Pulitzer prize for *A Long Day's Journey into Night*, and Samuel Beckett's Hamm insisted on playing out his exhausted hand in *Endgame*. Into this region of darkness and absurdity Evelyn Piper's fair, unsuspecting heroine, Blanche Lake, makes her way, searching for the daughter who vanished without a trace on her first day of nursery school. By day's and story's end, she will have journeyed deep into the black night in which the demented and mournful beings of midcentury modern imagining lived out their tormented existence.

Blanche, as her name suggests, hardly seems the type to seek, much less find, herself at home in the company of these creatures of darkness. She enters the novel fully expecting to make a place for herself—and, of course, for Bunny—in the insistently light and airy, brightly colored world of post-war urban America. Her first visit to Bunny's nursery school reassures her in these hopes with its cheerful spectrum of well-administered life: there are the friendly mothers in oxford-gray and bright-blue slacks, a caretaker Blanche calls Orange Smock after her sunny uniform, and even a teacher whose name, Miss Green, is happily suggestive of verdant growth. She is so convinced of the fundamentally benign order of the world that she talks—mainly to herself, but that

is when talk is a fairly accurate indication of state of mind—
as if the language of a four year old is all the language one
needs to brave the adventures and surmount the accidents of
life. The most ordinary events of the day occasion an almost
comic, even imbecilic astonishment: "She wondered if it
would be all right to ask Bunny's teacher—how ridiculous—
Bunny's *teacher*—how Bunny had taken her first day in
school. Had she made friends? (Made *friends*—Bunny!" (7).
She seems, in short, just the sort of young woman who
would translate Felicia—a name signifying happiness—into
the diminutive, huggable form of a bunny. How could she
suspect that the door to the nursery school, "modernized"
according to the most advanced educational and architectural
ideas, would prove to be, as the title of the movie playing
nearby advertises, The Gate of Hell, that she would soon be
speaking a language so urgent and despairing that those
hearing her could only take it to be the language of madness,
and that, unknown even to herself, beneath her mild if fret-
ful manner lurks a tiger who will be uncaged in the last pages
of the book?

Such playing against type—the high-class lady with low-
loin tastes, the murderous doctor, the psychopathic nanny—is
the trademark of Merriam Modell, writing under the name of
Evelyn Piper. The unassuming, ethnically unreadable pseudo-
nym disguises both her Jewishness and the insinuating strange-
ness of her unnerving satires on the culture of love, marriage,
and child-rearing in mid-century America. After graduating
from Cornell University in the late 1920s, she worked vari-
ously as a model and secretary (including service to a harmon-
ica quartet), joined the post-war migration of Americans to
Europe and lived in Germany until 1933, when she married and
returned to the United States. There is little hope and less
knowledge of this larger cosmopolitan world for the cloistered,
often timorous, and self-baffled protagonists of her master-

works, *The Lady and Her Doctor, Bunny Lake Is Missing* and *The Nanny*. As a writer, Piper reserved her sense of adventure, in the best modern manner, for explorations of the undiscovered or seldom visited territories within the mind.

In *Bunny Lake Is Missing*, the mind to be explored, first with bemused condescension, then with sympathy, finally with alarm, belongs to Blanche Lake, an unmarried mother who has recently come to New York to create a new life for herself and her child. When her daughter disappears, a search is launched and an investigation mounted that fails to turn up any sign of Bunny's whereabouts or even of her existence. The police, the school director and the psychiatrist summoned to assist and calm this understandably anxious female begin to suspect that Bunny is a figment of Blanche's imagination. Soon Blanche finds herself facing two related, but psychologically quite different, ordeals: finding Bunny and proving that she exists. The first ordeal tests her moral fitness for motherhood by thrusting her into the role of frantic mother. Maternal protectiveness, at least in fiction, is generally cloying, unless and until it is needed, and then it becomes heroic.[1] This form of female heroism is lamentably unsung, may even go unnoticed, a point made with startling and heartbreaking clarity by Elisabeth Sanxay Holding's masterpiece of ruthlessly protective mother love, *The Blank Wall* (1947; adapted in 1949 to film as *The Reckless Moment* and in 2001 as *The Deep End*).

Blanche's nervous concern for Bunny on her first day of school is understandable, indeed commonplace, but it does not recommend her to us as a possible heroine. If anything, it consigns her to the satiric ranks of doting mothers whose effusions tire everyone and are credited by no one except themselves. She arouses our interest only when Bunny cannot be found, and even then only because she surprises us with her fierce ingenuity in tracking down her child. Our interest is intensified when Blanche acquires a dark double, Mrs. Negrito, the greengrocer whose son, Eddie, patently infatuated with Blanche, is also missing (he, in fact, is the first "missing person" of the book). Blanche and Negrito, white and black, pale heroine and swarthy immigrant, are sisters under the skin (later we learn that Mrs. Negrito, too, has a colorful name, Rose). They are emotionally and narratively joined in a tireless search for their missing children. Each is desperate to rescue her child from harm, Blanche from the harm that may befall Bunny, Mrs. Negrito from the harm her son may do. But unlike Mrs. Negrito, Blanche, in her role as frantic mother, is compromised by the second ordeal to which she is quickly subjected, which tests her moral fitness not for motherhood, but for reality.

At first, it is not certain which charge is more damning— that she is a bad mother [2] or that she is a fantasist. What is certain—and startling—is how quickly Blanche is branded a bad mother even before Bunny is declared officially to be missing. When she returns to the school with a policemen to search the cellar where Bunny might have wandered, she is taunted by reproving bystanders: "And where was she when the kid got locked up? Late? Couldn't leave the television set! Call themselves mothers sending tiny little babies to school! All day long too!" (24). Although the voice of this accusatory chorus never rises above the level of ideological background noise, it does have the power to unnerve Blanche and bring her, emotionally, to the bar of Judgment. "If anything's happened it's a judgment, that's what I say! That's what they learn them in college—how to drop their kids and leave them for others to take care of—" (24). Judgment is rendered without making clear which offending sin is the more grievous—mothers relinquishing their children to the care of others or the education of women that puts the thought in their head. Blanche is made the scapegoat for modernity itself, with its new social arrangements, educated and working women, increased leisure time, and mass entertainments.

But however spiteful and retrograde, the actual idea and *prospect* of Judgment is never discredited, much less dismissed, as the explanation of why Bunny Lake is missing. Instead, the thought of judgment is internalized, where it takes on the authority and form of spiritual terror. Dr. Dennis Newhouse, the psychiatrist dispatched by his lover, the head of Bunny's school, to calm her anxious and apparently delusional client, reads Bunny's "disappearance" just this way—as a judgment Blanche has rendered against herself. With surgical skill, he extracts the secret wish that shadows her doting motherhood: "You see, before I was sure that Bunny was coming, I prayed not to have a baby. I was so frightened" (64). Armed with the unanswerable logic of his tribe, he confronts her with the dark syllogism he believes to have been crafted by her unconscious mind: She prayed not to have a baby; she had a baby; Bunny's disappearance is thus a delayed wish fulfillment, a finally answered prayer. Blanche turns "chalkily white" on hearing this pronouncement. Piper's wicked wit gives us this blanching Blanche at the very moment when her rosy maternal demeanor is drained of its color and credibility. The appalled Blanche is a pitiable figure onto which Newhouse projects the bleak truth unearthed by the modern science of mind: "No God so implacable as self" (59).

The God of self is a puritanical God ("No God, anywhere, so lacking in mercy") whose decrees have taken root in the American Psyche and still produce strange fruits:

> The old expression "the woman pays" flashed through Dennis's mind, because she did, of course. Because this was payment. Friend or no, lucky or no, broad-minded or not, this girl believed she was a wicked girl and that she *should* be stoned through the streets with a big red letter "A" on her bosom. (58)

Blanche, however, resists being cast as a contemporary Hester Prynne, not because Newhouse is right—for according to Freudian dogma, the truth of the Unconscious can be detected by the resistance it provokes—but because his diagnosis is too literary (and Bunny is real!), and because she is already beginning to suspect that the man who has come to ease her mind has become increasingly agitated in his own. His is a mind filled, as Freudian scriptures were filled, with Victorian notions of a woman's capacity to excite and to feel sexual guilt. He is too fond of the old expression "the woman pays," and too eager to confirm its authority. He is slow to realize that Blanche belongs to a new age, whose sexual motto is not "the woman pays," but that declaration of independence, "I am paying my own way."

Newhouse hears but cannot understand the terms of this emancipated idiom. He can only see Blanche as an anxious, self-condemning waif in a pantomime, her "little soft hands wringing like the hands of heroines in old-fashioned books" (59). His sexual tastes and gender paradigms thus make an irony of his name. Newhouse mentally confines Blanche to the old house of Victorian morality and its self-affrighting language in which girls are "wicked" and the mind can come "undone" by unrestrained longings. Yet it is not Blanche, but Newhouse who is undone by his own dark attraction to Blanche's soft and feverish body, her whiteness especially. He is drawn to her as once, as a medical student, he was irresistibly drawn to a cast of a dead girl drowned in the Seine *"so cold, so white, so . . .* Marble. Lips meant for marble (103, italics in text).

Amour was never more *fou.* Drawn to each other over the brink of the madness that awaits them both, the parties in this strangely matched couple confront each other at that proverbial crossroads where lovers declare their passion for each other. Their moment of reckoning is not just star-

crossed, but genre-crossed. Newhouse addresses her with
the tender but strict formality of a Victorian suitor, while
Blanche, "undone" but not unnerved by her ordeal, assumes
the fierce and vengeful mask of the female desperado
steadying herself for the final shoot-out with her lover, her
enemy. She waits inside some corral of the mind, curling her
finger around the trigger of the gun she has found and appro-
priated, waiting for the "next betraying, rotten, lying word
[to come] out of his mouth. . . . It would be easy, she thought.
They had made it easy, she thought. She wasn't the girl who
closed her eyes when there was going to be killing (even in
Westerns); she *was* a Western now; her trigger finger itched,
it *did*. She waited almost impatiently for this final betrayal"
(149, italics in text).

Blanche may not have yet stepped over the boundaries of
sanity, but she has crossed over the borders of convention, of
genre convention, that is, exchanging the soft voice, babbling
endearments, and doting affections of the beleaguered heroine
of Victorian melodrama (a central, palpitating figure in
Freudian storytelling) for the pitiless words and deadly
weapons of the gun-slinger, impatient for the satisfying
catharsis of blood. All of the concentrated moral force and
emotional impatience of the Western is compressed in
Blanche's itchy trigger finger. No God as implacable as self,
indeed, but now the self is no self-accuser but a dark avenger.
Her target is not just the man who has betrayed her, but the
"pure Victoriana" that casts her in the role of helpless, if
wicked, girl who must pay, who must wear a scarlet "A" on
her chest until she is redeemed by the forgiving love of a good
man. Her enemy *is* her rescuer, Newhouse, who has himself
come undone: "It was the tension and trembling of his voice
as he had said the formal 'Miss' that had undone him. Undone.
Yes. Precisely, the Victorian word was very precise. The thing
had been pure Victoriana: Miss Lake, may I ask you for the

honor of your hand in marriage? The formal address spoken into the soft night in a voice which had trembled appropriately had led to the 'I love you,' which was, when you understood it, perfectly rational" (149). What we do understand is that New-house's rationality is confounded by "the tumult and tumbling inside himself." Blanche's hand and her mind are perfectly steady, if itching to get on with show. The rational doctor trembles like a maiden, while the distressed and delusory female is virile in her singleness of purpose. No God so implacable as self, yes, but Blanche has become that godless figure, the woman who has no self, who has only a mission—to find her child and avenge her sex. She now despairs of finding her child since no one believes there is a child to be found. She may at least take revenge for the many betrayals of love on her rival, Newhouse's lover: "She'll suffer, all right. She'll suffer. She'll pay" (166). Having lost her self, she has lost her God. She will put her faith only in that dreadful Power of life and death that can be sighted along the barrel of a gun. It is to this savage belief that Blanche pledges her allegiance: "In gun I trust" (140).

This motto also serves as a passport admitting her into the raw and wicked territory of pulp. To plot a course through this dark, hard land she needs a guide. She thinks she has found him in Mr. Wilson, an unsuccessful writer and a neighbor who had once been friendly to her. Wilson should be able to help her since what she requires is part of his stock and trade as a writer—the means to make people believe in your version of reality. At first he, like everyone she encounters, dismisses her frantic ravings as fraudulent, if not lunatic. This may be ungallant, but at least he doesn't see her as a heroine in an old-fashioned melodrama. "Stop making like Pearl White!" (106) he sneers, evoking, in one of the better plays on Blanche's name, the silent screen's radiant icon of imperiled womanhood, literally so in her most famous role in *The Perils of Pauline*.[3] "You don't know what trouble is, Mademoiselle Blanche; you're not a writer. Sic—sic writer! Sick writer!" (105). All the more reason to believe that he is the man for the job! But on hearing her strange and improbable tale, Wilson thinks she has been sent by his wife to mock him in his writer's den and greets her with some high mockery of his own: "Of course I believe you! Nobody else would, but I do! If the rest of them won't, it's because they don't know that truth is stranger than any tired fiction" (107). He advises her to play out the melodrama to its conventional end, reminding her that in such desperate cases, the river awaits (he even gives her directions). Wilson is condescending and brutally dismissive; still he does not speak to her in the language one reserves for delicate or delusional minds. What he doesn't know is that he is addressing someone potentially sicker, and certainly more desperate than himself. Wilson's distress results not from missing something in the world, but in himself. In his own eyes, he is "a nothing since not [sic] good writer; a nothing because surely not a good man" (172). This is not a kind, nor is it an especially accurate, self-judgment. He will turn out to be, if not a good writer, someone who knows what a good—and credible—story is. In the course of the black night ahead, he will also prove himself surely to be a good man on whose fundamental kindness and writerly insight the resolution of Blanche's and Piper's story will depend. But in this first encounter, Wilson seems just another character in Piper's gallery of urban grotesques, "a nothing" with one eye smaller than another and a heart as cold as stone: "Newhouse thinks you're crazy but me, being a writer myself, you come to me? I'm supposed to have more imagination, is that it? I hobnob with queer ducks and queerer drakes? (106).[4]

This, last line, I like to think, may have inspired Penelope and John Mortimer in adapting and "updating" Piper's novel for Otto Preminger's 1965 film. Preminger's film shifts the scene from the tense streets of 1950s New York to an upscale London that, with its manicured town houses and cozy pubs, is as much village as modern metropolis. But what Preminger loses by forgoing the disquieting cityscape of American noir—the deserted el stations, darkened playgrounds and friendless streets—he recuperates by peopling his film with a lively and enthralling assortment of queer ducks and queerer drakes. The novel's physically disconcerting, gruff, but finally benign Mr. Wilson does not consort with queer ducks in Preminger's film—he is one. As deliciously played by Noel Coward, Wilson is not just a writer, or as he describes himself, "a poet, playwright and dropper of alcoholic bricks." He is also Blanche's sexually omnivorous, predatory landlord with distinctly sadomasochistic tastes. Given his "adults only" proclivities, Wilson can hardly bear the thought, much less the presence, of children, as evidenced in his lease contract, which stipulates, as he reminds Blanche on learning of Bunny's not yet contested existence, "no caged birds, no cats, no livestock of any kind." He is thus not someone who might help to dispel Blanche's nightmare; he is much more likely to lure her into one of his own making. He tries (improbably) to seduce her with his "melodious" voice and collection of "African heads, small pickled ones" and, when rebuffed, dismisses her in turn by proudly boasting of his more heroic conquests: "There are those at the BBC who bear, like medals, the bruises left by the love of Horatio Wilson." When the police come to question him, he proudly shows them his collection of whips, singling out his favorite "plaything," a whip "reputed to belong to the Great One himself," and politely asking if they would "care to have a bash." This not being Wilson's day, they decline the offer; undeterred he obligingly points out the skull also reputed to have belonged to the Great One—the Marquis de Sade—or so he was assured by the vendor who sold it to him in the Caledonian Market.

This droll, fundamentally comic conception of Wilson's degenerate character is an index of how differently the film

and novel understand queerness, taken in its more general
sense of personal oddity or moral exceptionality. This difference eventually declares itself in what they imagine a danger-
ously aberrant personality to be, that is, in how they fill the
role of malefactor (villain is morally too strong a word, given
that the evildoer in each instance is mentally ill, not criminally
motivated). Since this is an afterword and not an introduction,
I can reveal that Bunny does, in fact, exist but that her disappearance is attributed by book and film to two very different,
if similarly deranged, forms of queerness. In the novel, the
kidnapper is a disturbed woman, a former director/teacher of
the nursery school, herself childless, who is suffering, we are
informed on unimpeachable authority, from menopausal hysteria. In the film, Blanche is provided with a brother who
translates Piper's plot out of the dingy and withered region of
psychotic child envy into the more lurid, if equally over-
heated, realm of incest. Where the book explores 1950s anxieties around motherhood and feminity, the film takes up a
decidedly 1960s worry, the dangers of free and decidedly
unconventional love. The novel's culpable party, Ada Ford,
who is never seen but only referred to, nevertheless survives
the translation to film, where she is "upgraded" from
menopausal hysteric to "queerer drake." Her queerness is not
hormonally induced, but a permanent feature of her character
and imagination. As played by Martita Hunt, she emerges as a
benign eccentric, a white witch, living above the nursery
school, diligently at work recording the fantasies, especially
the nightmares, with which children populate their world. She
helps settle the film into a Dickensian vision of derangement,
a vision leavened by a humor that is often black but never desperate, as illustrated in the superb, campy wit of featuring the
Zombies in a cameo for the incidental pleasure of hearing
them sing the contemporary hit, "Just out of Reach." Zombies
lyrics filled with adolescent, gonadal yearning like "Our Love

Was Meant to Be" become sly and hilariously sick jokes on brother-sister love. Still, as one wag reviewer lamented, Preminger, for whatever reason, made no use of the Zombies song best suited for the situation, "She's Not There"![5]

With a brother to provide the (sick) love interest, the film can dispense with Newhouse, the psychiatrist, although it retains his name and gives it to the detective assigned to Bunny's case, a role envisaged and played out with just the right amounts of professional discernment, avuncular solicitude, and sly wit by Laurence Olivier. Olivier's detective is psychologically astute enough to solve the mystery of Bunny's disappearance, but also canny enough to understand that his job is not complete until he restores to Blanche her sense of moral security, as well as her child. The final words of the film, accordingly, belong to him. They are addressed to Blanche who, with Bunny finally safe and secure in her arms, is on her way home: "Sleep well, both of you, now that you exist." His is a benediction, however, that winks at rather than solemnifies Blanche's waking nightmare. Preminger's film is a black psychological comedy with a happy existentialist ending. Piper's fiction is something else, more fearful, queerer indeed, something that belongs to the tradition of pulp we might call glandular realism.

The last thing we might think to attach to the fiendishly clever tale Piper spins is the venerable term of realism. Glandular realism in particular may strike some as that linguistic oxymoron—a retrograde neologism. As such it would seem to add insult to impertinence, identifying women writers according to the endocrinal rather than intellectual character of their work. But if we recognize glandular realism as a literary mode rather than as a distinct sexual style, much of the sensation in sensationalist fiction by modern women writers becomes morally as well emotionally intelligible. Understood in this context, glandular realism is the expressive vehicle for modern women writers who wish to execute a sharp, pulpy turn on that literary mode Ellen Moers, in her groundbreaking work *Literary Women,* christened Female Gothic:

> What I mean by Female Gothic is easily defined: the work that women writers have done in the literary mode that, since the eighteenth century, we have called the Gothic. But what I mean—or anybody else means—by "the Gothic" is not so easily stated except that it has to do with fear. In Gothic writings fantasy predominates over reality, the strange over the commonplace, and the supernatural over the natural, with one definite auctorial intent: to scare. Not, that is, to reach down into the depth of the soul and purge it with pity and terror (as we say tragedy does), but to get to the body itself, its glands, muscles, epidermis, and circulatory system, quickly arousing and quickly allaying the physiological reactions of fear. (138)

Modern women writers imaginatively at home within the tradition of female Gothic live in a time, however, when reality has increasingly come to prevail over fantasy as a source of anxiety; it can even outwit fantasy for images of absurdity. They can find in the glandular realism of pulp fiction the same visceral intimacy with fear enjoyed in classic Female Gothic, from which it descends. It is a fear, however, aroused by the ordinary rather than extraordinary face of the world. In glandular realism, reality predominates over fantasy in keeping with the modern view that the commonplace is more fantastical than the uncommonly strange, the natural more terrifying than the supernatural. Still, the auctorial intent remains the same: to excite the helplessly compliant muscles, epidermis, and circulatory system, including and especially the whole respiratory apparatus—the quick breaths, panting, and sighs that signal the onset and discharge of anxious impulses. In the Age of Anxiety, glandular realism and its frissons become an emotionally truthful way of representing and reacting to the world.

This is a mode Wilson's wife, Marta, had urged him to adopt, a suggestion he dismisses with contempt until Blanche Lake comes into his life. Blanche brings with her the experience and knowledge of darkness. Wilson initially discredits Blanche's story as a "Gothic tale" he believes his wife has fabricated to shame him into a new understanding of reality (and into writing fictions with a chance for more popular success). He will eventually come to this understanding and try to represent it to the enamored, still skeptical Newhouse, with whom he joins up to find Blanche, who has despaired of them both: "Marta says what I'm writing isn't realism. She says, for Christ's sake, it's only in my book that nothing happens. She says, read the papers, turn on the radio. She says, by God, she'd *make* something happen if I didn't. . . . when [Blanche] comes to me as her only friend and tells me this Gothic tale, it never occurred to me that this wasn't Marta's childish notion of . . ." (133). Now, he tells Newhouse, he doesn't think the notion so childish; he recognizes that his intelligence has prevented him from seeing what was really there to be seen all along: "Maybe Marta doesn't think I can write, I thought, but she should certainly know I can read. It was an insult to my intelligence to expect me to fall for that story" (133). If we fall for the story, as we do, if we credit the Gothic tale told by Blanche and implicitly endorsed by Marta—and we should—then we must either accept the insult to our intelligence or admit the need for a different conception of reality.

Piper's good-humored jab at her own inventiveness in pulp fiction should prompt her readers, women and men, feminist or not, to make this admission and confess that the last thing we desire or expect in pulp fiction, whether written by men or women, is sober, plausible, documentary realism, the realism that presents us with the often shabby truth about the relations between people and about the social, economic, and political forces that condition, sometimes overwhelm, their individual lives—in other words, realism as a genuinely complicated, morally detailed vision of the world. What we seek in pulp fiction is *another* reality, intensified but also downgraded, a vision of the world that is lowdown, moody, salacious, and often unintentionally funny and as far from careful and sober reflection as we can get. We want, as Wilson's wife demands, something to happen, the sooner, the more terrible, the better. We crave the hormonal rush of glandular realism because the irresistible *sensation* of reality is represented in no other mode with such directness, recklessness or force.

The first three books in the Feminist Press's Femme Fatales: Women Write Pulp series—*Skyscraper*, *In a Lonely Place*, and *The Girls in 3-B*—illustrate the ways in which different pulp genres channel and deploy this force. *Skyscraper* (1931), the title of one of Faith Baldwin's pulp romances and its master image, symbolizes that force and the pulp world that is fashioned out of it. We understand from the novel's first page that the skyscraper, that "insolence of steel" as she calls it, is not just a building, but a society in miniature. As both structure and world, it represents, to Baldwin's appraising eye, the ultimate attraction in pulp fiction: "beauty, with menace at its core" (4). It is a beauty that Baldwin, the author of some eighty published novels, several of them best-sellers, celebrated for its dark and irresistable power. Pulp puts such lurid beauty on display, literally so on its traditionally garish covers. This beauty would soon tire the eye if it didn't come with a promise of menace beneath the surface and between the covers, a promise of stories which tell of the different forms menace takes in the modern world, stories about what love and money and power and loneliness are and what they makes people do, stories, as Baldwin catalogues them, of "greed and lust, of rescue and rapture" (4). Yet as Baldwin understands, pulp promises even more. In her opening pages she unleashes an avalanche of verbs to impress us with the fact that life for the characters in pulp is a life of imperatives. When the Seacoast Building opens its doors, she writes, it invites its workers within "to struggle, to attain, to fail, to succeed, to love and to hope, to laugh and to weep, to suffer and rejoice, to envy and wound, to hate and to pity. In short, to work for their existence" (5).

This onslaught of verbs captures the elementary grammar of pulp fiction, which renders life primarily as energy and force, in which emotions come in a rush rather than in quiet meditative arcs. Given how often pulp characters indulge their feelings, it is strange—and strangely exciting—how little real thought and time they give to understanding them. Time isn't wasted in pulp with long, clarifying descriptions of settings, institutions, things and the feelings they evoke. For fictions that take the complex hopes and hardships of modern life as their main subject, there is very little sustained account or explanation of modern finance or politics or social organizations. Even if there were, you would skip them as a maddening distraction, impatient for the next turn of events. We don't want to be detained by the heavy weight of things, so dense with meaning and complication. We want not so much to understand reality as to experience it in a heightened and compelling form. We can dispense with reflection, if only we can have more story, more twists and turns to surprise and startle the mind. We acknowledge this every time we confess that we are in the mood for a mindless entertainment. We know we don't have to pay dearly in mental energy for the quick and easy gratifications we seek—the cheap thrills of those fulfilling moments of "rescue and rapture," as Baldwin tickets them.

That is why, besides its low price and availability, pulp is so cheap. It doesn't tax the reasoning, responsible mind, but relaxes and sedates it, gives it over to the female fantasy of romance, the male romance of powerful superheroes (Spider Man and his mighty brotherhood of world-savers), the logical preposterousness of science fiction, the brightly hypnotic world of noir. That is why no pulp can be very long. The original flimsiness and disposability of the books' material form—cheap paper that quickly frays, spines easily fractured—urge and condition us to move through their pages quickly so we can lose ourselves in the fantasy before it falls apart. To read pulp—or rather to read and enjoy it—we need to put ourselves in the frame of mind of Dix Steele, the restless killer of Dorothy Hughes's mesmerizing noir thriller *In a Lonely Place* (1947): "He shut out thought, clamping it between his set teeth" (15).

I find this theme—the deliberate shutting out or shutting down of thought—a recurrent and defining element of pulp fiction written by women. It is a provision that allows the body to tell us what it knows: "Her body knew its treachery before her sleepy mind did," Piper writes of the betrayed Blanche, "and expressed its loathing primitively" (164). Glandular realism is a way for canny women writers to exploit their reputation for being instinctive and intuitive rather than disciplined thinkers. It permits them to think the unthinkable—child molestation and perversion in *Bunny Lake Is Missing*, nurturing lesbian attachments in *The Girls in 3-B*, insider trading and borderline prostitution in *Skyscraper*, serial killing in *In a Lonely Place*. Women who write pulp write about the body's way of knowing fully aware that their readers would rather be introduced to a new sensation than to a new idea, rather track a killer than a thought. Their fiction supplies us with images of life so pummeled by sensation that the mind itself becomes too bruised to react. This isn't my extravagant language, but Baldwin's, who reports at a critical point in her heroine's story that she felt as if "her mind had been beaten black and blue" (222). Baldwin's heroine mounts no effective protest to her mind being battered, as the saying goes, to a pulp. On the contrary, she takes it as a sign that she has experienced something not just brutal, but momentous, in such pulverizing sensation. Her response is paradigmatic. Characters in pulp fiction often feel caught in a nightmare that has spilled over into their waking life. So thinks Blanche, as she follows a policeman to the station where the search for the missing Bunny is being mounted: "What could be more dreamlike than this walk down the street with a tall policeman? And, as in dreams, the faces you passed, all strangers, all strange, turned indifferently toward you and then indefinitely away, and the policemen didn't speak again after he had asked where she lived, and she didn't speak, either, because what was the point in a dream when salvation only lay in waking up?" (34).

While the dream persists—and it often persists even beyond the last page of the book—pulp heroes and heroines survive primarily on impulse or terrified reflex. Characters must move and decide things quickly and they do so by instinct, not by the conscious and rational deliberations habitual to a mature moral agent. What might pass for thought in the mind of a crazed mother or demented killer is revealed to be little more than the reflexes of a threatened or twisted creature whose full human character may never be known to us. Annice in Valerie Taylor's *The Girls in 3-B* (1959) seems to understand the conventions of the genre she is in when she considers how little she—and by extension the reader of pulp—rationally knows about the characters of the novel. Speaking of a man she has recently met, she reflects (I use this term broadly) "As far as she knew, he might have been created the day they met." (122). That is as much as any of us can know of characters in pulp. They rarely present themselves as people with scrutable pasts and psychologies to be probed. Giving us a fuller picture of human character is the special province of the modern novel, with its techniques for rendering the slightest vibrations of feeling and thought. Questions that might take Dostoevsky two volumes to explore are dispatched in pulp with amazing coolness. So, you ask yourself while reading *In a Lonely Place*, what made Dix Steele a serial killer? The woman who knows him the best calls him Princeton, a label that refers to his alma mater and serves as conveniently as any other for the traumatic source of his homicidal hatred (though the admissions officers where I teach may groan to hear me say it). The reality, the pulp reality, as the opening pages alert us, is that he emerged out of the "unknown and strange world of mist and cloud and wind." In the universe of pulp, evil has no source and seldom suffers exegesis.

There is something elemental, then, something that lends itself readily to dream symbolism about pulp characters suspended in a trance of love or ensnared in a nightmare of loneliness and subjection. In female pulp fiction the dream of love usually takes the form of stupefaction. Heroines usually know they are in love when kisses leave them feeling, as Baldwin reports, "docile and amazed" (55). Baldwin herself, however, is aware that this stupefaction is best captured not through the mind of her innocent heroine, which we recall has been battered black and blue, but rather in the convalescent musings of the career women, who has survived the dream of love and lived to tell the tale: "She was remembering nothing. You do not remember the things that are in your blood. You put no names to them. They are. They exist, part of you. You question them no longer" (55). Newhouse, analyzing his own erotic subservience, observes that his feelings are "of course, traditional to the state, always this magnified consciousness of the other" (151). Blanche sums up this tradition less clinically in a Kafkesque image of that erotic subjection that can leave you feeling docile and amazed. Remembering

Newhouse's kiss, she suddenly has a vision of herself "as the hypnotized guinea pig in the biology lab, when the teacher had stroked its soft belly and it lay tranced on its back with its legs in the air" (165). So much for the dream—the stupe-faction—of love.

The chance to encounter or encounter anew female writers of pulp makes us wonder whether women writers dream a dream fashioned out of the longings and anxieties distinctive to female experience. Is the gratified wish different for women? Does the sense of menace originate in a different place in the psyche? Is a lonely place just a lonely place we all enter, or do women and men experience isolation differently? *Bunny Lake Is Missing,* like many of its sister fictions, raises these questions and by doing so also calls into question the social pieties and puritanical sexual mores of its time. Perhaps women writing pulp want us to feel (rather than rationally know) that the realities of the world are hard, hard enough to inspire and even demand unresigned counter-narratives of the way the world not only does work but *might* work.

But providing alternative descriptions of the world isn't what makes pulp so shocking to the uninstructed or unsus-pecting mind. It is in creating a new language for reality, lan-guage that seems to have seeped through the body's secre-tions, its fearful sweats and anguished tears, that female pulp makes us feel and learn something new, even startling, about the world. This even the rational doctor Newhouse grasps in trying to understand the "piquancy" of Piper's pulp heroine:

> Occasionally, the doctor thought, as, for example, it must have been with Keats, where the feverishness attendant on his T.B. added a special quality to his poetry, so with this girl; her delusion added to her piquancy. Her hysteria made her eyes notable and every motion of hers became exciting. When that

died down, he told himself, she would resemble the
others. (95)

This is both a psychiatric diagnosis and an invocation to the
muse of pulp fiction. Hysteria individualizes; it converts heightened sensation into sensational poetry. Coursing through the flat
plains of pulp prose we stumble across a seam of corded, twisted
language, the language of palpable hysteria, of feeling too insistently itself, too knotted to be beaten easily into pulp. Usually
these sudden spikes of feverish poetry come in that hard-boiled
form of one liners, like this unmaidenly retort to an offer of
respectable love from *Skyscraper*: "Can't stand men with honor-
able intentions and small incomes" (60). Such lines say more
about the hard choice between money and love that can warp a
woman's feelings in capitalist society than any sociological trea-
tise or creditably subversive, politically correct plot. And can any
didactic or incendiary tract protest more eloquently against the
violence and shattered promises of American life than the motto
of Blanche's dark faith, "In gun I trust"?

At other times the feeling captured is less practical and ide-
ologically serviceable, a feeling that seems to spurt out of
some abscess of the mind, lancing some hidden corruption we
were too squeamish to acknowledge. Such emotional abjec-
tion is captured with uncanny power by Taylor in *The Girls in
3-B* when she describes the appalled feelings of a young
woman who finds herself unable to resist the sexual advances
of a man who physically repels her: "She saw herself crawling, slinking to her hole like the other basement animals, the
mice that came out at night to feed from the garbage cans, the
slick quick roaches, and the scuttling thousand legged worms"
(79). This feeling of being "shamed, lost and doomed" is
known only to creatures of darkness and those writers who
illuminate their plight. Piper sees herself as one of these
chroniclers of the underworld, teeming with verminous life,

that lies just beneath the clean bright surface of the ordinary, brightly colored world: "The walls were brilliantly blue, but the paint was so lumpy that it seemed as if someone had simply painted the bright clean colors right over what had been underneath; that dirt, insects, mouse droppings were permanently fixed in the paint like flies in amber" (4). Piper enjoys stripping off the paint, exposing the dirt and subterranean life beneath. Her imagination gravitates to those places where she might create her own flies in amber. This is the literary ground of glandular realism. This, in the tradition of female pulp fiction, is as real as it gets, but it is enough. And it keeps us coming back for more.

Maria DiBattista
Princeton University
June 2004

Notes

1. The theme of the docile, babbling mother who is transformed into a heroine once her child is threatened is given another virile turn in *The Nanny*. There the delicate, sensitive, and self-doubting mother-wife surprises everyone, including herself, when maternal instinct reveals her capacity for heroism in the Hemingway tradition: "Now she was like—she was like—like that Spanish girl in the Ernest Hemingway picture, *For Whom the Bell Tolls*. Maria, wasn't it: The Fascisti had shaved that girl's head (and raped her) but she was healed, and up on the mountain top she became a heroine" (222–23).

2. Piper may be offering a homage to Melanie Klein, psychoanalytic portraitist of the "good" and "bad" mother as fantasized by the child dependent on her care, in the figure of Miss Klein, the teacher who skillfully, if impersonally superintends the children, and in the character of Officer Klein, the "kind" policeman assigned to look for Bunny but who Blanche later spots in a bowling alley. Piper seems fascinated by the way motherhood is defined and evaluated, since she returns to the theme of the wicked and good mother in her psychological horror tale, *The Nanny*. Klein's complex account of the child's relation to the mother is developed throughout her work, but is most succinctly and elegantly expressed in "Love, Guilt, and Reparation" (see *The Writings of Melanie Klein, vol. 1: Love, Guilt, and Reparation and Other*

Works, 1921–1945, London: Virago, 1988).

3. The titles of films that preceded and followed the twenty-episode series *The Perils of Pauline* (1914) suggest how Pearl White's character was indebted to Victorian notions of female conduct and destiny: *Home, Sweet, Home, Helping Him Out, Angel of the Slums, For the Honor of the Name* (all from 1911); *A Dip Into Society, Pearl as a Clairvoyant, Pearl's Admirers, Knights and Ladies, Pleasing Her Husband, Hearts Entangled* (all 1913); *A Lady I Distress* (1915). My favorite is *What Didn't Happen to Mary!* Still, intimations of a nascent modern womanhood can be glimpsed in the titles, if in nothing else of *The Lady in Pants, The Lady Doctor*, and (a tarnished Pearl perhaps) *The White Moll* (192). Filmography and selected list can be found on http://www.classicimages.com/1997/july97/white.html.

4. More imagination *is* it, actually.

5. Rightly criticizing the film's over-emphatic musical score, Neil Young goes on to comment: "As a breather from the muzak, top pop comb The Zombies turn up on a pub TV showing 'Ready Steady Go,' then later we hear their tunes blaring out of a transistor radio. Several Zombies cutes are played—perhaps the result of some deal between Preminger and their record company—so how bizarre it is that these *don't* include the band's most famous track, the all-too-appropriate 1964 smash 'She's Not There'!" Neil Young, seen in 7 December, *CineSide*, Newcastle-upon-Tyne, to be found on www.jigsawlounge.co.uk/film

Works Cited

Baldwin, Faith. *Skyscraper*. New York: Feminist Press, 2003. (Originally published by Dell Publishing Company in 1931.)

Hughes, Dorothy B. *In a Lonely Place*. New York, Feminist Press, 2003 (Originally published by Duell, Sloane & Pearce, 1947. Pulp paperback edition, Pocket Book, 1949.)

Moers, Ellen. *Literary Women*. New York: Anchor, 1977.

Piper, Evelyn. *The Nanny*. New York: Atheneum, 1964.

_____. *Bunny Lake Is Missing*. New York: Feminist Press, 2004. (Originally published by Harper & Brothers, 1957. Pulp paperback edition, Dell Publishing Company, 1965.)

_____. *The Lady and Her Doctor*. New York: Harper & Brothers, 1956.

Taylor, Valerie. *The Girls in 3-B*. New York: Feminist Press, 2003. (Originally published by Fawcett Publications, 1959.)

Films

Bunny Lake Is Missing. Dir. Otto Preminger. Columbia, 1965.

A daring new series uncovers the forgotten queens of pulp—and subversive new viewpoints on American culture

Femmes Fatales: Women Write Pulp celebrates women's writing in all the classic pulp fiction genres—from hard-boiled noirs and fiery romances to edgy science fiction and taboo lesbian pulps.

Beneath the surface of pulp's juicy plots were many subversive elements that helped to provide American popular culture with a whole new set of markers. Much more than bad girls or hacks, women authors of pulp fiction were bold, talented writers, charting the cultural netherworlds of America in the 1930s, 1940s, 1950s, and 1960s, where the dominant idiom was still largely male, white, and heterosexual.

The pulp fiction revival of the last decade has almost entirely ignored women writers. Yet these women were sometimes far ahead of their male counterparts in pushing the boundaries of acceptability, confronting conventional ideas about gender, race, and class—exploring forbidden territories that were hidden from view off the typed page. The novels in the Femmes Fatales series offer the page-turning plots and sensational story lines typical of pulp fiction. But embedded in these stories are explorations of such vital themes as urbanization and class mobility, women in the workplace, misogyny and the crisis of postwar masculinity, racial tensions and civil rights, drug use and Beat culture, and shakeups in the strict codes of sexual conduct.

The Feminist Press at the City University of New York is proud to restore to print these forgotten queens of pulp, whose books offer subversive new perspectives on the heart of the American century.

For more information and to order books, call 212-817-7925.

Small-town girls and big-city dreams collide in this 1950s pulp

THE GIRLS IN 3-B
VALERIE TAYLOR
Afterword by Lisa Walker

"A remarkable slice of bohemia from the 1950s. Valerie Taylor gives 'pulp' a good name and weaves a wondrous tale of love, lesbianism, poetry, and sex around three young women who leave their small town for the allure of the big city."

—**JUDITH HALBERSTAM**, author of *Female Masculinity*

232 pp., $13.95 paperback, ISBN 1-55861-462-1

Passions flare in this classic drama of a woman reborn—the basis for the famed film starring Bette Davis

NOW, VOYAGER
OLIVE HIGGINS PROUTY
Afterword by Judith Mayne

"At once tough-minded and terribly romantic, *Now, Voyager* sweeps us up in an ageless tale of love while foreshadowing today's notions of sexual liberation, emotional wholeness, and personal independence. Prouty is a wonderful writer, and her Charlotte Vale is a timeless and very sophisticated Cinderella."

—**PATRICIA GAFFNEY**, author of *The Saving Graces*

320 pp., $13.95, paperback, ISBN 1-55861-474-5

*A chilling tale of American machismo gone mad—the basis for the classic
1950 film noir starring Humphrey Bogart*

IN A LONELY PLACE
DOROTHY B. HUGHES
Afterword by Lisa Maria Hogeland

"A superb novel by one of crime fiction's finest writers. . . . Hughes's
atmospheric prose, keen characterizations, and unflagging pace lead
the reader on a nightmarish journey through the depths of one man's
disturbed mind."

—MARCIA MULLER, author of the Sharon McCone novels

272 pp., $14.95 paperback, ISBN 1-55861-455-9

A World War II spy thriller with a hard-boiled heroine

THE BLACKBIRDER
DOROTHY B. HUGHES
Afterword by Amy Villarejo

"Hughes writes brilliantly, from the heart, and at the very top of the genre."

—ALAN FURST, author of *Blood of Victory*

"Hughes is the master we keep returning to."

—SARA PARETSKY, author of *Total Recall*

256 pp., $12.95, paperback, ISBN 1-55861-568-0

Career—marriage—or intrigue with a dashing stranger? What's a girl to do?

SKYSCRAPER
FAITH BALDWIN
Afterword by Laura Hapke

"This charming 1931 romance declares that despite all challenges—
cultural, political, historical—women should insist on their right to
have it all."   —ALICIA DALY, *Ms.*

288 pp., $14.95 paperback, ISBN 1-55861-457-5

The Feminist Press at the City University of New York is a non-profit literary and educational institution dedicated to publishing work by and about women. Our existence is grounded in the knowledge that women's writing has often been absent or underrepresented on bookstore and library shelves and in educational curricula—and that such absences contribute, in turn, to the exclusion of women from the literary canon, from the historical record, and from the public discourse.

The Feminist Press was founded in 1970. In its early decades, the Feminist Press launched the contemporary rediscovery of "lost" American women writers, and went on to diversify its list by publishing significant works by American women writers of color. More recently, the Press's publishing program has focused on international women writers, who remain far less likely to be translated than male writers, and on nonfiction works that explore issues affecting the lives of women around the world.

Founded in an activist spirit, the Feminist Press is currently undertaking initiatives that will bring its books and educational resources to under-served populations, including community colleges, public high schools and middle schools, literacy and ESL programs, and prison education programs. As we move forward into the twenty-first century, we continue to expand our work to respond to women's silences wherever they are found.

Many of our readers support the Press with their memberships, which are tax-deductible. Members receive numerous benefits, including complimentary publications, discounts on all purchases from our catalog or web site, pre-publication notification of new books and notice of special sales, invitations to special events, and a subscription to our email newsletter, *Women's Words: News from the Feminist Press*. For more information about membership and events, and for a complete catalog of the Press's 250 books, please refer to our web site: www.feministpress.org.